SOME ANGELS DON'T SEE GOD

For Chidimma,

May all your heart desires
be yours today and in
Subsequent days.
I hope you enjoy this.

Ever Obi

04.09.2022

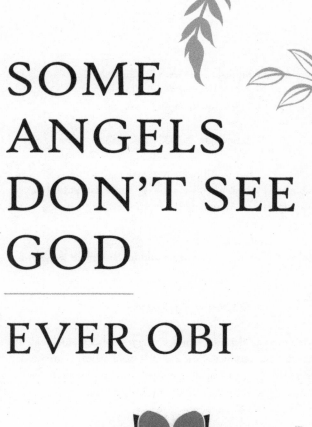

SOME ANGELS DON'T SEE GOD

EVER OBI

Abibiman
Publishing

New York & London

First published in Great Britain in 2022 by
Abibiman Publishing
www.abibimanpublishing.com

Abibiman Publishing is registered under
Hudics LLC in the United States and in the United Kingdom.

ISBN: 978-1-9989958-7-5

Cover design by Gabriel Ogunbade

For Lilian, my only sister.
They say no one comes in a complete package,
but I have never seen anything in you that spells
INCOMPLETENESS.

"The past beats inside me like a second heart."
—John Banville, *The Sea*

"The past is never dead. It's not even past."
—William Faulkner, *Requiem for a Nun*

Part One

I

It hadn't always been like this. There was a time when Peter's life was simple, when the little things in it were enough. Those were the days when love still protected him from the truths of the world, those days of innocence. Little things were enough to fill his leisure with joy. Little things like toys and cartoons; little things like killing mosquitoes

This Saturday morning, that joy returned when Peter swung his right arm to slap the left side of his chest, beside the bullet scar. He opened his eyes but his head ached from drinks from the night before.

The existence of mosquitoes was deeply unfathomable to Peter. He had often wondered their purpose, these tiny malaria-causing vampires. When he was a child, he would sneak out of the main building of his family home at sunset, with his younger brother, to kill mosquitoes in the garden. Over the years, mosquitoes had grown harder to kill. It was either his limbs no longer moved with the same precision as they did when he was a boy, or modern-day mosquitoes were simply faster.

Peter raised his hand. The minuscule carcass of the pernicious fly was flattened in his palm, a splatter of blood around it. Was it his blood or his and the slain mosquito's? Was his girlfriend's there as well?

Winnie was sleeping beside him, her left leg draped recklessly over his belly. Under the tweed blanket, he could feel the warmth of her naked body against his. He watched her for a few seconds, her mouth and eyes slightly open, like he had always known them to be in the early hours of the morning, whenever she slept. It always reminded him of 'Sleeping Open Eye', a song he knew from when he was a boy watching NTA 2 Channel 5. He would tease her about it.

He wanted to get out of bed but did not want to wake Winnie, so gently, he removed her leg from his body. Carrying his left hand as though it was broken—he did not want to stain his white bed sheet with the mosquito's blood—he sat up on the bed. He reached for the white singlet at his feet and with it wiped off the mess in his palm. The clothes on the floor brought a fuzzy memory of last night. They—he and Winnie—had sauntered into his apartment with an unspoken but mutual understanding of the only thing they wanted. They were having too much sex, Peter had always thought approvingly. There was something about her, something about her body, petite, plump and lush, and about her voice, a soft singsong, that made it hard for him to resist her. He was often turgid like a teenager, thinking about her. It surprised him how spontaneous their love life was. He knew stories of women who faked moans and orgasms to make their lovers happy and sometimes wondered if Winnie were one of such women because he could not believe how incredible he had become in bed.

What scared him, though, was how little they talked. It seemed their relationship was standing on sex alone for support. In private moments, thoughts of her were quickly overridden by the thought of sex with her. Happy or sad, stressed or relaxed, he wanted to be with her, to be inside her. She had never complained about the shallowness of where she stood with him, the limitations of what he was willing to give. Nevertheless, he wished they talked more. Some days, when they were out on dates, he found his mind racing, futilely searching for words, for conversations to initiate.

After work on Friday night, he had wanted to tell her about his conversation with his supervisor, but something suggested that there was no need. She had no solution to his problem. They went to Shaunz, a karaoke bar in Victoria Island, to drink in silence and watch others sing. Then they went home. Then they had sex. But his supervisor's words remained, so much so that he wondered whether they contributed to the pang lingering in his head:

"The bank has decided to redeploy a risk management expert to our subsidiary in Ghana, and I think you are the right man for the job. I have already recommended you to Human Resources. You have proven to me time and time again that you deserve this step. It's a big step with massive responsibility, but I know you are the man we need in Ghana."

His banking career had been a high-flying one so far. Just six months earlier, he had celebrated his fourth promotion in five years. He had improved himself and had given the bank his nights, his weekends, his sweat, his everything, and had been rewarded fairly.

"Give it a thought," his boss had said. "I am sure you will make the right decision for your career."

He was trying to make it look like Peter had a choice, but in the tone of his voice was something like blackmail: *You can reject the transfer, but you would be letting me down.*

Yes, he was dedicated to the bank and to his job, and the move to Ghana would be a major advancement in his career, but he was going to fight this transfer because he knew he wanted to remain in Lagos. He had earlier lied to himself that he wanted to stay because of Winnie. It was a self-deception that built a curtain wall of comfort around him, a sham reassurance that he wasn't such a bad boyfriend. It took just seconds for that fragile wall to come crashing down; the lie was too heavy for it to bear. He retrieved his reasoning and accepted the fact that the only reason he did not want to be transferred to Ghana was his mother. He did not want to be far from her. Family should always come first, he was taught.

As he stood up from the bed, he walked to his wardrobe, counting eight steps. Just beside the wardrobe, was a wicker laundry basket. He let go of the singlet he had used to wipe off the blood of the mosquito, and it rested on the border of the basket. He put on a pair of blue boxer shorts, then a black *jellabiya*. Alhaji Bala, one of his customers from the bank, had bought it for him, a gift from his last pilgrimage to Mecca. It had been oversized and looked like the black version of Willie-Willie's robe before he took it to his tailor.

Alhaji Bala wore a gold tooth and would not stop talking. The first time he met Peter, he was quick to notice that Peter was missing an upper canine. "Are you sure you don't need one of these, eh?" he joked, flashing his gold tooth. "But you will have to come to Mecca with me."

Peter liked to listen to Alhaji Bala, because through him, he satisfied some of his curiosities about the teachings of Islam. Alhaji Bala would tell him stories dating back to the origin of the long- standing feud between the Sunni and Shia Muslims, about the Battle of Karbala, during which Imam Husayn was killed. He would then complain about how some Muslims did not understand the age-long divisions and what exactly they practiced.

"But it is this understanding that breeds rift and violence among Muslims, don't you think?" Peter had asked him one day.

Alhaji Bala had thrown his hand in the air and said, "I used to think the most dangerous thing in life was ignorance, but it is not. Making excuses for ignorance is."

Peter stooped and began to pick up clothes from the bedroom floor. He roughly folded them and dumped them on the plastic chair beside the wardrobe. He headed for the door. He needed to get to the pharmacy to get paracetamol for his headache. Whenever he had a headache, he remembered his school girlfriend, Neta, who felt she was cursed because she had frequent strikes of migraines.

"Where are you going to, Pete?" He heard Winnie ask with a sleepy voice.

"To the pharmacy; I have a headache."

"It is food you need," she said. And when he turned to look at her, he saw that her eyes were closed and it was like she had not spoken at all. He left his flat and entered his car parked outside the compound, a 2004 model of Honda Civic which he had been driving for five years now. It was his first car and he had bought it off a senior colleague. His other colleagues at work would tease him and suggest that five years was a long time to have driven a car bought as second-hand, but he did not care. That it served its purpose was all that mattered. He drove through the tranquillity of early Saturday morning. Outside his estate would be chaos, he knew.

He spent the five-minute drive to the pharmacy, listening to early morning news on the radio. As usual, the stories were disheartening. Corrupt politicians accused of looting hundreds of millions; the economic struggles of the Nigerian real sector; a man raped his twelve-year-old daughter; a Roman Catholic priest accused of pederasty. Back when he was a boy, news like these would make his mother snap her fingers and say 'the world would soon come to an end'. That statement scared him. He expected an apocalypse, a total destruction of the earth by fire or water, like in biblical times. Though he did not want to die by drowning, it was fire that he feared the most. What if there was a heaven, as he had believed, and he had not done enough to make it? Did that mean that a harsher form of fire—with brimstone— would maintain eternal contact with his body and soul? He also wondered how it was possible for someone to be on fire, feeling the due pain, and not burn or degrade into ashes. He struggled with that mystery. What about other religions and denominations that did not believe in the idea of heaven and hell? Would their treatment be different on Judgement Day? And what if they were right and there was indeed no heaven or hell? The soul would die with the body and the body would rot away and be devoured by termites. No heaven. No hell. No afterlife. No reincarnation. Just nothingness. That meant he would have spent his entire life believing and swimming in falsehood.

There were more religious questions that he had had as a boy: Was Christianity the real religion, like his mother made him believe, and was Catholicism the right way to practise it? Over the years, given his experiences in life, he had come to his own conviction that nobody could claim understanding of these things. So these days, he did not bother anymore, having made his peace that nobody had the answers to these questions; people just believed what they believed, because it made them feel safe, it made them a part of something.

And nobody seemed to have the answer when a random mystic prophesied that the world was going to end at the beginning of the last year of the twentieth century. The rumour was that there was going to be three days of darkness, during which a total apocalypse would take place and the only people that would be left on earth were the righteous—the righteous with lit blessed candles, praying in their homes. Peter's mother bought white candles and took them to their parish priest to bless. When New Year Eve came, they put on candles around the house and prayed in fear. When NEPA cut off power supply, Peter could hear his mother's voice rise to great heights, fighting with his father's. And as he cowered next to the couch, folding himself up in fear, he remembered all those times he stole other people's pens in school, all those times he thought of and imagined naked girls, all those times he stole glances at his form teacher's cleavage. He knew he would not make heaven, and this knowledge made him sweat. It made his heart race in desperation; a desperation to see morning light.

Morning did eventually come, bringing year 2000 with it. The world had not ended. He was twenty-seven years old now, and the world was yet to end. Things had even got worse. Lootings were still done with impunity, even on a grander scale. Perverted men were still raping their own daughters.

When he walked into the pharmacy, his eyes searched through the shelf, ignoring the salesgirl whose attention was fixed on a book, her left leg draped over the left arm of a wooden seat.

"What can I get for you, sir?" the girl asked, springing to her feet.

She still had the book in her hand.

"Paracetamol." Peter took his eyes off the shelf to meet the girl's now smiling face. His eyes followed the movement of her hand as she placed the book on the seat she had been on. "Paracetamol and a bottle of Lucozade Boost."

His eyes remained on the book as the girl went to fetch the drug he had asked for. There was something he enjoyed about seeing people read novels.

"Here, sir." She had put a pack of paracetamol in a paper bag and extended it towards Peter alongside a bottle of Lucozade Boost. "Do you read?"

"In the past, yes." Peter collected the drug from her, reached for his breast pocket and handed her a bill of money.

"Why did you stop, sir?" the girl asked, groping the register for change.

Peter did not answer her question; he knew her type.

She was young, dreamy, and knew nothing about leaving home by 5.00am and returning by midnight every day, having little time to sleep. She could afford to sit around in this tiny shop, with all the time in the world, reading and waiting for customers to come to her. Now she thought everything was about literature. These little novels did not pay his bills.

"Can I see the book you are reading?" he asked her instead.

With the generosity of teenage boys passing a joint of weed around, she picked the book and handed it over to him. He could see that she quickly glanced through to memorise the page number she was on. There was excitement in her face. "The Angel You Know. It's interesting. It just got long-listed for the National Literature Prize for a debut novel."

He squinted in disbelief when he took a closer look at the book—*The Angel You Know. Neta Okoye.*

"Neta," he muttered. He turned the book over, but there was no picture. He checked the inner back page, no picture. But when he checked the frontispiece, there she was, her hair twisted into short dreadlocks. Same ol' glass-wearing Neta, with that smile that formed dimples on her face.

2

Peter had thought he had the best family. His father was a successful clearing and forwarding agent. Their family home in Festac Town had an outdoor pool and a flower garden. He and his younger brother would play in the garden and suck the sweet nectar from the *Ixora* flowers. His mother would smack them saying, "There are sweets in the house. Leave flowers for the birds."

Whenever Peter or his brother fell ill, their mother would take them to their family doctor, Dr Ogunike, a bald-headed man who was always quick to prescribe medleys of medicaments. Peter and his brother hated those drugs, how repulsive they smelled and tasted, how they made them nauseous, but they loved that their mother bought them Hi-Malt and evaporated milk whenever they were sick; the combination always soaked their tongues in grand sweetness. Peter always wondered why his mother associated *malt and milk* with sickness, a gift that came only after visits to Dr Ogunike's hospital, in the upsetting company of pills and colourful capsules. He did not understand why she did not buy malt and milk as casually as she bought candies and biscuits. Sometimes when their throats struggled in uncontrollable thirst of the mixture, they would fake a headache or fatigue, hoping that their risk would end in tablet-free refreshment. It never worked.

Their room was filled with all sorts of toys, both the ones they still found useful and the ones they had outgrown. Occasionally, their mother would invite her friend, Toy Woman, to collect the redundant toys and sell them as second-hand items in her shop.

"I have told their father to stop getting these toys for them," their mother once said to Toy Woman.

"How old are your boys now?" Toy Woman asked. "Six and seven."

"Six and seven?" Toy Woman asked with an incredulous look. "They still need toys then. Leave the man to buy toys for his children." Toy Woman was pretty. Her face glistened when she smiled, but Peter and his brother did not like her. There were some toys that they were emotionally attached to. Toys that, though they had outgrown, they did not want to let go of. Toy Woman took everything away. Peter and his brother once had a rubber teddy. Its body was yellow and it had a nose as red and round as a clown's. Peter and his brother christened it Karat China; *Karat* was their mispronunciation of *Karate*. They made Karat China their little hero and upon it, they heaped all the superhuman powers they saw in Chinese movies; movies filled with fights between men whose skills were so impossible that they danced and flew around like birds and disrespected gravity, dragging their grunts into songs as they moved in combat. Movies full of characters whose lips moved way ahead of the words they produced. They gathered all martial skills from movies like *Drunken Master* and *Snake in the Monkey's*

Shadow and heaped them on Karat China—little accretions of fantasies—until it became what they wanted. Their immortal toy hero. After watching Jackie Chan dance around and beat bad guys, they would recreate scenes from his movies, making themselves directors and stunt instructors, filling their scenes with toy characters that they needed to force into fights by knocking them against one another and inventing conversations. In these fights, Karat China was always the hero. He defeated and killed every toy that stood in its way.

Toy Woman visited one day and took Karat China away. Karat China's loss hurt Peter, and when he complained, his mother bought two beautiful teddies, fluffy and brown, each the size of a new-born. Their eyes and noses were smooth black balls, not red and coarse like Karat China's. His mother had missed the point: No toy made by a man or machine could ever replace Karat China. He did not tell her this because he knew that she would never understand.

Also, Peter once had a red tricycle with headlights that blinked and played tunes when turned on. At seven, it was no longer appropriate for his fast-growing limbs. His knees hit the handlebar when he pedalled, but he did not want to let it go. He enjoyed watching it, wiping dust off it and listening to the simple tunes it played. One day, Toy Woman visited and took it away. From the balcony, he watched her load toys into the boot of the taxi that brought her. The tricycle, his prized possession, was the last to be dumped in the boot. The taxi driver lifted it off the ground with one hand, his left hand, like it was nothing. Peter's lips tightened in childish rage as he watched Toy Woman hug his mother, enter the cab and leave.

Then he started sulking. When his mother said funny things, his younger brother would laugh. Not him. He wanted her to see he was indignant. But it was his father that had noticed.

"What is the problem, Peter?" his father asked him as they watched *The New Masquerade* on NTA in the living room. The soap's ensemble had been churning out part after part of hilarious performances, and Peter had not laughed like everyone else. "Is anything wrong?"

"Yes, Daddy," Peter quickly answered. He had been waiting for days, to be asked. He had made conscious efforts to make his frown prominent enough to prompt a question.

"What is it?"

"My tricycle," he said. "Mummy gave it to Toy Woman."

His father looked at his mother, and they both burst out laughing. "Is Prisca now Toy Woman?" he asked her.

She clapped her hands together. "I didn't know when she became Toy Woman." She shook her head and chuckled. "These children won't kill me. Which one is Toy Woman again?" She turned to Peter, the smile on her face changing into the look she always wore whenever she reprimanded him. "So, that's why you have been folding your face as if someone died? Over a tricycle that you have outgrown."

"I love that tricycle," Peter said.

"Peter, come," his father called. "Come and sit beside me." He joined his father on the big sofa. His father put an arm around him. "You are a man now. You should not be riding tricycles. Tomorrow, I will get you a proper bicycle."

The glower vanished. "Really?" Peter asked.

"Yes, of course," his father answered. Whenever he said 'yes, of course', he kept his promise.

It was then that his younger brother took his eyes off the TV to say, "I want a bicycle too."

"I thought you did not like bicycles?" Peter asked sharply, as if a second request would change his father's mind. "Is it not football that you like?"

"Football or bicycle, everybody gets what they want," his father said.

The next day, he returned with two bicycles like he had promised. Every Tuesday, after school, Peter's mother would let him and his brother ride their bicycles with other children in the close. On Saturdays, whenever she was gone to the market to buy foodstuffs, Peter would invite his friends over to their house to play football. Their compound had the needed space. They played *Felele,* a ball made of soft plastic and took little effort to propel. Whenever they heard the honk of his mother's car, they would scamper to safety. His mother did not like them playing football. She thought it was a rough game. The ground was concrete and they pushed one another a lot. One could easily break one's bone or hit one's head. And Peter's brother had once collapsed in school while playing football. It was a risk she was not willing to take. She allowed them ride bicycles and play hide-and-seek in the compound. But when they felt like playing football, she would ask the other boys to go home. Peter and his brother would stay in and play snakes and ladders, Monopoly and other board games. Their mother spoke highly of Monopoly; she said it made people smart. She said the same thing about books and would sometimes force them to read.

Reading bored them, but they had no choice. Their mother was more assertive and less indulging than their father. She treated them with great love and care, but when she wanted them to do something, her voice was so strong that they obeyed without protests.

Peter's father was no ordinary businessman. He also was, in his own way, an artist, who could play the guitar and write songs with musical notation. Some Sundays, Peter and his brother would beg him to play for them. He'd shrug and reach for his acoustic guitar, and when he started making it sing with his red plectrum, Peter and his brother would dance to the peace and joy he created with his own renditions of songs by Evi Edna Ogholi, Bright Chimezie and Joe Nez.

Other Sundays, when their father was not entertaining with his guitar, their neighbour, Mr Sweet, would visit with his wife and daughter. The two families would dine together and have long conversations. Mr Sweet was a clearing agent, too, and a good friend of their father's; he liked to call Peter *Peero*. Mrs Sweet and their mother were friends, too. Peter liked their daughter, Anita. Their parents would call them husband and wife. He liked her tiny lips and her dimples. Because of Anita, he loved to have the Sweets around.

But something bothered him about the Sweets. It was a puzzle that sent his young mind to work anytime he was around them. He questioned their sanity, really. Why would a family allow themselves to be called 'Sweet'? So one day, he asked his mother, "Why is Anita's surname *Sweet*?"

"They had a surname they did not like. They were formerly called Nwosu. Do you know what that means?"

Peter shook his head. "Do you even know what *Osu* means?" There was a slight contortion on her face, which showed she did not expect him to know what the word meant.

"No, Mummy," he answered. "What does it mean?"

She explained to him that Osu, according to the Igbos, were a class of people who had, in the days of the old and inter-communal wars, sought protection from the gods. These requests were special, because for the gods to devote their time and attention, to protect a specific family, a price had to be paid. And the gods, being what they were—jealous and greedy—demanded total ownership of a lineage, of living family members and unborn offspring. These families had sold their freedom and their descendants were seen as properties of the gods. Peter's mother called them *outcasts*. She also told him that some Osus were humans whose ancestors had committed crimes against humanity and the gods, and were ostracized forever.

"It is something the Igbos take very seriously," she said. "People don't marry Osus; they marry among themselves."

When Peter asked her if Anita and her family were Osus, she said to him, "Don't concern yourself with such nonsense. There is no such thing as outcasts and there is only one true God. There are no gods, and no one is their property."

Peter liked to have Anita around. He liked that she was known as his wife and he her husband. It was a joke that he never saw as a joke. It was the main reason he fancied growing up. He dreamt of them—himself and Anita—as married grownups living in a house that was picturesque and bigger than his father's, playing with their kids and no dogs. Dogs were what prevented him from visiting the Sweets as often as he would have loved. He hated dogs and the Sweets had two. An Alsatian, Stefan, that understood simple English, and a Rottweiler, Riot, that had once chased him down the stairs. It had taken the intervention of Mr Sweet to make Riot retreat.

"Don't be scared, Peero," Mr Sweet had said with a smile as he led the dog away. "He was never going to bite you."

Peter did not believe him. *He was never going to bite you*? And he was named Riot? The Sweets were incredibly awful at choosing names, Peter thought. To Peter, dogs were created only to bark and bite. He did not like their smartness, he did not like their slobbering and he did not like their snarl. He decided he was going to tell Anita, when they got married, that they were not going to keep dogs.

As they grew into their teenage years, the innocence in his thoughts towards her began to yield to the pressing curiosity of his adolescent mind. He began to care less about her smiles, about her dimples. He was more interested in her lips; he wanted to kiss them. He was more interested in her breasts which were becoming more prominent; he wanted to see them bare, touch them. When his friends in school started having girlfriends and talking about sex, he knew that Anita was the only girl he wanted as a girlfriend. He wanted to experience all his fantasies with her. He wondered if she too wanted him as her boyfriend. She was comfortable with him. She laughed at his jokes and fixed gazes at him when they talked. Whenever they were alone, watching TV together, she would lean on him, her breasts pressing against his arm. Then, he wondered if she had any real awareness of the effect the physical contact had on him, or was her mind still that innocent that she snuggled up to him whenever she felt like, like they were still eight?

But he never got the chance to know how she truly felt, he never got the chance to ask her to be his girlfriend. Two days before his fourteenth birthday, he overheard his parents having a conversation in the living room.

"Did they even ask Anita if she his father asked. "They should have allowed the girl finish secondary school."

"Anita is only a child," his mother said. "Her parents know better. And education in the US is way better than the pathetic system we have in this country."

"No." His father shook his head, wagging his finger. "I don't agree with you. I still think that we have some good schools in this country. People can't afford these schools, that's all."

"You are lying to yourself. I only agree with you when you say they should have let her finish secondary school here. It is better for her to leave the country as an adult. That way, she is more mature, and knows the value of respect. Those kids in America lack respect. They do as they like, and their parents do not have any control over them. A lot of people who leave this country as kids return with painted bodies and drug issues. Look at Greg, King of the Palace."

Greg was a boy from their neighbourhood who was sent abroad as a teenager. He got involved in crime and drugs, and was brought back to Nigeria by his parents, with serious mental disorders. He wore his jeans way below the waistline, had a scorpion tattooed on his right bicep, wore earrings, rapped when he walked and smoked weed at every corner in the close. Parents did not want him around their children. The landlords held several meetings to discuss him and the danger he posed to the children. In the early hours, as the neighbourhood still slept, he would scream from the balcony of his father's house, his arms spread out in the air, "I am the king of this palace!"

"Boys piercing their earlobes open, it's pathetic," said Peter's father "But it also depends on who she will be living with."

"I asked her mother. Anita will be staying with her elder sister. She says the woman is a no-nonsense disciplinarian."

"Good." Peter's father nodded. "Good"

"I hope you are not planning on going back on your word regarding our boys' education?"

"And what would that be?"

"They will leave this country once they complete secondary school."

"Once it comes to the boys' education, you have the final say.

What does a businessman like me know about education?"

Peter had heard his parents laugh, but what really bothered him was what he had heard about Anita. She was travelling to America and didn't say anything to him about it. It broke his heart.

She left Nigeria without saying goodbye to him. She was not going to be his girlfriend. They weren't going to get married like he had imagined. There would be no big house with children playing— not any they owned together.

Then his father was killed in a car accident, and everything changed. They lost the house to the bank and life became difficult. It shocked Peter's young mind, how dramatically things changed. The reason it all happened remained elusive to him. During his funeral, Peter watched his mother and his younger brother shed unending tears. He wanted to cry, too, to pour all that burdened his heart out through tears but did not find any. It confused him, because he had cried during his paternal grandmother's burial, six years ago. His grandmother to whom he was not close. He had cried simply because he saw his father cry. He did not understand why he couldn't bring himself to cry for the man whose mere tears had been enough to break him down.

It was the first real tragedy they faced as a family; an unfortunate rub accompanied by financial struggles. They moved into a smaller apartment, and their mother, who had resigned from her teaching job while her husband was alive, had to step out from the unproductive comfort of being a housewife, into the strenuous venture of retailing. Toy Woman introduced her to a friend who was a clothier that sold cheap second-hand clothes in Yaba. She joined that line of business, but it was not enough.

Peter's mother sought financial refuge from Mr Sweet, who was reintroduced into their lives not as a boisterous Igbo man that laughed as he discussed business with Peter's father, but as a frequent benefactor who appeared in times of desperate need. He paid their house rent occasionally and sent cheques to their mother for their school fees. Some Sundays, he visited their cramped apartment with his wife.

Peter noticed that his mother's attitude towards the

Sweets changed. There was then a regardful touch in her expressions when they were around. She nearly dipped into a curtsy to greet Mr Sweet and nodded to his wife's statements with differential courtesy. It was then, the attitude of a woman who should be, and was grateful for the kindness the Sweets periodically extended. Looking back, Peter knew that Mr Sweet was the only reason he was able to finish school, to have this life he had now. Earlier in life, he liked the Sweets solely because of their daughter, Anita. But after his father's death, he found another reason. Whenever Mr Sweet visited, he refrained from asking about Anita, how she was doing, how education in America was. Sometimes Mr Sweet would tell him, "We spoke to your wife over the phone. She is doing okay." For once, he never said what Peter wanted to hear: *She asked about you, she sends her greetings.* When it came to Anita, he wanted to hear something more personal to him. It would have comforted him, knowing that she still thought of him after all these years. Maybe she now had an American boyfriend. Then he would hear Mr Sweet tell his mother, "We would be traveling to America next month to see Anita, we miss her a lot." They never said anything about Anita returning to Nigeria. Maybe she visited and they just did not mention it; they did not think it was important to bring her to see *her husband.*

Another facet of Peter's life ushered in something personal, and it was not about Anita. It was something that hit him like another tragedy, a personal tragedy. Events of that day remained in his mind, just like the date. It was year 2004, the seventeenth day of January, and a poky day at school. The Further Math teacher, Mr Ukoh, surprised everybody in class. He walked into the classroom during his period and shocked the students with a test for which there was no advance notice. It was on vectors and differential calculus,topics Peter needed extended study and prior notice to be able to pen something reasonable.

When the teacher walked in and said, "Tear out a sheet of paper, we are having a test", the class became frantic. Peter himself, sometimes, wondered what he was doing in the Further Math class—like ordinary Math wasn't enough. It was optional; he had had the liberty of choosing French instead, but he did not. He had been a French student in Junior Secondary and had not liked it. That day—just like other days when he sat hand to cheek, deadpan as Mr Ukoh's teachings became a Greek rumble of signs and derivations— was one of those days he wished he had chosen French over Further Math.

Of course, he performed badly. He spent most of the test time looking up the classroom ceiling, like the answers were there. He did not prepare for the test, and there was no way he could magic the ability to do better. He wondered what Mr Ukoh hoped to achieve. And it was mere rubbing of salt in the wound when he said, "Ladies and gentlemen, this is what we call a pop test." He left the classroom, shaking his head. He was proud of what he had done.

When Peter returned home, he had to do some chores: he fetched water and warmed the bitterleaf soup his mother had prepared three days ago. His younger brother was in a boarding school in Ikot Ekpene. He, too, had been in boarding school in Lagos, but had become a day student after his father passed way, to give his mother some company. His only friend then was his classmate and neighbour, a boy named Paul, but his mother did not like him spending time with Paul after school. She said Paul was a bad influence. Consequently, Peter's life after school hours was forced into a routine of chores and helping his mother at the store.

That night, after they had dinner, as Peter tried to conceal the chagrin that remained in his heart as an aftershock of the pop test, his mother dropped what was the most shocking combination of words he had ever heard. Her revelation left a distressing surge in his spine. It hung in his stomach like a heavy meal, the memory of her preliminary words effaced by it. She had started by saying something about how she loved him so much, about how he would always be 'their son'.

"You were adopted," she said to him. "Your father and I had agreed to tell you this when you turn fifteen. You are fifteen now. It has been difficult for me to say, but I would not want you to hear it from an outsider. You were adopted. But we will always be your parents, your father and me. It was difficult for me to get pregnant. The doctors kept assuring us that all was well with us medically, but your father was adamant we adopt a baby. When I suggested we wait and hope on God, he smiled and said to me: 'When God answers our prayer, we would have two. There is nothing wrong with that, is there?'." She paused to smile. "When we saw you at the orphanage, I already felt like a mother. You were a sweet chubby-faced baby. Just three weeks old." She pressed her palms against her cheeks, like she was drawing some warmth from them. "Your eyes looked innocent but curious. It was like you knew what was happening and wanted us." Another pause. "Three months after we adopted you, I found out that I was pregnant. We were happy to have you both. You are my son. Telling you the truth doesn't change it." She shook her head, and waited for him to say something or express a feeling.

It surprised Peter. It surprised him more than Mr Ukoh's pop test. An array of emotions suffused his veins, but none was expressed on his face. He had an impassive look similar to the ones he wore in Mr Ukoh's classes.

"I am sorry, Peter," his mother spoke further, afraid that his silence and blandness suggested anger. Then she turned away her face. "I wish your father were here. He would have done this better." She covered her face with her hands and started sobbing. Peter moved closer to her, wrapped his arm around her shoulder, and still without saying a word, he rubbed her hair gently. He was now the man of the house; whenever his mother cried, he had to console her. Many years had passed and he had never met his birth parents.

He did not like to think about them; he had no real pictures of them in his mind. When he was younger, he dreamt about them, but their faces in his dreams were silhouetted profiles. The unconditional love he got from the parents he knew was enough for him. There was no room to think of *what would have been*, if he was raised by his birth parents. They never loved him; they did not want him. His mother could easily have been a teenager who got pregnant for her street boyfriend, or, worse, an indiscriminate prostitute who did not even know who the father of her child was.

He was grateful for the life he had, despite his family

tragedies. He was grateful for the Sweets. He would give anything to be seven again, for one more day, to be back in the house they lost to the bank with his family, seeing old Nollywood movies all over again. To have his father around once again; to watch Toy Woman from the balcony, as she left with their toys. To hold hands with Anita in pure fondness and ask about the Sweets' crazy dog, Riot. There was always an unsettled wrench in his gut; he felt he did not cherish those moments enough. If it was possible, he would take it all back, to enjoy the comfort of that environment greedily—the way he felt he should have but did not.

3

Sunken was the only word Neta could think of as she sat in front of the white dresser in her room, getting ready for her book reading. She squinted into the square mirror which had borders festooned with plastic butterflies, her left index finger running through the depressed flesh that encircled her eyes. The image of her face, as always, saddened her and she hated that she had to wear her thick-lensed glasses each day she stepped out of the house. The glasses hid the hollowness around her eyes, but they brought about it in the first place. And the more she wore them, the more her eyes sank, the more prominent the dark circles around them became. Her condition, she always thought, was akin to the struggles of a drug addict who, despite being aware of the dangers drugs posed to well-being, still could not live without them. The difference was that while the drugs were a temporary trip to the land of euphoria for the addict, the glasses did not give her that kind of satisfaction.

The first time Esther, the only person she called friend these days, saw her without her glasses, she had screamed. "Your eyes…" Esther wagged her finger, searching for the right words. "…they have gone inside."

"It's the glasses," Neta said, replacing the frame atop her nose, her attention partly back to the book she was reading. "But you look like I'll go blind tomorrow."

"The problem is these books you read. You read too much."

Neta forced a smile. "The books have no business in this. It is the glasses."

"But the books are the cause of the defect, to begin with."

Then Neta took her eyes off the book to look at Esther, expecting to see a smile, something that suggested she had made the comment with her tongue in cheek, but she was surprised to see Esther's face puckered and serious. "It is not books," Neta said with an exaggerated pout and a light frustration at Esther's incredulous assumptions.

"What is it, then?"

"Myopia. Progressive myopia."

"Progre-*what*?" Esther asked, her face contorted in puzzlement. Neta ignored her. "If the glasses are the reason your eyes are sinking, you need to start using contact lenses then. They will make your eyes to come out again. I don't like the way your face looks without your glasses."

Neta listened to her and purchased a pair of contact lenses. But she soon found that she could never get used to them. First, she imagined that she would poke her own eyes one day while trying to put them on in the morning or retrieve them from her eyes as sleep came calling. Also, having to take them off every night was a burden. Whenever she had them on, the consciousness was irrepressible; she could not stop thinking that she had something in her eyes. Some days, her eyes felt water-logged. Other days, it felt as if she had wood splinters in them. When she complained to Esther, she said to her: "It is in the mind. You need to consciously stop thinking about it." Soon, she started forgetting to remove them before closing her eyes to sleep, eventually making up her mind to quit using them when she heard rumours about a young man in Abuja that went blind because he forgot to take off his before going to bed. She did not want to put herself in that position where she had to risk irreversible blindness because she wanted to make her eyes to *come out*. Never again. She also realised that, surprisingly, she had missed her glasses, those eye-sinking demons.

Knowing that she had a somewhat helpless dependence on her glasses frustrated her. Some days, it was a quiet anger, just simmering under the surface and making her pensive. But on days like this, as she applied a light makeup in preparation for her book reading, she felt like breaking something. Like picking up the snow globe next to the desk lamp to her left and throwing it at her reflection in the mirror. She just wanted her sight back, unaided.

She looked away from the mirror and caressed the sphere of the snow globe. It had the image of a father reading to his daughter seated on his lap as they were adorned by a depiction of falling snow. She could not remember the number of times she had touched this globe; these days she seemed to do so every morning before leaving her apartment. It was not just a toy to her; it was a relic of memory that she had had for over twelve years now. It always left a bitter- sweet taste in her mouth, reminding her of her father, Jikora, and his constant encouragement, ensuring she held on to literature. But it also reminded her of the time he came home with her very first pair of glasses, a set of round nerdy lenses with the ends of a black rope hanging from each arm, confident that it was going to correct the then emerging defect. Although his expectations about the corrective ability of the lenses were terribly misguided, the literature lover he saw in her were nascent manifestations of the writer she would become. Now, the glasses were the pain while the snow globe was emollient.

4

That day, twelve years ago, Neta's father, Jikora, knew that he needed to leave Victoria Island earlier than usual if he was going to beat the evening traffic. Carrying his briefcase, he walked through the office halls, waving and smiling to his colleagues, excitement on his face.

"Hello, Biodun," he greeted the receptionist on his way out. "Good evening, sir," Biodun responded, smiling back. "Are you on your way home already?"

"Yes, I am," Jikora replied. "My kids have returned from boarding school for the long vacation."

Biodun's grin widened. "That's lovely. They must be great kids." Jikora nodded proudly. "Yes, they are."

"When you—"

"By the way..." Jikora cut in but stopped when he realised what had happened. "You were saying?"

"Never mind, sir," Biodun said. "I hope to see them someday." "You will." Jikora quickly switched topics. "Once Dele gets back to the office, tell him that I've gone, that he should inform the team of our meeting on Monday."

"OK, sir."

"Have a great weekend," Jikora said and walked away.

Biodun watched him from the reception. She kept her eyes on him as he chatted briefly with the security guard who carried his briefcase to his car. She watched him get in the car and drive away. Biodun always felt something electric whenever she spoke to Jikora. At first, she tried to convince herself that all she felt for him was respect in a *boss-subordinate* kind of way, but when she started thinking of him before choosing what to wear to work, she knew that what she felt was something as complicated as sexual love.

Jikora always acted like he never took notice. He was good to her though, but that did not count, because he was good to everybody. He was polite to her, but he was polite to everybody. Maybe he thought her young—she was just a twenty-two-year-old intern, waiting to get a call up from the National Youth Service Corps, and he was a forty-year-old banker with a wife and teenage children.

A wife—that could easily be his reason for ignoring her little advances. Biodun hated to think of Jikora's wife, Edna. They had met once, and Edna was angelic. Her beautiful face and unblemished skin radiated a youth that had passed. The shape of her body, her height, and the elegance in her appearance made Biodun conclude that she had either been a model or a beauty queen when she was younger.

She was almost right. Edna had been the epitome of "beauty and brains" at the university. Lecturers knew her. Every boy wanted to date her. She was envied by other girls: they thought she lacked nothing, this intelligent girl with a full head of natural hair.

After school, after meeting and marrying Jikora, after a set of twins, she got a job at Lead Bank. To other women,

Edna's friends, she and her husband were the *perfect* couple with the *perfect* jobs and the *perfect* children.

Sixteen years into marriage, Jikora still opened doors for his wife. When he walked with Edna, he made sure she walked on the inside of the sidewalk to shield her from traffic and the odd splash from a puddle. At forty, he remained attentive to his body. And at work, he was an exceptional corporate banker.

For how dedicated he was to the demands of his jobs, it was inevitable that the only time he and his wife spent with their twin children, Jeta and Neta, came on weekends. Jikora made the most of the little time he had with them, whenever they returned home on vacation from boarding school.

As a father, he did an entirely different job compared to the way he was raised by his own father, who believed in the "spare the rod spoil the child" principle. His father did use the *rod*: sticks, leather belts, fists. Jikora's memory of his childhood was greatly attached to the strictness of his father; the fear he felt when he was around. The fact that he was an only child did not save him from his father's punishments. His father was a different man. While other parents treated only children with great indulgence, his was the opposite. At first, Jikora thought his father hated him; years later, he wasn't so sure. In Form One, news got to his father that he had skipped class. That day, after dinner, his father raised a cane to administer punishment for truancy. He ran behind his mother who begged for mercy on his behalf.

"Truancy is a serious offence," his father said. "You are spoiling this child."

"Dike, you will kill my son for me oh!" his mother screamed. "This is my only child."

"One day," his father said, "one day, he will thank me for this.

He is my son too."

From that moment, Jikora made a personal resolution to be a better child, to behave better, for fear of the rod, and for his parents. His mother was instrumental in developing the qualities he had grown with. *Respect* and *manners* were her favourite words. She would say things like: "Respect is reciprocal", "Jikora, come on, greet; don't you have manners, this boy?" Or she would combine both words in one sentence: "I raised you with good manners, you should respect people".

Years had passed since both parents' death, but Jikora knew that his lovable disposition was owed to his mother, and to his father, he owed his professional shrewdness.

Jikora often thought things would have been different if his father had been more educated. But that didn't matter now; he had a great childhood, growing up in Aba, under the caring eyes of his mother, and a father who was determined to turn him into a good man. A good strong man. Two wonderful people who worked long and hard amid financial deficiency to see him through school.

His days in the University of Nigeria, Nsukka were tough. His mother sold her jewellery and clothes, and to solve the school fees problem for good, his father sold his only land. There was no silver spoon sticking out his mouth when he was born, but he knew he was fortunate to have had parents alive to their responsibilities. His academic years were filled with a sincere desire to make them proud. He was a bright student; reason enough for his parents to ensure he graduated from the university. Their hard work and Jikora's academic determination were subsequently rewarded as Jikora's banking career kicked off once he left school. Then he met, fell in love with, and married Edna, the most beautiful woman he had ever set his eyes on. Electing not to have a lovechild, they had decided to get married, after Edna told him she was pregnant. They were young but knew what they wanted.

One day, Jikora stood in the hospital ward with his boy-and- girl twins in his arms. He had never been prouder of himself and of Edna. His parents were proud of him too; they had always wanted grandchildren. So much that even when Jikora was a boy, his mother would always talk to him about marriage and grandchildren.

Jikora drove down to Lekki Phase One, relieved to have evaded the rush hour. He would soon be home. However, his excitement was not just about being home. It was about seeing the children— they called his office line and told him they were already home. On the back seat were a neatly folded football jersey for his football- loving son, Jeta, and a pile of novels, for his literature-loving daughter, Neta.

His two children reminded him of his parents so much. His father was passionate about football. Jikora clearly remembered how his father's support for the Aba local club, Enyimba FC, gave him some comfort after the death of his wife. He remembered how his father followed their struggles, their relegation, and their record- breaking quest to gain promotion in the early '90s. Whenever he visited him in Aba, all they talked about was Enyimba and football, as though they were both deliberately avoiding the topic of his dead mother. Jikora saw that the club made the old man happy, so he went with him to see their games when he visited. The club seemed to be the only string holding him connected to life.

But 1997 turned out to be a disappointing year for Enyimba and for Jikora. A poor run of form had immersed the club in a struggle against time and relegation, and Jikora's father was hit by a stroke that left his right limbs paralyzed. Jikora brought him to Lagos to receive adequate medical attention, but it wasn't enough—he died. The words he mumbled to Jikora a day before he died still rang in his head: "You never get over the loss of a loved one. Eight years after the death of your mother, I still feel the same way I felt the night I heard about her death." And before Jikora said anything, he held his hand and said. "My boys will be relegated again, don't you think?" Jikora shook his head and said, "Your boys will be fine, and so will you." But he died the next day. Jikora wished there was a way he could let him know that Enyimba escaped relegation that year; he wished there was a way he could inform him of how the democratically elected governor of Abia State had changed the fortunes of the club with financial support; he wished he heard the sounds of victory from the grave when Enyimba won the Nigerian Championship Title and the Super Cup. But the dead do not hear.

So, it was impossible for his mother to see how Neta, her granddaughter, had grown into a beautiful young woman that loved reading just as much as she did. His mother did not get much education but was literate and fascinated by books. Jikora still blamed himself for her death. After the birth of the twins, he sent money to enable her fly down to Lagos for omugwo. From the moment he went to pick her up from the Murtala Muhammed Airport, she complained about how nauseated she was and how she felt uncomfortable for hours.

"Mama, you didn't fly for hours," Jikora tried to correct her overstatement.

"Well, that one is your business," she said with a playful hiss. "I just know that I'm going by bus when the omugwo is over."

Then she asked how the babies were doing. His mother spent the next one month taking care of the infants like they were her own. She bathed them and changed their diapers, she prepared ji mmiri oku for the family; she never allowed Edna do anything. And if Jikora suggested she was overworking herself, she'd take care of him too.

"You are looking lean," she would say. "Are you sure you eat lunch? Let me get some food for you to eat."

When it was time for her to return to Aba, Jikora gave her cash, bought her jewellery and expensive Hollandais wrappers, and suggested she travel by air, but she disagreed with him. "I did not enjoy flying. My heart was in my mouth, and I thought my head was going to explode. My ears were clogged. I will go by bus."

When Jikora offered to hire a car and a driver that would drive her, she said,

"My son, you like wasting money. Because you have your small bank job, you now want to spend the whole money on me. I will board a bus at the park, don't worry." Jikora gave in and lived to regret it.

En route to Aba, their bus was attacked by armed robbers, and during their sporadic shootings, a bullet caught her neck. Jikora never forgave himself; he should have insisted she travel by air. He thought grandchildren would make his parents happy, he had imagined the children playing in the field with their grandparents, but everything changed dramatically. His mother spent just a month with them before her death, and his father showed no real interest in them; he spent the remaining eight years of his life supporting Enyimba, following their progress in the professional league. And somehow, Jikora still blamed himself for everything. He still believed that things would have been different if he had been able to persuade his mother to travel by air after the omugwo. Perhaps she would still be alive now; perhaps his father would not have had a stroke, and the twins would have known their grandparents better. But persuade, he could not, and death, he could not reverse. All he could do was accept, enjoying whatever blessings he could count. The blessings of a good wife, and the blessings of great children, as he believed he had in Jeta and Neta.

As he stepped down from the car, the gate man locked the gate and strode up to greet him.

"Welcome, sir," he said.

"Thank you, Oko." He opened the backseat door and carried out the pile of four books with the football jersey folded on top of it. Oko extended his arms to help. "Don't worry, Oko."

"Okay, sir," Oko said and withdrew his hands. "I heard Jeta and Neta are already back."

"Yes, Oga. They are inside."

"Okay," Jikora said, extending the car key to Oko. "There is a small bag in the boot. Help me get it." Oko took the car key and walked off briskly.

Jikora walked into the house and found the help in the kitchen. He could see the surprise on her face—she always left before he got back.

"Good evening, sir," said the middle-aged woman, with a curtsy. "Good evening, Madam T," Jikora answered. "I can see you are making dinner already."

"Yes, sir. You are early."

"I couldn't wait to see the kids."

Oko walked into the kitchen and handed a tote bag over to Jikora.

Jikora received the bag with his left as his right was already occupied. "Thank you, Oko."

"Neta and Jeta are in their room upstairs," Madam T nodded in the direction.

Jikora started sneaking up the stairs; he wanted to surprise the twins. When he got to their room, he silently opened the door.

"Surprise!" he said, but there was no response. His eyes fell on the bed and he could see that they were sleeping under the blanket. He dropped the gifts on the table beside him and tip-toed to the bed. He grabbed the blanket and gradually, he pulled it away. Oblivious of his presence, the twins slept on. Jeta was on a pair of boxer shorts, and Neta, on a pink nightgown, lay beside him with her head placed on his bare chest. Jikora put out his hand to wake them but changed his mind and left the room.

WHENEVER THE TWINS were home, Jikora insisted the family eat together during weekends, so the next morning, they—Jikora, Edna, Jeta and Neta—were having a breakfast of sandwiches and tea in the dining room. They were eating and chatting. Neta seemed uninterested in the conversation as she tried to eat and, at the same time, read Dorothy Wimbush's *Professor Q's Secret*, one of the books her father had bought for her.

"Neta," Edna called. "Please, put that book away. You can continue when you are through with breakfast."

Neta glanced at Jikora, as if she expected him to say, *come on, let the girl read*. Jikora didn't. Instead he smiled and drank from his teacup. But he spoke when she dog-eared the page she was on: "Why are you folding the page?"

"So I can easily go back to where I am." She closed the book and put it aside.

"Then get a bookmark or memorise the page number."

"Memorise?" Jeta asked in disagreement. "That is stressful."

"That's what I do," Jikora said with a playful grin.

"Daddy!" Neta called, disbelief ringing in her voice. "Take it easy."

Jikora shook his head and turned to his wife. "Tell them," he said. "These kids never believe anything these days. They think my brain is too old to memorise a page number, when I had already started dealing with numbers in banking operations before they were born."

Edna pulled her cup away from her mouth to burst into

laughter, and the twins joined her. Jikora shook his head again. "You all gang up against me," he said. "I'm the man of this house." They laughed more and ate for a while in silence.

Jikora raised a sandwich to take a bite, but paused midway, his eyes fixed on the twins as they whispered, giggling and falling on each other's shoulder. It took him about three seconds and a touch on the shoulder from his wife to realise that she had called him 'Honey' twice.

"Yes, love," he responded, looking at Edna.

"Eat your bread," she said with an almost commanding tone. "OK," Jikora said with a nod and took a bite.

"Mum, would you be making vegetable soup anytime soon?" Jeta asked.

"Aunty Chidinma will make that for you next weekend," Edna said.

"Is Aunty Chidinma coming?"

Edna turned to Jikora. "Chidinma called," she told him. "She said she will be coming to The Island to spend next weekend with us."

"Aunty Chidinma is really coming?" Neta asked. "Will she come with Small Ben and Samantha?"

Edna smiled to the twins. "Yes," she said. "She is coming to spend next weekend with us, with her children."

The demands of their banking jobs only meant that Jikora and Edna had little time to spend with the twins as they grew. So as babies, until they got into secondary school, it was Edna's cousin, Aunty Chidinma, that took care of them. Aunty Chidinma and the twins shared a special bond. She was good to them and they loved her. Growing up, they preferred spending time with her than their parents. She was a big sister, treating them with love and kindness. Edna and Jikora were totally comfortable with Chidinma. But on Sundays, Edna made sure she prepared the food herself; she had a small fear that her husband would get used to Chidinma's cooking and prefer it to hers. On such days, she would take charge of the kitchen, allowing Chidinma to help with things that required little culinary skills. She would say, "Chidinma, help me pound the crayfish and pepper. Cut the vegetables for me. Fetch me some water. Wash off the mortar and pestle." She would call Chidinma and teach her basic things about cooking. Although Chidinma already knew what she taught, she would nod, as if she understood Edna needed to prove that her absence from the kitchen did not mean she had become a lousy cook. Many a times, she would dip a cooking spoon into the pot of soup, hit the head of the spoon on her palm and lick it, closing her eyes and nodding, as if to derive optimum savour. She would call Chidinma and say, "*Ngwa*, bring your hand". When she did, she gave her some to taste as well. As Chidinma licked the soup off her palm, she would smile at Edna and say, "Agadi nwanyi anaghi aka nka n'egwu oma agba: An old woman is never too old to perform a dance she had mastered in her youth." This, Chidinma knew, boosted Edna's confidence.

As the family gathered to eat, Edna would boil with eagerness to hear Jikora's comment. She would push him to comment if he didn't say anything: "Is the pepper too much?"

Jikora would shake his head and say, "Just the right amount, my love. This food is delicious."

That was all Edna needed to hear, but Jikora yearned for Chidinma's food.

Then came Benjamin Nwakire, Big Ben. A wealthy businessman in Alaba International Market. Big Ben was from Agulu in Anambra State, and so was Chidinma. He travelled to the village to meet Chidinma's parents.

"The first time I set my eyes on her, I knew she was going to be my wife," he said of Chidinma. "But she was still a small girl, so I waited for her to come of age before doing the proper thing." Chidinma's parents gave Ben the permission to visit Jikora and Edna when he returned to Lagos. Chidinma's father also wrote to Edna in very few words:

> *A suitor for Chidinma will be visiting you soon. His name is Big Ben, and he is from our village. We like him, and we know he can take care of our daughter. When he comes, please receive him and allow him talk to Chidinma. Assess him and give us a feedback.*

When Edna read the letter, she smiled at the words, "we know he can take care of our daughter". She knew it was a righteous way of saying, "He is rich!" When she introduced Jikora to her parents before they got married, her mother had taken her to a corner and whispered: "Hope he can take care of you?" Even then she understood that what her mother really meant was: "Hope he has money?"

So when Big Ben visited two weeks after Chidinma's father wrote, he looked no different from what Edna had expected: rich and ostentatious. Edna had always had a firm contempt for Igbo businessmen with little or no education. She always thought them crass, brash, arrogant and boastful. She had once complained to Jikora: "They always try to make points that don't make sense and expect you to listen and agree with them because they have money. They are always quick to say 'My business. My money.' They are so arrogant. I turned down dozens of them, before we met."

But when Big Ben walked into their house—although everything about him, from his name to his appearance, spoke of the typical Igbo businessman Edna had in her head—he was different. He listened and talked calmly. When they all sat at the dining table to eat, Edna invited Chidinma to join them. Edna asked prying questions to get Big Ben to prove her feelings about Igbo businessmen right, but he kept surprising her. She asked him about his business, but instead of talking about how much money his business made for him, he said, "We are trying. God is in control." And when he learnt they were bankers, he talked about his "excellent account officer", and not about how much money he had in the banks or about how bankers pestered him daily to open accounts with them. He surprised Edna to the point of exasperation. He even said "excuse me" when he burped. When Jikora noticed what Edna had been trying to achieve, he tapped her knee under the table to make her stop. Edna then allowed Jikora do the talking. She just watched Big Ben with undistracted interest and a consciously fortified nose to discover whatever she was missing, but all she could see was the stealthy manner with which he stole glances at Chidinma. When there was nothing to notice, Edna began to find fault in his grammar; how he coined a word from two similar ones—how he said *prettiful* instead of saying *pretty* or *beautiful*, how he said, "This food is *nouritous*," instead of either *nourishing* or *nutritious*.

After the meal, Jikora and Edna allowed him some minutes to talk to Chidinma alone.

In the room, Jikora asked his wife, "What were you trying to do out there?"

Edna replied, "He is making conscious efforts to hide things.

They are always hiding things."

"Well, I like the man. Give him a break." "He is too old."

"He is just 32. I have three years on him."

"Well, you already have kids nearing their teens, and Chidinma just turned eighteen. The age gap is too wide."

Edna gave up the fight when Big Ben left and Chidinma said she liked him with a smile on her face. Chidinma's parents liked Ben, Chidinma liked Ben, and Jikora liked Ben. Edna knew she had to like Ben too. So, she picked up a pen and wrote to her uncle, Chidinma's father.

Ben is a good man, and we believe he will make a good husband for Chidinma.

And he did, at least for the past five years. They had been married and blessed with two children. Big Ben adored Chidinma. He opened a boutique for her in Surulere and bought her a car. Though she visited them in Lekki occasionally, Edna missed Chidinma's presence in the house. It was after Chidinma got married that they decided to send Jeta and Neta to a boarding school where they could grow with other children.

"Is she coming with the kids?" Jeta asked, repeating Neta's question.

"Yes, she is," Edna answered. "I already told you."

"I can't believe Aunty Chidinma is coming," Neta said excitedly and threw herself at Jeta who put his arms around her, and they remained in a hug. Jikora's eyes narrowed with the same curiosity he had watched them with all morning. He was not sure what bothered him, he was not sure what he was curious about, but he was sure that he wanted them separated at that point.

"Chukwunetam," he called Neta. And they broke the hug. "Get your food, and come sit by me." He tapped the empty seat by his right. Neta obeyed and took the seat by his side. "How are your eyes?"

"They aren't fine, Dad. In school, I still struggle to see the board.

When would my glasses be ready?"

"They are ready," Jikora said, enjoying the excitement that appeared on Neta's face.

"Where are they?"

Jikora snapped his fingers at Jeta. "Go to my room and bring me the red bag on top of the table. Don't look in, just bring it."

Jeta left and reappeared with the bag and handed it over to Jikora with a coy smile that showed he had looked. "He got you a toy," he mocked Neta. "Are you a baby?"

Neta quickly dipped her hand inside the bag and brought out a snow globe. Her eyes widened in excitement.

It had the image of a father reading to his daughter seated on his lap as they were adorned by a depiction of falling snow. "This is beautiful. What is it called, Dad?"

"A toy," Jeta quipped through a stifled laughter.

Edna reached for Jeta's right ear and pulled it, causing him to yelp. "Coconut head." She turned to Neta. "It's a snow globe."

"A snow globe," Neta said, nodding. "Snow globe." She turned to Jikora. "And this is you." She pointed at the man in the globe. "This is you reading to me."

Jikora nodded. "That is me reading to you." He dipped his hand into the bag and brought out a glass case. "Now try your glasses."

Neta put on the glasses and dashed off to look in the mirror.

After breakfast, in their room, Edna asked Jikora, "Is anything the problem?"

"What are you talking about?" Jikora said.

"I don't like the way you look at the twins these days," she said plainly.

"Nothing is the problem, love," Jikora said and went into the bathroom.

The next day, Jikora watched from the balcony as Jeta and Neta chatted under a shade in the compound, smiling, hugging and holding hands. He walked into the living room where his wife sat in front of the TV, watching Pastor Chris Oyakhilome preach to his congregation. He sat next to her and said, "We have empty rooms in this house. Why are the kids still sharing one?"

Edna took her eyes away from the TV and looked at

Jikora as though he just asked the most ridiculous question. "I don't understand you."

"We are under-using rooms, and it doesn't make sense. Let's put the children in different rooms."

Edna picked up the remote control from the table and lowered the volume of the TV. "This isn't about the rooms," she said. "What are you worried about?"

Jikora was quiet for a few seconds before he spoke. "I think…I think they are too close."

"This is ridiculous, they are twins," Edna said. "Is there anything wrong in them being *too close*?"

Jikora started to speak but struggled to find the right words. "Forget it," he said finally.

CHIDINMA'S CHILDREN WERE a source of mixed emotions for Edna. Their presence brought memories of her own twins when they were little, how they played with abandon. But whenever she carried Chidinma's one-year-old son, Ben Jr., Small Ben, as Neta called him, the smell of his hair, the delicacy of his skin, and the innocence in his smile reminded her of the babies she was willing to have but could not. And with that came a sting. Samantha, four, was pretty, but played like a boy. If Chidinma complained to Edna about Samantha's boyish nature, Edna would say, "It is something she would outgrow, don't worry."

A couple of years after she had her twins, Edna became pregnant again, but her joy was short-lived as the pregnancy ended through a miscarriage which the doctor claimed was as a result of work-related stress. She had hoped she would be pregnant yet again, but that didn't happen, even as the doctor insisted that nothing was wrong with either of them. So they prayed, waited and had sex, but the babies never came. It took them several years of frustration to accept the truth that Jeta and Neta were going to be their only children.

"What are we doing?" Jikora had asked. "We already have wonderful kids; there is absolutely no need to keep pressuring ourselves."

On that day, twelve years ago, Edna sat on the kitchen chair with Small Ben on her laps, as she chatted with Chidinma who prepared dinner. Small Ben attempted to wriggle out of Edna's hold.

"He wants to join his people in the room," Chidinma said, pouring some liquid spices inside the cooking pot. By 'his people', she meant Samantha, Neta and Jeta.

Edna dropped Small Ben to his feet and he started toddling away, towards the kitchen door. "Tell Jeta to give you some biscuits," Edna said to him. He nodded and walked away without looking back.

Edna turned her attention back to Chidinma. "You have lovely kids." Chidinma smiled, stirring the soup. "I have never met kids as lovely as Neta and Jeta," she said. "I just want my children to be like them. You are a great mother, Sister. You did a great job in raising them."

There was a smile on Edna's face. It was a source of pride to her, whenever people referred to her as 'a great mother'. She had been able to combine her career and the responsibility of motherhood quite well, she liked to think. "Your contribution in their lives was immense. I am sure you are well aware of that," she said to Chidinma.

Chidinma sat on the seat beside Edna, dropping a tray

of oranges and a kitchen knife on top of a stool. "And I remain grateful to you for trusting me." She took one of the oranges and started peeling it. "Thank you, for giving me the chance to be part of their lives."

"I couldn't have trusted anybody else. You are like a sister to me."

"Thank you," Chidinma said, squinting to prevent the orange peel liquid from squirting into her eyes.

"Tell me, how many babies do you want to have? Have you and Big Ben talked about it?"

"Big Ben? That one wants to have five. Sister, I told him without mincing words: After this baby I am carrying, that is it. I am not having more than three children."

Edna's eyes narrowed. "Are you pregnant again?"

Chidinma cut the skinned orange open and extended it to Edna. "Yes, I am. I was going to tell you."

Edna took the orange with her left hand, taking Chidinma's hand in her right. "How many months?"

"Two, Sister."

"I am so happy for you, Chi-Chi."

Chidinma was blessed; she could have a baby anytime she wanted to. All she had to do was go to bed with her husband. "Congratulations."

"Thank you, Sister." She took another orange from the tray and started peeling.

Edna sucked from her orange and spat out seeds into her hand. "You know, sooner or later, you will need a help that will take care of the kids as you go about your business."

"God forbid!" Chidinma said, shaking her head. "I don't trust all these housemaids. I don't want anybody spoiling my kids. I will take care of my children myself. I will combine it with running the boutique; it is not that demanding. Ben suggested the same thing and I told him *no* straight away. Housemaids are evil."

It made Edna feel grateful, once again, that she did not have headaches about "evil housemaids". For her and her kids, it had been Chidinma all the way. She had peace of mind, knowing that her kids were with Chidinma. When she got married to Big Ben, and the children were sent off to boarding school, Madam T was employed as a non-live-in help whose responsibility was just to clean the house and make food.

"I understand," Edna said, nodding her head and sucking more juice from the orange.

Chidinma finished peeling the orange she was holding, dropped it back in the tray, and stood up to check the pot she placed on the burner.

"Where is this girl? Chukwunetam!" Edna called.

Neta quickly appeared in the kitchen, standing by the doorway with a look of a criminal awaiting verdict. "Yes, Mummy."

"What are you doing in the room?"

"Nothing," said Neta. "I'm just relaxing with Jeta and the children."

"You are relaxing? Stay here with me and your Aunty."

"Sister, let her be," Chidinma intervened. "Neta, you can go.

The soup will be ready in no time."

Neta glanced at her mother, like she sought her permission to leave the kitchen. Edna looked away, took the orange Chidinma had dropped in the tray and cut it open. Neta snuck back to the room.

"She is growing into a pretty woman, you know that," Chidinma said, covering the cooking pot. "Just like her mother."

Edna chuckled and shook her head. "Are twins not meant to be close?" she asked, sucking the orange.

Chidinma retook her seat and picked the last orange. "Of course, they are. That's why they are twins. Why do you ask?"

Edna sighed. "It's my husband," she said, her words decelerated. "He is worried about them being too close. He wants them to have separate rooms now."

Chidinma was still for some seconds, the orange and the knife in her hands. "Why?" she asked.

"I have no idea, Chidinma." Edna's voice had dropped to a whisper, but it was yet heavy with concern. "When he looks at them, there's this strange look I see. I can't explain it, and it scares me. I have been seeing it for a while, but it is getting worse now."

Chidinma started peeling the orange again. "You worry too much, Sister. Maybe he is just stressed out at work." She cut the orange in half. "He will be fine," she said, extending one half of the orange to Edna, not minding that she had not finished eating the one she had.

5

Are you sure he is going to like this hair?" Biodun asked, dressing her new braids at the mirror.

Ginika stood up from the bed. "I'm telling you, the hair is amazing, but you need to stop worrying about this man. He is old enough to be your father."

Biodun held her braids together. "And you think I have not tried?" She put on a hairband. "Ginika, I have tried."

"He is distracting you."

"From what?" Biodun asked, now on the bed.

"From Tunde, of course. You are going to lose him over someone you will never have."

Biodun sighed. "I just can't get him off my mind." "But he doesn't know how you feel!"

There was a little silence before Biodun spoke again: "Ginika, I need your advice. Please tell me what to do. I feel like I'm going insane."

"Shut up," Ginika said in a low tone and joined her on the bed. "You are my best friend, Biodun, and I would always tell you the truth. You must forget this man. You and Tunde were such a wonderful couple in school. People would kill to have what you guys had."

"That was school," Biodun said firmly. "We need to grow up." "And you think developing a crush on an older man who doesn't know you exist is growing up?"

"He knows I exist," Biodun said quickly, as if making that point would change Ginika's thinking.

"You are wasting your time. We all had crushes. Remember Corper Mike in secondary school. Then I used to dream we would be husband and wife. But all the feelings died once he finished his Youth Service and left."

Biodun smiled. "You cried for a week. Every night, you cried." "And you consoled me. Thank you."

"You have already thanked me enough over the years. And besides, who wouldn't understand? Corper Mike was hot."

"The reason I failed chemistry that whole year. I never listened in class as he taught. I just stared at the movement of his lips." She looked into Biodun's eyes. "But that was then. You can't be doing this now."

Biodun shook her head. "This is different. I think I'm in love with him."

Ginika did not intend to, but she laughed. "I said the same thing about Mike."

"Mike's case was different. You were a teenager, naïve and eager to explore, and live things you were feeling for the first time. I'm an adult now. I have had boyfriends. I understand feelings now, and I'm telling you, I love this man."

"It is going nowhere. What exactly do you want from him?

Marry him?"

"I just want him."

"He is married. Don't pursue this, you will embarrass yourself. Yes, I was a teenager then, but this is no different from my case with Corper Mike. And it is going to end the way all crushes do. The crush never cares. Even when he does find out, he is going to call you and counsel you like a little girl or ignore you…" She looked away. "…the way Mike ignored my letter."

"You wrote Mike a letter?" Biodun asked, surprised.

"Yes, I did," Ginika said, scratching her hair theatrically. "The day he left, I sent a letter to him and poured my heart out. I told him exactly how I felt and begged him to write me back from wherever he would end up."

"I'm guessing he did not."

"Of course, he didn't. He saw me as a small girl, a little sister. I was just a stupid girl."

"That is the point! I am not a small girl." Biodun jiggled her breasts with her hands. "I have all it takes to be his woman. Jikora would want me."

"He would want to have sex with you! See wetin you carry for your back, see your chest. He would sleep with you but not take you seriously. Chop and clean mouth. We are going for NYSC next month. Please complete this final month and leave with your dignity. Don't embarrass yourself. Or is it just sex you want with him?"

She winked.

"Leave me *jor*." With that, Biodun walked out of the room. "Chei!" Ginika screamed. "Ikebe Super! See what you want to give that old man on a platter of gold."

"He is not an old man," Biodun said from the door.

MR NITTIN WAS one of the reasons Edna wanted to quit banking. In all her years in banking, he was by far the most difficult customer she had managed. He was stubborn and demanding. Each time he needed something, he wanted it attended to in record time and never expressed any form of gratitude. He was a *special* customer. One of those who, at the slightest failure to meet his demands, threatened to close his accounts with the bank.

But he was an important customer. His companies brought good business to the bank and presented them with an attractive source of free, investable funds. He knew this and used it to his advantage. As a result, the bank needed someone to manage his fickleness and ensure it did not slip into irreversible disloyalty. They needed someone to coax him when he had second thoughts about doing business with them. They needed someone to placate him when he threw tantrums about delayed cheque book delivery. They needed someone to schmooze him when he threatened to close his accounts because of delayed fund transfers. Edna was that *someone*. Unfortunately. He would shout at her and insult her. She hid her thoughts behind a fake, professional smile.

Once, he told her, "You are a lazy banker. Very, very lazy. I will close my account because of you." Then, he called her stupid, and her wall cracked. He did not call her stupid exactly, but that was her interpretation of it. It was her chance to release a smidgen of her accumulated irritation.

"Why did you do something so stupid?" he said. "That's it, I am closing my account."

In a spur-of-the-moment reaction, she had talked back

at him. "I need you to close your account today," she said calmly. "I keep going out of my way to please you. We keep cutting corners, making special provisions for you, trying to keep you happy, but you don't appreciate any of it. You must close your account today and look for another bank that can give you what it is you are looking for, because I don't have it, and neither does Lead Bank." She could see the shock on his face, his mouth slightly open, his teeth clenched like those of a dog that really wanted to bite back but was too afraid to do so. But Edna was not done. "And the next time you refer to me as stupid..." She left the words hanging, took her eyes away from him and started writing in her journal, expecting to hear him—with his fragmented English—say something, voice more abuses maybe. But he did not say anything. He sat still for a while, then stood up and left her office. So Edna was surprised when he called her and said jovially, "Edna, please, I need you to stop by my office today." She wondered what he was up to. But when she got to his office, he was friendly, acting as if nothing happened. Instead of complaining about banking services, he chose informal discussions about Nigerian foods, the ones he had tasted and the ones he would never try. Then he talked about his family in Maharashtra, his wife and young daughter, about Hinduism and the caste system. For the most part of their conversation, Edna did not say anything. She listened, her smile tight. She was not used to having casual conversations with him. Her relationship with him had been strictly professional. She did not understand why he was friendly, when she expected him to be upset. "Why did you invite me over, sir?" she asked politely when he ordered his secretary to make her coffee. "Is there something we can do for you?"

"I am sorry," he said, drumming his fingers on his desk. "For yesterday, I am sorry. I will never say stupid to you again."

Edna did not respond. The repulsive, impudent Nittin had become warm and silken. She did not understand how this was possible.

"It's okay, sir," she said. "I am sorry I talked back at you. I did not intend disrespect."

He threw his hand in the air. "I have a cheque for you," he said.

Edna left his office, happy like a child who just stepped out of a birthday party with a pocketful of lollipops. She hoped this new Nittin would live past that day.

Before she got to where her car was parked, a call came in. She picked it, thinking it was someone from the office or another customer.

"Madam, na me."

It was Madam T's voice. From the noise in the background, she knew Madam T was calling from a local phone centre, her voice hurried to avoid spending more time and paying more.

"What is the problem, Tolu?" Edna asked. She knew there was one whenever Madam T spoke pidgin. "And why didn't you call me with the phone at home?"

"I no go work today, ma." Madam T was speaking very loudly. "You are shouting, Tolu," Edna said. "Why are you not in the house?"

"My pikin get Malaria, ma. I dey take care of am. But I go come tomorrow afternoon."

"Are you saying that no food was made for Jeta and Neta? They have not had lunch?"

"Madam, I call them. Small stew remain for fridge. I tell Neta make she boil small rice. That one go do them for lunch."

Edna heaved a sigh. "Carry your pikin go hospital, you hear?" It was only Madam T that made her speak pidgin.

"I hear, ma." There was a drag in her voice and Edna knew she wouldn't visit any hospital. She would not waste money when she could easily get cheap malaria drugs from a local pharmacist.

Edna sighed again when Madam T hung up. Madam T not coming in meant work for her. She had to prepare dinner when she got home. She glanced at her watch; it was past four. She decided against returning to the office. She would drive home and start making dinner immediately. She dialled her office.

BIODUN LOOKED INTO the tote bag like she did not already know its content. She wondered if Jikora would like the white office shirt. From under her computer keyboard, she slid out a neatly folded piece of paper and dropped it in the bag. She hadn't told Ginika of her plans. It was her last month as a receptionist. She did not want to spend the rest of the year wondering what would have happened if she had overcome her fears and be open with Jikora. So, she bought him a shirt and—knowing that she might not be bold enough to use words from her mouth—wrote him a letter, just as Ginika did Corper Mike.

She brought out a small hand mirror and looked in it, praying that Jikora would see her as beautiful as her reflection suggested. She had made her braids into a bun and blushed her cheeks. In recent months, because of Jikora, she spent her salaries buying new clothes and shoes. She revealed a little cleavage and made her gowns tighter, so that her curves would shock Jikora's senses whenever he saw her. When her boyfriend, Tunde, complained about her sudden vainness, she told him nonchalantly, "Every woman is vain." Her attraction towards Tunde was beginning to thin. She found many reasons not to be with him. Suddenly, she did not like the way he kissed her, she did not like the way he snored when she slept beside him. These were habits that were never an issue for her, until she developed whatever it was that she felt for Jikora. When Tunde touched her, she imagined it was Jikora. She wanted to go on dates with Jikora. She wanted to be alone in a room with him.

It was time for her to make her move, before Jikora left for one of his meetings. She replaced the mirror and, reaching for the letter once again, she had a final thought about it.

The idea of a letter is not stupid, it is not childish, she tried to tell herself. It would be awkward walking into his office to blab about love and attraction; she did not have enough courage for that. So she sighed and walked to the door of his office, tapping at it and waiting for a response.

"Yes?" she heard him say. She took a deep breath before walking in, a smile on her face. "Biodun." He raised his face from his computer screen.

"Good afternoon, sir," she greeted.

"Good afternoon. Is someone here to see me?"

"No, sir," Biodun said. She was making a great deal of effort to stay calm, to prevent her voice from breaking. "I am here to see you, sir."

"Please, sit," Jikora said, and watched her sit. He noticed the bag in her hand. "What is it you have in the bag?"

"It is for you, sir." She wished she could talk to him without having to include the word 'sir' in every sentence. She dropped the bag on the table.

Jikora moved the bag closer and took a peep. "A shirt," he said and smiled. "Why would you get me a shirt?"

The smile on her face was steady and unnatural, like that of a model posing for an uncomfortable photo shoot. "To say thank you." "Why would you say thank you to me?" His voice was friendly, but curious.

"This is my last month here, sir. I am leaving for NYSC."

Jikora tilted his head backwards. "I see. But you did not have to spend your little money to buy this for me. I do not know what I did to deserve this."

"It's nothing, sir. You are a good man. You have been good to me."

Jikora thought for a while. He did not know if it was right to reject the gift. "Biodun, before I leave the office today, come meet me. I will refund you the amount you spent getting this shirt for me. I appreciate the gesture, but I will give you the money back."

Biodun shook her head. "I don't need the money, sir."

Jikora nodded and smiled. "Well, thank you. You have

done well." There was a line of seriousness in his voice. "But make sure you see me before you leave today, okay?"

She gave a light shrug and stood up to leave. "Thank you, sir." "I should be the one saying that."

As she walked towards the door, she tried to exaggerate the movement of her hips, for Jikora to feed his eyes on what he was missing, if he was interested. When she heard him call her, she paused, thinking he had already found the letter. "Yes, sir," she said, turning to her side.

He was quiet for a few seconds. "You look very beautiful today," he said carefully.

Her smile, this time, came naturally.

"Thank you," she said and left his office.

SHOOTINGS FROM AN action movie scene was the only sign of human presence when Edna walked into the house. She wondered why her children left the TV on when they were not watching it. She placed the plastic bag of foodstuffs and her handbag on the centre table and turned the TV off. She dropped the bag in the kitchen and headed upstairs, her fingers unbuttoning her shirt. She changed into a loose blue gown and removed her jewelry, placing them in a box. The memory of her visit to Nittin's office still left a good feeling; she found herself humming a song. She left her room and started walking towards her children's room to check on them—to reprimand them for leaving the TV on—before cooking dinner.

She grabbed the doorknob and pushed the door open. "Chukwujetalum—"

She froze. Her children sprang from the bed, clumsily

picking up their clothes from the floor and forcing their limbs through. She hoped what she had just seen was a dream.

I AM NOT sure this is exactly the right way to do this. But it's all I have got, my only voice. The only problem is: I don't think it would come close to expressing, to the right extent, what I feel for you. Countless times, I have seen you when I close my eyes to sleep. I have imagined your touch. My breath ceases when I am in your presence, I can't help it. You are a source of happiness to me, but there is sadness in my heart, knowing that I cannot be with you. All this sounds desperate, I know. But the truth is: I don't even know what I am desperate for. It is certainly not to be with you in the way I want. I'm trying to come to terms with the truth that it won't be possible. Maybe I just needed to pour out my heart to you, to let you know how I really feel.

I apologise if my letter offends you, I don't mean any disrespect to your marriage. It is just that when I am gone from here, it would be comforting to me knowing that you remember me as the young girl captivated by your warmness, your charm, rather than another receptionist. Every morning, I stand in front of the mirror longer than necessary. Every night I sleep, holding my pillow. It's like a part of me has been lost to yearning for you. I don't want to call this love, I am too scared to do that. But I know that it is something like it.

I might never get to have you, but I have a part of you; I have your smile. One sees me through two weeks, and I have received enough to last me a lifetime. That again is comforting.

Have a great life. I wish you all the best, you, your wife and children.
—Biodun

Jikora glanced over the letter, raising the corner of his mouth. It was not the first time a woman was declaring affection for him. It was almost like they did not care about his marital status, and that the ring on his finger had been nothing more than a meaningless band of metal. However, Jikora knew that it would be unfair to blame Biodun for feeling the things she had sincerely confessed in her letter. Her life was really just starting and she was still filled with dreams and the fire of youth. He also knew that she was a pretty and shapely young woman. She had breasts and hips that had always got in the line of his vision. He had always looked away and did not think much about it.

He shook his head when he realised he was actually plunging deep in thoughts about her. He had never cheated on his wife and would not do it with Biodun. He sat, trying to figure out the best approach to handle this, whether to have a brief conversation with her about the letter and tell her that he was not what she needed at this time, that what she needed was someone her age, someone who would love her and have time to give her the required attention, or to ignore her and act like nothing had happened and he had not seen any letter. He had not made up his mind when his phone rang. He opened his desk drawer and brought out his Motorola cell phone. It was an incoming call from home. He immediately flipped it open, expecting to hear Neta's voice, reminding him to visit the bookshop for a book he had promised her, Helon Habila's *Waiting for an Angel*.

"I need you home right now." It was his wife's voice instead.

It was commanding, and it was serious.

"Calm down, Honey," he tried to speak calmly. "Is everything okay?"

"No, nothing is okay." Her voice shook this time, like she was trying to hold back tears. "I now understand your fears."

"What fears?"

"I need you to stop me. If you don't get home now, you will meet three corpses when you eventually do. I will kill our children, then hang myself." She hung up.

Jikora quickly stood and frisked himself down for his car key. He dashed out of his office, through the reception, zapping past Biodun like she was not there. She got on her feet and watched him from the glass door as he entered his car and drove off.

EDNA SWUNG HER arm to slap Jeta across the face, but he tried to duck away and her elbow caught his face. He squatted, holding his face. She knew she had hurt him, but she did not care. To hurt him was exactly what she wanted. She was too disappointed, too angry. She descended on him, slapping and landing blows, while Neta stood by the corner of the room, shivering and whimpering.

"You," Edna said, pointing at Neta, moving away from Jeta who quickly got to his feet. "For how long?" She started walking towards her.

"I am, sorry, Mummy," Neta blubbered.

Edna grabbed her arm, pulled her closer and slapped her back. "Answer my question, you stupid girl!" She kept raising her fist without striking, making Neta flinch. There was something in her subconscious that restrained her. She would kill her if she continued hitting her. "I am disappointed in you." She left her and attacked Jeta again. She needed a physical expression of the rage that had encapsulated her, and Jeta was the right victim. He did not beg like his sister. All he did was cringe and try dodging her flailing hands.

She hit him with whatever energy she had in her, but still felt she did not hit hard enough. She was acting like a madwoman. Never in her life had she thought that, after fourteen years, she would be hitting her twins for the first time; her sweet babies.

She soon got tired and pulled away, dropping on the bed, gasping for air and talking at the same time. "You children have killed me." She put her hands on her head. "You have killed me."

"Sorry, Mummy," Neta said, her voice apologetic, and her eyes teary. "It won't happen again."

"Sorry for what?" Neta's words annoyed her and gave her a fresh energy. She stood up and swung her arm at her, but Neta stepped back and avoided it. She moved closer to her and slapped her face. Then turned to Jeta again and smacked him a couple more times. Neta's apologies infuriated her, but Jeta's silence did worse; it filled her with rage. She turned to Neta.

"So you are no longer a virgin? You allowed your brother touch you?"

Neta did not answer her question. It broke her heart that it was *really* true. They had gone all the way, under her roof and under her nose. She sat back on the bed, feeling that her world had crumbled. "Your father will come home and meet us here."

She sat on the bed, shuddering, shaking her head and snapping her fingers, waiting for her husband to come home. She had nothing else to do to them; it was beyond her. She felt powerless and ashamed. She had a lot of questions to ask them, but all she could do was stare at them in wonder.

Twenty minutes later, she picked up the phone to call her husband again. It rang through the first time and nobody picked. So she dialled again. "Jikora, pick up!" she screamed.

"Hello," a gruff voice answered. "Na who be this?"

She withdrew the phone from her ear to be sure she had dialled the correct number. "Who are you?" she asked. "Where is my husband?"

"Okay, na you be the wife?"

"Please, hand the phone over to the owner, my husband." Frustration was evident in her tone.

"Madam, accident happened in VI."

Edna dropped her phone. Her world had really crumbled.

6

These days, Neta did not know how to feel about book readings, her own book readings. It was okay when she was not a published writer. Then she could attend readings of authors she admired, take a backseat and enjoy the peace that came with them. Whenever it was time to ask questions, she never raised a hand; she never said anything. It was easier and more relaxing to just listen to the answers writers gave to questions asked by other people from the audience. It always fascinated her how incredibly humble the writers she met were and how, somehow, they always knew how to say things that seemed and sounded right.

It was this fascination with the modesty and radiant expressiveness of writers that formed a halo of nervousness around her at her own readings. She had been to readings of, and met, some writers like Teju Cole, Chika Unigwe, Eghosa Imasuen, A. Igoni Barrett and Binyavanga Wainaina.

Often, she would attempt to shrug it off, look herself in the mirror and mutter self-assuring words: "You are awesome. Keep being you". But it was always a different story whenever she took a seat in front of an audience to read and discuss her book.

The actual readings did not bother her. All she needed to do was create a world, her own world, barricaded by her words and allow herself to be lost in the freedom of the sound of her voice. Though she knew little about Islam, she had concluded that the liberating depth that came with her words when she read from her book was akin to what muezzins describe as their feeling while calling for worship.

It was the questions that came after the readings that always ruptured the bubble. She felt the pressure to say the right things, pressure not to bore people. Although she understood that people who went for book readings were largely people like herself, people with somewhat distorted idea of what boredom really meant, she also knew that too much of anything—whether enjoyable or not—could have unpleasant effects. Her friend, Esther, having followed her, years ago, to listen to Eghosa Imasuen read from his second novel, *Fine Boys*, struggled to understand how it was possible for people to derive pleasure from attending author readings. She had once called it "the most pathetic and mentally-draining activity one can engage in". And then she called it "an incredibly boring gathering of people with dead social lives". Before she had agreed to go with her to see Imasuen, Esther had asked with irrepressible wonder in her voice: "You mean you would just sit and listen to some nerd on glasses read from a book containing made-up stories?"

"That is not the only thing readings are about," Neta had responded. "And it is not all writers that wear glasses. Eghosa Imasuen does not wear glasses."

"What else are they about?"

"There's questions and answers. Book signings and pictures.

Personal discussions with the writers."

"And how are these fun?" Esther had asked, defiant bemusement written on her face.

Neta later made up her mind to stop discussing literature and books with Esther. She would never understand the beauty of words when made into art and how that art lifted the spirits of people like her.

After her actual reading at Terra Kulture, she sat at the stage, facing Fabian Dani-Moore, an upcoming spoken-word artist and freelance copyeditor, who served as the anchor for the day. Dani- Moore was pointing out interested people from the audience to present their views and ask questions that Neta would entertain.

Neta was not entirely sure that she was giving appropriate answers to the questions being asked, but she noticed that a particular girl had developed so much interest in her book that she kept asking question after question. It made her impressed by her own story, by the attachment it seemed the girl had developed to the book.

The girl put up her hand again and stood to speak when Dani- Moore gave her a slight nod to proceed: "Neta," she called, her voice shaking with excitement. "I don't know why, but I feel that you are part of this story. The character, Ruth, has so much in common with you. Your description of her physical features could easily pass as a description of yourself. When she smiles, dimples form on her face, just like you. And to make it even more convincing, she wears glasses, just like you."

"But you have glasses on, as well," Neta quickly cut in, drawing low and short-lived giggles from the audience.

"Well, well." The girl pushed the bridge of the oval-shaped glasses she had on. "I can totally do without them. And the eye wires are not round like yours, like Ruth's." She sat down and ended her statement: "And when you described her temperament, I cannot help thinking it is you."

"How do you know my temperament?" Neta asked, this time, the smile she had transformed into a curious contortion of her face. She genuinely wanted to know what would make a stranger believe she knew her personality. She did not think she had become that transparent, that open to be read.

"Intuition," the girl responded with a shrug.

Neta soon found herself attempting to convince the audience that the book had nothing to do with her:

"Have you read Adichie's Americanah?" she asked Dani-Moore, and he nodded. "When people read Americanah, they concluded that through Ifemelu, Chimamanda was trying talk about herself. We wanted to believe that, I wanted to believe that. But in reality, I don't think she was writing about herself. Ifemelu is not her."

She took her attention to the girl where she was seated, cross- legged, face beaming with a grin. "I understand what you mean; I get these feelings too. When you write fiction, the truth is that at some point, the line between your story and reality breaks. To the writer, the story no longer feels like fiction; it begins to feel like a true story, a memoir of some sort, that only the writer witnessed, and is pressed to tell it. It is possible that as you write, a part of you falls off, into the pages. It could land on a passing subplot or on a character, but this does not necessarily mean that the character has become you. I guarantee you, one hundred percent, Ruth is not me. And *The Angel You Know* is absolutely a work of fiction."

Neta was just catching her breath when Dani-Moore pointed to a middle-aged woman sitting in the front row. Her hair was entirely grey. Not the traditional kind of grey that waffled, growing between black and white. It was the kind of decisive grey that knew what it wanted, that knew that it wanted to be white. To Neta, it was white hair, not grey—it was hair people associated with well-educated people and professors, like Wole Soyinka. But then again, there was Chekwa, Neta's late maternal uncle. He had white hair but had no formal education. He could not even spell his own name.

When the woman spoke, that age-long sentiment was confirmed. Her English sounded like a song, her pronunciations accurate and clear. "I love what your book teaches," the woman said. "It teaches about the two-sidedness of love. How love can build and destroy at the same time. How it can bring peace and heartbreaks, at the same time. It teaches a lot of lessons."

Neta smiled, rubbing her palms together.

"It is true, the things you say about love, very true. It feels good, whenever people pick out lessons from the book because I honestly did not write the book to teach anything. I once read an interview Christopher Okigbo granted in the sixties, and he said something very interesting. He said, *I do not have any function as a writer. I merely express myself, and people can use these things for whatever they like.* When I write, I just aim to express myself, to tell a story. But it is good that you have seen and pointed out lessons. It makes me proud. It makes me happy."

A hand went up once Dani-Moore asked if there were more questions and Neta nearly sighed in something resembling disbelief. It was the girl again, the excited one. "If you say this book…" She raised the copy she had. "… isn't about you, what then inspired you to write it?"

Neta drank from the glass of water resting on a wooden stool to her left. "You know, when people ask me, 'What inspires you?', I usually don't have an answer. Because as a writer, your sources of inspiration are countless. There is no single source. For me, I get my inspiration from anything and anywhere. I get inspired by the things I see. I get inspired by my own experiences and the experiences of others. I get inspired by the things I hear, by the things I smell. I get inspired by what I feel; by what I see other people feel. There are no limits, Sweetheart." She saw the girl's face light up and she knew it was because she had called her "Sweetheart".

"Would there be a sequel?" the girl asked.

"No." Neta drank more water and replaced the glass on the stool. "No sequel. That is the extent to which I know the story." Neta watched her as she grinned and nodded. "Do you write?"

The girl heaved a sigh, the smile on her face widening. "I try to write. I don't consider myself a writer yet, but a storyteller. I share stories about myself and my thoughts on Facebook and other online platforms. People say these stories are good, but I don't feel them myself. It is funny that I enjoy reading books so much, but when I write, my words lack the magical effect of good prose. Sometimes, I feel like I need to be guided."

"It is good you consider yourself a storyteller," Neta said to her. "This means that you know the kind of writer you want to be, so you have clarity. And you are still young. You have the two important things you need for this journey: youth and clarity. But storytelling is an art broader than those think pieces we post on Facebook. Do you understand?" The girl nodded and Neta continued. "Writing is my life, and the biggest thing it has taught me is that I am my own best teacher." Neta pointed at the girl. "You are your own best teacher. And reading is the first step. Since you know the kind of writer you want to be, then you know the kind of books you should be reading. Get and read as much as you can, fiction, creative non-fiction, poems. These are the works that beautify the art of writing. But this time, adopt another approach while reading them. Don't read them to enjoy them, don't read fast. Read to learn. Read to understand. Read to grow as a writer. The way you read these works should be different from the way others do. You need to understand that others are fun-seeking spectators in this game, but you are a student, learning the ropes. Read to learn. That is how I learnt, that is how I am still learning. Reading this way will answer a lot of questions about writing for you. Do you have any book you have started working on?"

The girl shook her head. "Not really," she said. "Nothing important enough to be mentioned."

"Start writing then. If you want to get published, start working on an actual book. Remember, it is the books that live forever, not the Facebook posts." Neta winked at her and she grinned. "You need to make writing a part of you. Let writing become what you cannot do without. And as you go on this journey, don't write whenever it is not flowing. Take your time, rest when you can. When it comes, take advantage. Don't rush your stories. Make use of your creative liberties. Play with your words, use your metaphors. Apply the things you learn from the books you read. You are still young, but let the fact that life is too short fuel you with a sense of urgency, to start telling those stories before whatever we are all doing here comes to an end."

"Thank you so much, Neta," the girl said, her eyes blinking in gratitude.

Neta had time to take more questions. Some about her book and characters in them, some about her personal life. She did not understand why people would come for a book reading and ask questions about things personal to the writer, things totally unrelated to either the writer's work or to literature. A man from the gathering, in his thirties, well-dressed, bearded and good-looking, asked her when she was getting married. The question was both unexpected and ridiculous, but she swallowed her feelings to say, "That is no discussion for today", hoping that her tone had not been as colourful as it would have been if she did not control herself.

But the man was not done yet. "Are you currently dating?"

It was then that Dani-Moore intervened. "I think we should not regress from the reason we are here. We need to take more questions about the book, *The Angel You Know*."

The man smiled and took his seat. There was an awkward aura about him, something that suggested he knew exactly what he was doing and was deliberately looking for trouble.

When the questions came to an official end, it was time for

book signings. Neta enjoyed this more than having to answer questions. It was easy, scribbling her signature on the front matter of a book; it was relaxing, even. At her first ever book reading, she just scrawled away her bland signature. Then her publishers told her that she had to make the signings more personal to the book owner. "These people make out time from their busy schedules to be here with you, to listen to you, to buy your book," they said. "Courtesy demands that you make the signing more personal to them. That is what all writers do; it is like a standard now." Then she started asking people for their names when they brought books for her to sign.

When the same girl who had bombarded her with a myriad of questions walked up to her, wearing an infectious smile and holding a copy of *The Angel You Know*, she said "Remind me your name, dear" as she stretched a hand for the book. The girl had said her name when she asked her first question, but Neta had forgotten.

"Arese," she said with a huge smile. Her excitement was so infectious that Neta could almost literally feel it as a current passing into her. Her glasses were of a more fashionable form and the colour was oxblood, to match the sling backs she had on. Neta could not tell if they were needed support to cover a defect, like hers, or just part of the efforts of a young woman making a fashion statement.

Arese, she wrote on the book. *May your life continue to shine, like hope made of gold, one that will bring all beautiful things your way*. And she signed.

As Arese received her book from Neta, she asked: "When I start working on my book, can I send chapters to you to review and comment?"

Neta smiled at her. "I would love to Arese, but it depends on how free I would be then. It is hard, but you need to also learn how to review and criticize your own works. Try to feel your own story. When you write a tragic scene, don't leave the page if it does not break your heart. When you write a sex scene, don't leave it until it turns you on." She watched Arese smile. "Review, criticize and rewrite."

"Okay," Arese said, fiddling with her cellphone. "Thank you, Neta. Please, can I get your number?"

"Of course," Neta replied and called out her number as Arese saved it on her phone. "Send me a text later so I can have yours."

"Anything else I should know?" It was obvious Arese did not want to leave yet.

Neta shrugged. "Learn how to stay away from your phone and how to turn off your internet. We are all getting addicted to our phones, aren't we? But you cannot finish any book if you don't have the discipline to stay away from your phone, except you are writing with it. I don't know if I have more to say. Just call me later. We shall talk more."

Then through smiles, Arese told her how excited she was to meet her, how *The Angel You Know* was the best work of fiction she had read in recent years, how the book spoke directly to her. Neta wanted to ask, 'how exactly did the book speak to you?' but she did not. At the time, she did not have the patience to prolong the discussion. There were others she needed to pay attention to. But before Arese left, she said something that warmed Neta's mind.

"You are the future of African literature," she said and

hugged Neta. The words did not make Neta smile, but the genuineness in Arese's voice did. The sheer weight of the title 'Future of African Literature', not Nigerian, made her head feel bigger and dizzy at the same time, it covered her like an over-sized coat.

"You are very generous," she responded. "Thank you."

It soon seemed she was through with the signings and interactions with people. She sat with Dani-Moore and two of her publishing editors, discussing the success of the reading and her recent nomination for the National Literature Prize. Then she noticed someone drop a book on the table in front of them, apparently asking for an autograph. Still talking to Dani-Moore, she dropped her hand on the book, without lifting her head to take a look at the man standing in front of her.

Then the man spoke: "Please, can you sign my book?"

Even before she looked up, she already knew whose voice it was. There stood Peter, wearing a smile she knew was not a smile. The smile on her own face immediately disappeared.

"Peter," she called, her voice crashing into a whisper, her eyes widening like she had seen a ghost.

"Neta," Peter responded. "Can you please sign my book?" "Sure." Neta reached for a pen resting on the table to her right and scribbled her signature. Handing the book over to Peter, she said: "Thank you for coming."

"I need a moment with you." Peter's voice almost sounded like a command, like Neta had no choice.

"Excuse me," Neta said to Dani-Moore, stood up and followed Peter to a corner of the hall.

"I need to see you, away from here," Peter spoke again.

"Not now, Peter. I am busy."

Peter spoke further, ignoring what Neta had just said. "There's an outdoor restaurant down the road. "Food Land, it is called. I would be there."

"Peter, I will be here for a while. And…"

"I will be waiting," Peter interrupted her. "Even if it is going to get to midnight, I would wait. And you would come see me."

The confidence in his voice made her heart thump. And as she watched him trudge out of the hall, like a hired killer who had just executed a job, she knew that she was going to see him.

Two hours. That was what it took for her to show up. Two quick hours that felt like just a quarter of it to Peter. He had not intended it as a joke when he said he was willing to stay till midnight. In fact, he was willing to stay beyond that. It was an indication to the level of patience he was willing to allocate to the possibility of seeing Neta. It was something close to desperation. Not the kind of desperation that made one's limbs shake, that caused unrestrained impatience, but the kind that compelled a conscious relaxation of the mind and body. He had waited and endured for six years; six years of yearning to see her. Two hours, or a little bit more, actually meant nothing. It was just like a drop of water into a river.

After he met the salesgirl at the pharmacy reading *The Angel You Know*, his life had not remained the same. He could remember having asked shamelessly: "Can you sell this book to me?" He could remember the incredulous look the girl gave him. "You could pay a visit to the bookstore," the girl had said. "I can recommend one and give you directions, if you want." Then she spoke further. "And she would be reading at Terra Kulture in a fortnight. You could go and pick up a copy there." Attending the reading sounded perfect to him. Neta would have no hiding place, after succeeding at cutting him off all these years.

As he sat, drinking fruit juice and intermittently picking groundnuts that the waiter had served in a silver goblet. The waiter had dropped a menu and had returned several times to take his order. Each time, his response was the same: "I will call you when I am ready." But when the waiter kept coming back every ten minutes like a programmed robot, Peter got frustrated. So when he spoke again to the waiter, he was as polite but firm. His tone betrayed his fragile patience.

"Alvan," he said. He had read the tag just abo breast pocket. "Please, don't come again until I call you." He smiled; the waiter returned the smile and walked away.

When he saw Neta walk in wearing a sleeveless Ankara gown, something happened to his heart. It was the same feeling from nine years before, when he first met her at a friend's birthday party in school. As it was then, he could not describe what he felt; his heart was either getting bigger or it was attempting to move to the right side of his chest.

After she pulled a seat to sit across to him, they sat in silence for a few seconds. Then Peter signalled to the waiter.

"What do you want to eat?" Peter asked.

Neta shrugged. "I am not sure I am hungry. I ate small chops at the reading."

"Well, the last time I checked, small chops wasn't food," Peter said. "What do you want to eat?"

Neta gave out a helpless sigh and looked up at the waiter. "Get me anything simple." She wagged her index finger at him.

"Small portion, please."

The waiter had a pen fixed on one spot on the notepad. Seeking precision, he suggested: "Something as simple as Jollof rice and goat meat?"

"Jollof rice and some greens," Neta said. "Fish. No goat meat."

"You should try our goat meat, ma," the waiter said. "It is peppered goat meat."

Neta shook her head. She did not understand how the mention of pepper was supposed to imply an improvement on goat meat. It reminded her of an episode with her friend, Esther. They had taken a cab to a spot in Lekki Phase One, where they sat next to the sea. Out of curiosity, Neta had ordered things on the menu she had never had before. First, she ordered Bloody Mary. Apart from the mirror-appearing legend, the only Bloody Mary she knew before then—from books she read in her secondary school library—was the former queen of England and daughter of Harry Tudor, King Henry VIII. She wanted to know why the drink was called Bloody Mary. When the drink came, she found it horrible, a bad concoction of blended tomatoes and vodka. Then she ordered something on the menu known as *Asun Toh Bad*, but soon understood that it was just goat meat with a *great* amount of pepper. Pepper that set her tongue on fire. And when the Bloody Mary drink was doing a terrible job at saving her tongue, she had gulped one full bottle of water. It had taken a while, and a full glass of yogurt, for the burning sensation to show mercy. That day, she learnt two lessons. One: Drink only familiar drinks. She was never going to try Bloody Mary again, or any drink that had 'Mary', or 'blood' or any other lexical compound that had the word as one of its parts, in its name. Two: Nothing good comes from excess pepper.

"Grilled fish, no goat meat," she said. "*Non-peppered* grilled fish." Peter ordered rice and stew with plantain and beef.

They sat through a six-year-old awkwardness and more silence before Peter spoke.

"You wrote a book. *The Angel You Know*, huh? You wrote a book." He paused, searching for a reaction. When she showed no emotion, he was compelled to speak further. "You wrote a book about us? You wrote a book about me?" His voice was now rising. "Who gave you the right to write about us?"

It was then that Neta spoke. "Peter, that book is a work of fiction."

"Bullshit!" Peter's right hand had clenched into a fist. "That was what you told that girl at the reading: 'I guarantee you a hundred percent, *The Angel You Know* is a work of fiction'. How could you lie through your teeth? How could you lie to the world? It breaks my heart. I feel disrespected that you could ever think of saying that to me. It is bullshit."

"Peter, do not curse when you talk to me."

Peter banged his fist on the table. "This is not school. This is not Unizik, Neta. You cannot control me. Those days are over, so I curse when I want to curse. And I am telling you, this is bullshit. This is not fiction; you wrote a book about us." There was real anger in his voice. "This book is about me. This book is about you. This book is about Derek. This is my life, our lives. You told the world our story without my permission." Peter found himself banging the table again. "You think you are the only one who has a voice because you can write?"

Neta's eyes suggested that she was startled, a little bit surprised at Peter's anger, but when she spoke, her voice was calm and composed. "What upsets you in this book, Peter?"

"It is my life," he said. "I did not give you permission to write it. There are private things that you alone know about me. You wrote about them in this book."

"I cannot remember a character named Pe "Daniel is me. Ruth is you. Bernard is Derek. What are you trying to achieve? Why did you write this story?"

"I wanted to tell our story. It is a story I felt I owed the world. It is a story that..." She paused and sighed like she was exhausted. "I was merely expressing myself."

"You were expressing yourself?" Peter's anger had rescinded. "One would have assumed you wanted to put me in the past after you left me in that hospital, on a sick bed, years ago, without looking back. One would have assumed that you wanted to put us in the past; that you wanted to put everything that happened in the past. You cut me off, you changed your phone line. You made it clear you did not want to see me. Why choose to express yourself now? It simply means that all along, all that happened between us has been on your mind. Why have you hidden yourself from me? What did I do wrong? You told me that you were going nowhere. You promised."

Neta tried to speak, but the waiter interrupted as he arrived with their orders. He carefully placed everything they ordered on the table and left.

"Let us eat, Peter," Neta said, with a tone intended to plead. She reached for his hand and gave it a slight squeeze. "And I promise you, we will talk." She wanted to calm him down. It was difficult for her to talk through his anger, through his frustration, through the occasional banging of the table.

Peter obeyed and they ate, mostly in silence.

When they were done eating, Peter drove her home. The drive to Surulere was a largely quiet one, but Peter could feel a hot force of questions pounding against the wall of his chest, like squash balls against concrete. But he remained silent, as though Neta had cast a spell on him when she touched his hand at the restaurant. A spell to hold it all in. And when Neta spoke, it was to give him directions on how to navigate his way to her apartment.

"This is where I stay," she eventually said, pointing to a yellow two-storey building on Bode Thomas.

As Peter controlled the car to a halt, the spell broke.

"Why, Neta?" he asked. "Why did you leave me? I made many attempts to reach you, but you were always one step ahead, ensuring that I am shut out of your life. You frustrated my efforts and now you write a book?" He paused and continued when Neta remained silent. "You have no idea what I have been through these past years." The tone of his voice was now soft and emotional. "There were times when I could not sleep because the thought of you just won't let me. And when I managed to, I am awakened in the early hours of the morning by dreams about you. I was going crazy. I am stressed out, Neta. It has been incredibly difficult for me to love another woman. You made me complete." It surprised him that he was talking through tears. Neta leaned closer towards him and he, just like a baby seeking to be consoled by its mother, dropped his head on her shoulder. She began to stroke his head. She, too, now had tears in her eyes.

"Why did you find me, Peter?"

"After all these years, you still make me cry."

"Why did you find me?"

Her tone demanded an answer, almost like she was angry at Peter for finding her.

"Why did you write a book? People who do not want to be found do not write books."

Then some seconds passed. "We are dangerous together, Peter."

"No, we are not."

"We hurt people." Neta's voice was now shaky. "We hurt each other. A lot happened between us, Peter. I figured it was impossible to get over what happened. I decided it was best we put it all in the past."

"You wanted to put it in the past but you could not. You cannot put us in the past. We are meant to be together, Neta. Six years have passed and I still have all these feelings for you, you still make me cry. The things I felt with you…I have never been able to feel them with any other woman. What am I supposed to do about that? Keep living like this?"

"Peter," Neta called without speaking further.

"Tell me that all these years, you do not think about me. I think about you every day and deep in my gut, I know that you still think about me. And I was wondering how it is easy for you to move on. But then I figured that you are a coward. I am facing these things. I want to keep living with the acceptance that whatever happened has happened. I would not make my heart suffer for past mistakes."

"It is easy for you to say, Peter. The blame is not on you."

"I was equally responsible for everything that happened. But we cannot afford to pause our lives because of mistakes we made when we were just kids."

Neta withdrew her hand from Peter's. "I am going in," she said. "Are you coming in or not, Peter?"

They stepped out of the car and she led him to her apartment and to her room.

That night, they slept in each other's arms but before they gave in to the force of sleep, she asked him, "You have stopped wearing your denture, why?"

"When I leave that space open, I remember Stica. When I wear a denture, I remember you. I prefer to remember Stica. His memory does not carry pain, unlike yours."

In the morning, when Peter woke up, Neta was nowhere to be found, but he found a note on the dresser.

I am off to church, she wrote. *I do not want to believe that after all these years, you still practise paganism. But I did not want to wake you because I know you do not have a change of clothes. In the kitchen, you would find bread. You can make tea, if you want. If you can stick around for me to come home, then I would make good food. But if you decide to leave before I get back, keep my key under the foot mat outside my door. 08057953829 is my number now.*

And before I forget, I signed your book again.

Peter reached for his copy of *The Angel You Know* resting on the dresser and flipped the front matter open. He smiled when he saw the writing: *To Saint Peter*. It had been long since she last called him that name. So long that he had forgotten how good it felt.

"Saint Peter," he muttered, his fingers over the text.

But his smile was cut by the sound of his ringing phone at the bedhead. He reached for it and shook his head once he saw it was Winnie. She had called four times last night and each time, he had ignored it. He dropped himself on the bed, his eyes blinking in resignation. He knew from that moment, that everything was going to change and he would not be able to do much about it.

7

Peter's phone rang again. Again, he ignored it. He did not think he could have a conversation with Winnie. He was not exactly sure why he had been avoiding her calls; he did not even know what he felt now, but he knew it was not guilt.

As he put on the TV, hoping to catch a program and distract his thoughts from Winnie and from the incident of the day before, he caught Robert Redford making his indecent proposal to Demi Moore and Woody Harrelson over a pool table. He changed the channel. He knew that movie; he hated that movie. Not because he did not enjoy it growing up, but because it reminded him of his father's death. It was only amnesia that could make him forget. He could remember exactly where he was and what he was doing, when his mother's phone rang from the kitchen. He was in the sitting room, seeing *Indecent Proposal*. The movie had heightened his anxiety and curiosity about sex. It must be something very valuable that a man was willing to pay a million dollars for it.

When he heard his mother's phone ring, he did not know what the caller had said until he heard a loud scream from the kitchen. It was the scream of a madwoman; it was

97

the scream of his mother. She hurried into the sitting room, disorganised and screaming repeatedly: "Peter, give me car key." The haste in her voice and the repetition confused Peter who sprang to his feet and picked the remote control before dropping it to pick up the car key from the centre table. They—Peter and his younger brother—watched her run out. They heard her start the car and zoom off. They had never seen her like that. All she had on as clothes were a black sleeveless top and a wrapper tied around her waist.

When Winnie would not relent, he knew he had to take her call, or she was never going to stop. He sat up and frisked his jacket lying on the other side of the bed. He gazed at his cell phone, expecting the caller to, somehow, be another person. He sighed when he saw that it was still Winnie.

"Hi, Winnie," he said.

"My mother is in town, Pete," Winnie said quickly, sounding excited.

"Really?" Peter asked. He was expecting her to complain about the missed calls. He was expecting her to be mad and ask "Where have you been?" But for some reason, she had not.

"Yes, Pete," she said.

"How is she? When did she come?" Peter tried to let the conversation flow with the calmness she had established.

"She is good, Pete. I want you to meet her today."

Peter's heart skipped a beat and he started stuttering. "I..I..I need to…Okay, okay."

"Please, love. This means a lot to me." "Okay, okay. I will try and come around." "Thank you, love," she said.

"You are welcome."

And when she paused, Peter knew exactly what was next. "And why have you been avoiding my calls since last night?"

"I was tired, Winnie. I was tired."

"Too tired to take my calls?" she said in that same voice that Peter had not been able to decide whether it was genuinely playful or dangerously sarcastic. The kind of sarcasm that overlaid anger.

"I put my phone on silent; I did not want to take work calls. I apologise."

There was another pause and Peter knew she still had questions to ask. But he also knew she would just let it go. It was either she did not feel she had enough ownership over him or she valued what they had to a fault, to the point of ensuring it is free from avoidable squabbles. He did not want to believe it was just her nature. There was always something calculative about her, even in her liberalness.

"Okay," she said. "I will just wait for you."

"Okay, dear," He said and hung up. A part of him wanted to be back at Neta's. She gave him an option of sticking around for her to make food when she returned from church. He did not have a particular reason for choosing to leave before she got back from church, but he also was not sure if he would have found a logical enough reason, free from the trappings of his feelings, had he decided to stay.

NETA LAY IN bed, tossing and turning. Like Peter, it had also been impossible for her to put the events of yesterday off her mind. She held an old picture of her and Peter; it was taken at a fast-food restaurant named Chuckies the first time they went out on something resembling a date in

Unizik. The picture held memories that mixed happiness and sadness. She wondered if Peter still had a copy of it.

When she returned from church and found the key to her apartment under the foot mat, where she had told Peter to keep it if he decided to leave, she was a little disappointed. Not finding Peter at home made her think momentarily that maybe, it had all been a dream and she never met him, that yesterday just did not happen.

She undressed and took another shower. Then she headed to the balcony to feed T.T, her Congo African grey parrot, groundnuts and diced watermelon. Seeing Peter now made it impossible for her to spend that Sunday alone at home. Her apartment, in which loneliness had become comfort to her, could no longer hold her. T.T, being one of those parrots that did not speak, did not offer the kind of company she sought. She needed to be around people, not birds, to keep her eyes and head occupied, and think less of Peter. When she put a call through to her friend, Esther, she told her that she had gone to see her boyfriend, Declan, a married man who she had warned her many times to leave. Then she decided to visit Aunty Chidinma and spend time with her three children. She shared a special bond with them and had fond memories of when they were but toddlers. They had grown into teenagers and Small Ben was not that small any longer.

When she returned from Aunty Chidinma's house, she went into her study, one of her rooms that she had cleared. All she had in it were a table and chair, a bookshelf by the corner filled with books that cut across literary genres, and space—enough space to think and create. It was in this room that she put finishing touches to *The Angel You Know*. She sat and powered on the white HP laptop. She opened a blank MS Word document with the intention to just write, anything. As she stared at the blank page, the only thoughts she had in her head were of Peter, and she could not control the urge to attempt to write something about him, about him and her.

Strings from the past, she first wrote. Then she deleted 'the past' and changed the title to 'Strings from an Old Love.' But before she could drop her fingers on the keyboard again, she heard her phone beep with the receipt of a message and she knew it was Aunty Chidinma, in her usual fashion, asking her if she got home safely. But when she made her way back into the bedroom and picked up her phone from the bed, her heart raced when she saw the message from Peter. She had not saved his number, but she knew the message was from him.

I cannot keep you off my mind, the message said.

She sat on the bed, looking at the message and trying to decide what to do. Everything in her wanted to send a reply, but the cautiousness of her memory restrained her. *Maybe this is a bad idea*, she thought.

Eventually, she responded. It was like her fingers had now developed minds of their own, acting against her self-control. *Neither can I*, she typed and sent.

Can I come around?

It is late, Peter. I don't want to stress you. You've got work tomorrow.

But do you want me around?

Of course, Peter.

Then I am around. I am at the door. Your door.

A strong chill ran down her spine. She wanted to reply and ask "are you serious now?" But she knew Peter and she knew he was not joking. So like an enchanted woman, she walked into her living room, to the door, and opened it slowly. There, was Peter in a black hoodie. They stood staring at each other like zombies. Then she moved to her right and rested on the doorjamb, making way to invite him in. He walked in and watched her bolt the door before they both walked into the bedroom.

"Peter," she said in a whisper. "You should have told me before coming."

Ignoring her words, Peter moved closer to her and immediately planted a kiss on her lips. She did not push him away. With their lips still locked in passion, he slowly lowered her to sit on the bed. Still without saying a word, he took his lips to her neck. When he spoke again, he was whispering endearments: "You are the love of my life…" And when he looked at her face, her eyes were closed and her lower lip held in a bite. Then he slowly removed her glasses and kissed her face and the hollowness of her eyes. He dropped the sleeves of her red silk nightgown to reveal her breasts. Her nipples were now like short spikes. When he tugged at the nightgown by her waist, she moved her hips to allow him undress her down to just her white underpants.

Then he started to undress himself too. When he came at her again, to touch and kiss her breasts, his penis had risen, responding to the sensualities of his body and mind. Soon she dropped on the bed and he on top of her, reaching for her underpants.

After they had sex, he held her from behind, listening

to her paced breathing and scenting shampoo from her dreads.

She turned around to face him, and touching the scar on his chest, she asked, "Do you think of him sometimes?"

"Who?" Peter asked, the tone of his voice suggesting that he knew who Neta had asked of.

"Derek," Neta said, her voice heavy and dull at the same time.

"Every day," Peter replied. "Every single day."

8

The first time Peter laid eyes on Neta was nine years ago, at a friend's birthday party, when they were both sophomores in Unizik. That friend was Derek, one of the gifts of friendship that Peter's stay at the university inadvertently gave him. The other being Amandi, his confidant and roommate, both of them gifts that Unizik snaffled away as quickly as it gave. These days, whenever Peter looked back, he ascribed his losses, the end of his friendships with Amandi and Derek, to that birthday party at Elite Hostel, to his first meeting with Neta. That meeting was the first of the events that would ultimately drive a wedge between Peter and his friends.

The problem was that Peter had had a conversation with Neta immediately after they met, telling her that he felt a connection to her. Then, he learnt that she was Derek's girlfriend. The problem was that even with this knowledge, he had allowed himself to keep falling. He called it *love* and accepted that he lacked the capability, the emotional strength, to fight it. This acceptance, this unforced submission to the dictates of this love, only made it bigger and bigger, until Peter was bold enough to pursue it, ignoring Amandi's warnings. The problem was that this love was not supposed to happen. The problem was that she had loved him too.

She had loved him but had attempted to stay away. Though she knew that a lot was absent in her relationship with Derek, though she saw that Peter's love seemed like it would attempt to fill the emptiness she always felt, she wanted to avoid him, to avoid more mistakes that were only likely to add to the weight that bothered her conscience. But it was difficult to stay away from Peter.

Peter needed Neta because she was everything he had been searching for. She made him feel the same things he had felt as a boy, with Anita Sweet, the same things he had felt in secondary school with Oluchi. How his heart danced, how helpless he always found that he was. Neta was everything he had been searching for since he broke up with Oluchi after they both had been admitted into Unizik. It was a search that had led him to a series of unprotected sex that caused him more problems than pleasures. First, there was Udoka, his next-door neighbour at Royal Garden Hostel, the one he had lost his virginity to. Then there was Senno, the medical student that had been smitten by him.

It was his relationship with Senno that had brought Stica, a dreaded cultist in school, his way. Stica, who had been interested in Senno himself, had, with the help of his gang, abducted Peter. They had beaten him to the point that he lost a tooth. This attack had happened before Senno told Peter she was pregnant with his baby, throwing him into months of immense mental stress as they went through the risks of an abortion. The abortion had happened and, though he had been relieved, he was not proud of it. He believed he had disappointed God. He believed he had failed his mother and all the lessons she had tried to teach him.

So when he met Neta, he had already made promises to himself and to his God, promises that wove into months of abstinence from sex, months of loneliness and masturbation. It was true that he was searching for something when he met her, but he was lost himself and needed to be found. He believed that she found him as much as he found her. When he kept coming back, when he would neither take *no* for an answer nor see the logic in her reservations, her concerns about Derek, she gave it a chance, this relationship that seemed like a mistake but felt right at the same time.

During their final year in Unizik, it was easy for them to bond and give their love a chance to grow. It was easy because Amandi, Peter's roommate who had been against this betrayal, went missing from school, after he was diagnosed of an HIV infection. It was easy because Derek broke his leg during a football match and had to miss what was left of the first semester, recovering in an orthopaedic centre in Abeokuta, where his father had moved him to, after the specialist at Igbobi had made comments suggestive of an amputation. Peter loved Neta dearly, he was certain. She made him better.

She bought him a denture for the tooth he lost to Stica's gang, and taught him to write in cursive. She drew him closer to literature and corrected him whenever he made simple grammatical errors. When she learnt of his admiration for the actor Saint Obi, she nicknamed him *Saint Peter*. And when he learnt that her middle name was Angela, he started calling her *Angel*. He believed she was an angel, that he did not deserve her, and was willing to keep improving, to be fit to have her love for as long as possible.

When Derek returned to school, he could not take what had happened; Neta had broken up with him over the phone, while he was still in Abeokuta, to be with Peter. It was a betrayal Derek could neither recover from nor accept. Peter believed that their love, what he shared with Neta, was worthy of this sacrifice. He believed this because he did not fully understand Derek's state of mind; he did not know what he would do next. He did not know that Derek would eventually visit them, him and Neta, as they spent the night together. When they opened the door to let him in, they thought he had only come for closure. They did not know that he had a gun with him; he was not supposed to be capable of that. When he shot Peter in the chest, just before his eyes closed to unconsciousness and whatever waited ahead, Peter did not understand it. Derek was not supposed to be capable of this.

Part Two

9

Neta's gaze remained on the words inscribed on the outdated calendar hanging on the wall of Debola's office:

Ignoring problems do not make them go away. A problem left in the head can lead to mental problems. Sharing them with friends and family even makes them grow bigger. Sharing them with your pastor gives you false hopes. Tell your problems to a godsend professional counsellor, a psychological mind surgeon and see them disappear. Remember: your secret is safe with Dr D.

Debola was not a doctor, not of any form, but he liked to be called 'Dr D'. He called himself a mind surgeon and said there was no way one could be a surgeon without being a doctor. He was a clinical psychologist at the psychiatric hospital in Yaba, treating victims of drug abuse.

Neta had never thought her friend Esther to be a generous person, but Esther had surprised her by introducing her to Debola and paying for five therapy sessions for her, only the second gift she had given her, after she had bought her a parrot on her last birthday. When months rolled by and the parrot did not speak, Neta had said to her: "I thought parrots were meant to talk, mimic voices at least."

Esther had said confidently, "Don't worry, it is still getting used to you. It will talk. Continue to speak to it."

But after several months, the parrot had remained mute, only occasionally squawking and whistling in bird languages that Neta did not understand. It had caused Neta to start reading about parrots and other species of talking birds. She had read somewhere that their chances of repeating spoken human words depended on their abilities to trust humans. She also read that some parrots never learn to get to that level of communication with humans. After more weeks of saying simple words to the parrot and not getting anything in return, she gave up. She had picked up her phone and dialled Esther's number. "Why did you even get me a parrot?" she had asked her.

"You like staying alone," Esther had replied. "I see that, so I give you your space. But even when I am not around, I need to make sure you have company. You need that noise, you need the parrot."

"I love having you around, Esther." "Not all the time, Neta, but it is fine."

"It is just that I need to write sometimes, so I need to be alone." "Then enjoy the company of the parrot as you write."

"Esther, it is not even talking. All it does is try to shrill my ears out and hit the cage with its beak."

Esther had laughed. "It will, Neta. Parrots are supposed to be active. It is probably making all that noise because you are not giving it enough attention. They need attention. They communicate to you when they are hungry or uncomfortable."

"No. I don't think it would. It is tongue-tied. It is not all parrots that talk. Get me a book next time."

"No way!" Esther had shouted over the phone. "These books will make you run mad one day. They are making you more reclusive. You are withdrawing yourself too much from normal people. And besides, if I decided to get you a book, how do I know you have not even read the book?"

"You could always ask me."

"Then where is the surprise in that? The element of surprise is important in giving gifts. It amplifies the gesture. Manage the parrot, Neta. It is an African grey; I owned two when I was growing up."

Esther then told her more stories of the parrots her father had bought for her when she was a teenager, Pascal and Hector, and how good they had been at mimicking sounds and knowing people's names. She said she had planned to name them Paris and Hector, after the Trojan princes, but her father started calling them Pascal and Hector, so much that one of the birds was then saying *Pascal* all the time.

"I had them for two years, until my mother mistakenly killed them."

"What happened?"

"She locked them up in a car without ventilation and they suffocated. She travelled with them, from Awka to Oguta, to visit her mother. When she got to Oguta, she locked the car, forgetting she had not brought them out, and went to greet friends. *Na so the birds take die.* It pained me because they were part of the family already. Neta, parrots are intelligent birds. They hardly fall sick and they eat little, easy to have. All you need to do is give yours more attention and you will enjoy it, I am telling you."

Neta had accepted the parrot the way it was. She even

gave it a name, 'TT', representing 'Tongue-Tied', and loved it regardless. She fed it nuts and fruit crumbs, and still talked to it without expecting anything in return. And surprisingly, TT and its songs provided a kind of non-intrusive companion that human beings could not give. Esther had been right.

So when Esther gave her another gift, Neta had hoped that she would be right too.

Her first meeting with Debola was somewhat disappointing. Debola appeared as an unprofessional loudmouth who liked to blow his own trumpet, referring to himself in third-person, and yapping about how the right attention was not being given to mental health in Nigeria because of pastors and churches.

"People do not know the difference between psychological problems and spiritual problems," he said. "They take cases they should bring to Dr D to their pastors who are not trained to handle such matters. Now, these pastors are supposed to tell them the truth and direct them to Dr D, but they always fail to do that. They like to be important, and they like the money, so they entertain anything that would keep their congregation attached to them. They end up making these cases worse. Go to Yaba and ask about Dr D. They will tell you that he is number one in addiction treatment."

Neta felt a need to point out to him that she had not come because of an addiction, but because her friend thought she was showing signs of depression, because she herself knew she had been battling depression, or something resembling it, for years now. The word *depression* seemed to do justice to it; there was nothing else to call it. It was a near-total lack of happiness. Debola spoke further. "Not just addictions; depression and all forms of mental and psychological challenges."

At the end of that first session, Debola gave Neta an assessment form and a printout that contained five hundred and sixty-five objective questions on feelings, mood and priorities. He asked her to fill out the form and answer the questions as honestly as possible. He also told her to do a rough sketch of a human being of any gender on the back of the form. "Take them home. I know it is a lot of questions, but be honest in answering them. They are important to what we are trying to achieve. Take your time and come for the next session when you are done."

"What are you doing with the sketch? I'm terrible at drawing anything."

Debola smiled and said proudly, like a flamboyant magician preserving his tricks, "What I need it for should not be your headache. Just know that you have come to the right place."

That evening, after she got home, Esther called to know how it went, what she thought of Debola. "I don't know what to say, Esther," Neta said. "I think he talks too much. Are therapists not meant to listen more?"

"Neta, your problem has always been lack of patience. I am sure he was just trying to break the ice. He was meeting you for the first time. Debola is a professional; his subsequent sessions with you are going to be more helpful."

"He gave me an assignment of more than five hundred questions!" Neta pointed out. "Five hundred, Esther! I am probably going to spend the entire night solving them."

"Come on, Neta. You say *solving* like they are some hard secondary school mathematics questions. I am sure these are simple questions about your life and opinions, questions you don't even need to think through before answering once you are being honest with yourself."

"He also said I should draw a person. This is not fine arts. Are you sure this man knows what he is doing?"

Esther sighed over the phone. "First, I got you a parrot, and you complained that it does not talk. Now, I have recommended Debola, who actually talks, and you are complaining that he talks too much. You are already blocking him off. Neta, I paid good money for those sessions. I beg you, have an open mind. Let him do his work. You need help, don't you think so?"

"You sound like I am already mad."

"Neta, you seem not to have interest in anything else apart from your books and writing. You don't even want to give any man a chance in your life, you are not connecting with people anymore. You are not happy, I see that. I don't know what it is, but you are carrying a burden you don't want to share. I beg you, let Debola do his work."

To show her appreciation for Esther's efforts, she stayed up all night with an HB pencil, ticking her answers from the options provided in the form. She drew a man because men were easier to draw. She examined her drawing and smiled at how she had got the legs wrong, short and curved. She took more pleasure by adding a beard on the face of her creation. *A bow-legged and bearded dwarf.* Just perfect, she thought sarcastically.

She submitted the printout to Debola, and he invited

her two days later for a second session. This time, Debola did not talk about himself. It seemed like his face had been covered by a professional veil, more serious than it had been during their first session together. He spread out a graph sheet on the table. Somehow, he had converted Neta's answers into graphs and numbers.

"What is this?" she asked.

Debola pointed to the curve of the graph and traced it to a number on the Y-axis. "The graph checks for depression, OCD, and some other complexes listed here." He pointed to the left side of the graph that had a listing of mental illnesses with points attached to them. "You can clearly see that the test for all the things we are testing returned either negative or negligible. All, except depression." He paused and raised his face. "You are depressed, Ms. Okoye. As a matter of fact, you have been depressed for a very long time now."

Neta's mouth tightened. "How do you know it has been a long time?"

Debola quickly turned the paper over to its other side. "You see, there are three stages of depression." He pointed at the stages listed on the paper. "There is mild depression, moderate depression and severe depression. You could see here that each of these stages has point ranges assigned to them. And from the answers you supplied to those questions, one could see that you are at the brink of severe depression. In some cases, people jump from no depression to severe depression, depending on the gravity of what they have experienced. But in most cases of depression, it takes years for people to move from mild depression to moderate, and even more years, sometimes decades, to slip deeper. You have had persistent, untreated depression. When it becomes severe, it could lead to suicidal tendencies." He folded the paper and pushed it aside. "Now, it is time to listen to you, to know you. What is your story, Neta Okoye? Start by telling me how you feel at the moment."

Neta shrugged and said, "Good. I feel good."

Debola wagged his index finger at her. "No, you don't feel good. You would not be here with me, if you felt good. How do you feel? Be open to me; I am here to help."

Neta sighed and clasped her hands. "I am not sure how to describe it."

"Just describe it, anyhow. I will understand."

Neta sighed again. "Sometimes, I feel unhappy. Other times, I feel nothing at all. No happiness. No sadness. Just numbness and emptiness. And a lack of understanding of what the point of all this is. Just nothingness."

"Point of what?" Debola's voice had gone soft. "Neta, I need you to trust me. I promise you, we will achieve great results if you trust me. Point of what, Neta?"

"Point of life." Neta sighed, and decided to open up to Debola, for her sake and for Esther who had paid money for this *experiment*. "Most times, I feel this need to be alone because I feel like I don't have much to offer to people. I cannot give happiness because I don't have it. I want to, but I cannot give what I don't have."

"And why do you think you don't have happiness?"

"Because my head is filled with the pressures of life and my heart is heavy." She held her head, then ran her fingers down her hair. "Sometimes, it is melancholy but other times I can't describe it. It feels like I am floating through life, like my body wakes up without my soul. It is a scary feeling that affects everything I do. My mind is filled with thoughts. Thoughts that make sure I do not get enough sleep. That I do not enjoy the simple things of life. When I see people seemingly happy, beaming and enjoying life, I feel a longing, a desire to be equally happy. But it is hard for me."

Debola opened his drawer and brought out a journal. He opened it and began to write. "So you do want to be happy?" he asked.

"I'm not going to lie, I want to be happy. I want to improve my eating habit and feed more than once in a day, but I struggle to keep my appetite. I want to sleep better. I want to be that girl that goes out with friends and drops all worries. I want to but I cannot. I cannot control these feelings, this pensiveness. There is a constant fear in my heart."

Debola scribbled in the journal. "What are you afraid of?"

Neta shrugged. "Everything. I fear everything, from the simplest of things to the most serious." Debola fixed his eyes on her, wanting to hear specifics. "I fear that I would never get to read all the books I wish to read. I fear that I would never be able to create as much as I would love to, to write and birth all the stories that I'm pregnant with. I fear that the characters would lose faith in me and no longer trust me to tell their stories. I fear they would stop talking to me and turn to another storyteller, someone who has a pen in hand, waiting for a story to write. I fear death, that I will die without leaving a mark and be judged for talents unused and for passively living in potential for the most part of my life. I fear that I will die young. I don't know how I feel about heaven, but I fear that I will never do enough to make it."

Debola nodded and ran his left fingers over one of the pages of his journal. "You know, it is interesting that you mentioned books and writing. Esther told me that you write, that you recently had a book published," he said. "She is worried literature is making your state of mind worse."

Neta smiled. "She keeps saying that. Esther is a good friend, but she does not get it. She does not understand the role of literature in my life."

"Tell me: What is the role of literature in your life?"

A smile returned to Neta's face. "Literature is my drug, my life, the only thing that makes me happy."

"The only thing?"

"I can't think of another. My book is doing well. It just made the long-list for the National Literature Prize. That makes me happy."

"You have a book out. Why are you being hard on yourself? It is progress, isn't it? Why do you feel you are not doing enough? If you have been handed this gift, a key to your happiness, why then have you not immersed yourself in it?"

"I feel like I am not writing enough. I am a fiction writer, Doc." She saw the smile on Debola's face as he received the word "Doc".

"But whenever I pick up a pen, I am always directed towards writing my own story, and with that comes some form of holding back."

"But if the story keeps you awake, why not tell it?"

Neta fixed a look at Debola. "Is everything we discuss here confidential?" she asked.

Debola put a hand in the air. "I forgot to mention

that. Your stories are safe with me. It goes against the ethics of my profession to share whatever happens in this room with anyone else. Feel free and talk to me."

"I have neither told nor admitted this to anybody. My book is not entirely fiction. It is about me."

Debola adjusted in his seat with interest. "What is the title of this book?"

"*The Angel You Know*," Neta answered. "It is about my experiences in school. All I just did was change names." She sighed. "It is incredibly difficult for one to write about oneself because it demands a level of honesty that comes with admitting to your past, to your avoidable mistakes and immersing yourself once again in the pains and tortures they bring. In *The Angel You Know*, I had to write about the men that I hurt, a friendship that I destroyed. It took me a long time to complete it. Sometimes, while writing it, I would just pause and break down in tears. Sometimes, I went months without writing anything. It was a heartbreaking book to complete."

"Tell me that story," Debola demanded. "I want to hear it." Neta shook her head. "It will spoil the book for you." Debola chuckled. "Don't worry about that."

"It is a long story."

"Do I look like I have something more important to do?"

Neta gave in and told him everything she could remember about Unizik, everything she had written in her book. About herself and the once admirable friendship of Peter, Derek and Amandi, and the trail of misfortunes that ripped them apart. She told Debola that she had been one of those *misfortunes*. She told Debola about that night Derek walked into her room with a gun, how he had shot himself and Peter; that was the end of *The Angel You Know*. The novel did not say what happened next, but Neta had continued, telling Debola how she had managed to pull herself out of the state of shock to be able to call for help from her neighbours.

By the end of her story, tears were running down her cheeks, but her speech was still clear. Debola handed her a white handkerchief, almost like he was prepared for her tears, like he had expected them, like he had been donating handkerchiefs for a long time.

"Your story is touching, Neta. I understand why it was difficult for you to write it. You feel responsible for their deaths."

"Peter survived. The bullet to his chest missed his heart." "That is good to hear. You feel responsible for Derek's death?" "I am responsible. I broke him. I drove him to do what he did. And when it mattered the most, I did not listen. I should not have opened that door. Peter warned me, but I was an idiot."

Debola reached for her hand on the table and tapped it, withdrawing immediately like physical contact was abominable. "Do you feel you need something, forgiveness perhaps?"

"I made avoidable mistakes."

"But you were in love. Regretting your actions would mean regretting that love. Do you regret that love, what you had with *this* Peter?"

"I am not sure. Was it worth it? What we paid was too great a price to pay for anything. I shouldn't have loved Derek's friend."

"We don't choose whom we love."

"But we can control our feelings. I was in control of it, but Peter kept coming. His resolve weakened my reservations and I gave in to my feelings. I lost the battle. That was a big blow to Derek. Yes, I feel like I need forgiveness, but I am not sure who from. God or Derek? Sometimes, I feel like I don't deserve forgiveness, so I don't bother to ask. Maybe I am being too harsh on myself, maybe I judge myself unfairly, but the truth is that I have my demons from the past and there is a constant battle between me and them. Some days, I win, but mostly, they win, they are powerful. I want to be closer to God, but I am not. I want to spend more time writing, creating and publishing books, but that is not the case. More stories from my past would not let me write fiction the way I want. I think about them every day, every single day, the boys whose lives I destroyed."

"You are too hard on yourself. You did not destroy any life," Debola said, writing in his journal again. Neta swallowed an urge to ask him what exactly he was writing. "Peter? Where is he now?"

"I don't know. We have not seen since 2009, since we left Unizik. He has made several efforts to reconnect, but I have made it impossible. I feel he is better off without me, that we are better off without each other. Our pasts are tied together and filled with bitterness. We cannot share the present without sharing that bitterness. I don't like that bitterness."

"And do you think staying away from him has helped?"

"I don't know. I don't know if I would have been better off or worse off with him in my life. But what I know is that there is a void in my heart that even literature cannot fill."

She sniffled. "Or maybe it is time to stop this disorganised speech. It is time to stop talking about voids like they are a bad thing. Life is all about voids, right? And we are all looking to fill something, right?"

Debola smiled. "You have a problem we need to solve. I am not going to help you deny it or write it off as a normal, general problem.It is your problem and we need to solve it." He closed his journal. "What about love and dating? Have you tried to give another person a chance, someone who does not remind you of your past?"

"I have tried. I have, but I failed woefully, over and over again." "And why do you think you failed?"

"It is always my fault. I struggle to give attention, almost like I am incapable of feeling certain things now, things like love. I have met good men who loved me, but I just could not love them back. I don't understand it. I don't understand me. I don't understand this life. I don't understand anything."

"Don't you think that a part of your happiness lies in love? Don't you think having someone you love would contribute to your happiness?"

"I don't understand this thing called happiness, not at all. I have heard stories. Stories of the way it satisfies, the way it heals. The way it lifts people into the best versions of themselves. But this is not my story. The times I felt something like it, it did not feel like happiness in the stories I heard. It was never steady, never firm."

"You need to discover other sources of happiness. Only literature is not enough. You need to open up your heart to love again."

"These things are not that easy." "You have to try."

"I have, Doc. I am tired of trying."

"I am here now. Let me help you. Neta, for you to heal, you have to forgive yourself, if you think you need forgiveness. You have allowed this guilt to become a part of you. Derek is not here to forgive you for the wrong you think you did him. Forgive yourself."

"How does one even forgive oneself?"

"I will help you through it. I would have asked you to speak to

Derek, if he were alive. Right now, only you can do this for you. Let me help you."

"But Derek is not the only life I have destroyed."

"You did not destroy Peter's life. He is alive, that is all that matters."

"No, not Peter."

Debola glanced at his watch. "Who, Neta?"

Neta removed her glasses to wipe tears off her face. "No," she said, like she was fighting herself. "I can't tell you that now. It is about events that happened way before I gained admission into Unizik."

Debola took another glance at his watch. "We have to round up now. We have spent more time than we should. We shall continue next session. You will tell me about your family and this other boy whose life you think you destroyed. You also need to do two things for me: When you are coming next, write a letter to yourself, pouring out your heart, but forgive yourself in it. Secondly, write down three things you want this therapy to do for you."

Neta nodded and stood up. When she got to the door,

she stopped and turned around to ask him, "The sketch, what was it for?"

Debola smiled. "That test isn't for you. I just wanted to see if you had another hidden talent."

"Apparently, I don't," she quipped and they both laughed.

THE THIRD SESSION happened after she met Peter at her reading, after he slept over at her place. When Debola walked in, Neta asked him why he had a calendar that was outdated by three years.

He mumbled a response and asked Neta for the letter he asked her to write and the note on what she wanted the therapy to do for her. She gave the papers to him. He scanned through the letter and nodded. Then he opened the other note and read the words:

> *At the end of this therapy;*
> > *I want to be able to hold on to a solid form of happiness*
> > *I want to have inner peace, ridding myself of this weight*
> > *that has forced itself on me.*
> > *I want to redevelop the emotional capacity to give back love.*

Debola adjusted his chair and placed both forearms on the table. "The effectiveness of my treatment depends on your cooperation. We can achieve all this, once you open your heart to the therapy."

"I met Peter," Neta cut in.

Debola's face brightened with excitement. "Are you serious?"

"I met him and the feelings are still the same. I still love him, almost like my feelings did not even change."

"And does he still love you?"

"I cannot speak for him, but it appears so. He still wants me, after all these years."

"What is the next step now?"

"I don't know, Doc. I want to allow him set the pace."

"Neta, I have a strong feeling that a huge part of your happiness lies with that young man. Go and take it. Please, do not push him away, for your own good."

They talked more about Peter and about her book and readings, and the national tour her publishers were planning for her. Debola told her that he was happy all these were happening at the same time. He said it was good for her treatment. When he asked her about her family, her face instantly grew sad. "I don't want to talk about my family."

"Why?" Debola asked. "Why do you keep avoiding the topic of your family?"

"Because I will have to go back to the beginning, to the very story I have been avoiding to write, to growing up, to all the mistakes I made, to my family tragedies."

Debola reached for her hand. This time, he held it tightly and spoke to her. "You need to talk to me. Please, talk to me."

She did not know how he did it, but Debola possessed some authority. She had barely known him, but she had shared with him more than she had ever shared with anybody. He made her feel light and she felt she could trust him. So she told him about her family, about her father who died in a car crash, about her mother who was now remarried and based in America with her new husband. She stopped there.

But Debola pushed further. "Are you an only child?" She stood up and started pacing the room back and forth, breathing heavily and sweating, like she was having a panic attack. Debola stood up and approached her. "Do you need water?"

She nodded. "Yes, please."

Debola fetched a glass of water from the dispenser and gave her. She took a sip and handed the glass back to Debola. "Sit down and catch your breath, Neta."

She obeyed him and sat with her face raised to the ceiling, and tears rolling down her temples. Debola sat on the table, beside her. "I am fine," she said.

"You must not talk about this today, if it upsets you this much." She dropped her face and opened her eyes. "It is fine," she said.

"I am fine." She wiped tears off her face. "What was your question again?"

"Are you an only child?"

"No," she said. "I have a brother. His name is Jeta."

"Where is he? What happened to him? What have you been carrying in your chest?"

"He is alive," Neta answered, stroking the beads of her bracelet. "He has been in prison for over a decade now, for manslaughter. He is one of the other boys whose lives I ruined."

Neta's parents had thought Chidinma was a blessing. For Edna, having a cousin available to take care of her children, like they were her own siblings, and keep her home, as she skidded through the strenuous requirements of her banking career, made her feel lucky and beholden to Chidinma. She never called her a housemaid, like other women did their helps, and did not accept it when someone else did. "She is my cousin, not my housemaid," she would always say.

She had heard stories from women who were her neighbours about *evil housemaids*. In these stories, these housemaids had poisoned families; these housemaids had kidnapped and disappeared with children they were supposed to protect; these housemaids had snatched husbands from the grasps of their unsuspecting mistresses. During those years, these stories sparked a silent campaign against these housemaids, a campaign that wore a garment of maltreatment and wickedness, a wickedness glazed and straightened into normalcy amongst wives and mothers. A housemaid to a friend of Edna's and neighbour, Mrs Mbanefo, used to wear only one dress all year round, year after year. One day, at a hairdresser's salon on their street, as the two women sat, getting their hairs washed, Edna asked Mrs Mbanefo, after the housemaid had come to deliver a message to her, "Why does she always wear that particular gown?" She had been looking for an opportunity to ask this. Mrs Mbanefo's husband was a prosperous distributor at the Trade Fair Complex, dealing in cosmetics and personal care products. Mrs Mbanefo herself was the headmistress of a primary school in Lagos Island. It was difficult for Edna to understand why a girl that lived with them was always seen on the same black and raggedy dress.

Mrs Mbanefo hissed. "These maids," she said. "They are better off like that *oh*. I don't want to hear stories, my sister. These maids are terrible. It is not only in movies that they snatch husbands. You need to keep them unattractive, to a point that they cannot tempt your husband. It is one dress per year for her, and before I hand over her new dress for the year, I collect the former."

"Why collect the old ones? Even if you wish to buy her a dress per year, why not leave her old ones for her?" Edna asked.

Mrs Mbanefo shook her head. "No. It is too much. I must collect them. It is either I burn them or I turn them into rags for cleaning my floors."

Edna's jaw dropped. "Haba!" she exclaimed. "That is not good *nah*."

"Edna, you need to open your eyes. That girl you are taking care of and allowing her look that fine, that your maid–"

"She is not a maid," Edna pointed out. "She is my cousin."

"Be deceiving yourself there. Don't allow that girl to

grow wings. You will regret it when she does. Cousin or not, you need to keep people in their place."

But Edna knew that as insensitive as Mrs Mbanefo sounded, she was a world better than her other neighbour, Catherine, whose husband was a high-ranking police officer. The story was that Catherine's housemaid, Ugochi, did not eat the same meals as the members of the family she served.

In the mornings, when the family ate buttered bread and drank hot tea rich in powdered milk and Bournvita, Ugochi would eat her own bread with clear and tasteless water. During lunch, when the family ate rice with chicken stew, embellished with scented leaves, Ugochi would eat parboiled rice mixed with palm oil, the same meal as the family dog. The family dog even had it better; his was always served with chicken bones from the family's leftovers. Ugochi only ate after everyone had, after she had fed the dog, and her meals did not come with meat. When Ugochi got tired of eating poorly prepared food without meat, she started eating some of the chicken bones meant for the dog and grubbing on remnants from the family plates. She would hide in the pantry and scrape the meat off bones with her teeth, like a scavenging bird suffering from starvation. She always had to eat whatever she could during the day, whenever she could, because she knew that there would never be dinner for her. At nights, as the family ate ẹ̀bà, something her late grandmother used to call *utala* when she was still in the village, she would either be fetching water or cleaning the kitchen and thinking of her grandmother. She wished her grandmother could resurrect temporarily to see how this woman she called *madam* was depriving her of utala which she willingly made for her three times in a day, when she was alive. The family always ate ẹ̀bà with soup in which various categories of fish—stockfish, dry fish, smoked fish, and fresh fish—swam to their second and final deaths. The aroma of the stockfish was never kind to her; it constantly invaded her privacy, reminding her of what she was missing, the nutrimental deprivation she was suffering. Catherine said eating at nights would make her tired and lazy come morning.

Also, Ugochi had neither shoes nor the kind of flip-flops they used to call *bathroom slippers*; the ones that even beggars on the streets had. She would walk the streets barefooted to run errands while Catherine's children pranced around in their expensive sets of footwear. One day, she walked onto a path where a careless hospital had disposed of used syringes and needles, and a needle caught her right sole. She sat on the floor, holding her foot and crying for no one in particular. A Good Samaritan who had seen what happened took her to a nearby chemist to be treated against tetanus. The man bought her a pair of bathroom slippers and paid for her drugs. The mistake she made was that she accepted, not the drugs now, but the footwear. She should not have. She was a housemaid. And according to her madam's definition, she was not fit to eat square meals and wear proper clothes; she was not supposed to plait her hair and look pretty like other young girls, and she was not supposed to wear footwear.

The next day, Catherine was rummaging in Ugochi's bag, as she would periodically, searching for something she herself did not know. She came across the bathroom slippers and a burning rage instantly seared through her chest. She summoned Ugochi, screaming her name.

"Where did you get these?" she asked. "So you are now stealing money from me. You are stealing from me to buy slippers, ehn?"

Her question and the fire in her eyes shook Ugochi into a confused state, and this confusion pushed her into making the wrong decision. In this case, telling the truth was the wrong decision. She told her that a man had bought the footwear for her, thinking that it was better than being called a thief. Catherine had jammed her hands together and snapped her fingers. "You are now jumping from one man to another under my roof. You want to get pregnant so the world will say that I, Catherine, pushed you into prostitution. I feed you and clothe you. What are you lacking? What do I not give you?"

"Everything," Ugochi answered, immediately wishing she could reach out and grab her words back in the air and send them back, down her throat. She did not know why she said it; she should not have.

"What did you say?" Catherine asked, gradually giving in to the incipient anger that was rising in her stomach. "That I don't give you anything, you ingrate? God will punish you, this girl. By the time I finish with you, I will send you back to that your miserable village in Eziagu, so that your wretched kinsmen can give you the moon and stars."

Before the little girl could open her mouth to her defence, to at least lie and say that she had meant to say *nothing*, Catherine started battering her face, raining down slaps and punches. A kick to her belly had her down on her knees, holding her belly, but Catherine was not done yet; as a matter of fact, she was just starting. She rushed into the kitchen and ground red and yellow peppers in a handheld mortar. She scooped the mixture into her right hand and hastened back into the room. Ugochi was still on her knees when she rubbed her pepper-soaked hand over her eyes. The girl went mad and jumped up, screaming and covering her eyes. Catherine slapped and kicked her, sending her to the ground again. She held her down, overpowering her as she attempted to react to the sting in her eyes and, at the same time, free herself from Catherine's hold. With the viciousness of a witch, Catherine raised Ugochi's dress and smeared her private parts and every other orifice she could find in her body with pepper. Then she let go of her, watching her as she screamed on top of her voice, hopping around and heading for the bathroom. Her screams attracted the attention of their neighbours who, after knocking without answer, kicked in their door and rushed Ugochi to the hospital.

Tales of Catherine's wickedness and what people came to know as the *pepper treatment* spread through the neighbourhood like forest fire. It was then that Edna started hearing that Catherine was not the first woman to have used it in their neighbourhood. It was a common practice that her fellow women employed to punish their housemaids. Mrs Mbanefo even admitted to her that she too had tried the pepper treatment, when she was certain her housemaid had stolen from her. "She confessed, you know," she told Edna. "People are talking about Catherine because she did her own too much. I heard that she even mixed yellow and red peppers."

Edna was disappointed. These women, all of them, had

deceived the society to think that they were good women, good wives and responsible mothers. Nobody would have thought that Catherine, with her angelic and demure appearance could hurt a fly. Nobody would have thought that Mrs Mbanefo, a model headmistress and a leader of the Catholic Biblical Instructors Union in church, could treat another woman's child like a slave bought at an auction. Then, Edna became fully convinced that, even with all her flaws and frailties, she was better than all these women; she was a better mother and a better human being. She would never—she could not even imagine it—treat Chidinma with such cruelty.

Chidinma would not snatch Edna's husband, as Mrs Mbanefo had feared and warned—but she would do something that would remain in her home, hanging in the air like a foul smell even after she had married Big Ben.

Edna had forgotten something: Chidinma was adolescent and imperfect. Being imperfect meant that her mind was no longer innocent of carnal thoughts and curiosities. Being imperfect meant that she, like normal teenagers, was adventurous, unavoidably prone to mistakes and bad decisions. Her puberty had come with its fire and hunger, an almost unquenchable need to be with a boy. Matthew, one of the boys who lived with and worked for Mrs Mbanefo's husband as both a houseboy and an apprentice in one of his shops in Trade Fair Complex, was the first boy ever to kiss her. He had been making passes and winking at her with every opportunity he got. She started winking back and smiling at him, desiring to be alone in the dark with him, for she knew that the illicit desires that burned her heart could only be quenched in the dark. One day, after he had made sure no one was watching, he led her under the staircase of his master's house, kissing and fondling her. It felt good, even better than she had imagined. She wanted more, to go further, for him to blindfold her and lead her down this road of teenage sinfulness.

"Let us do it," she told him. Her voice ordered but her facial expression pleaded.

He looked at her in disbelief and scepticism; he had not expected her to make this demand of him. Even during those days when he eyed her up and threw risqué smiles from the balcony of his master's apartment, he had only thought about this which he currently had with her, to hide in dark places, like unwanted rodents, and share kisses.

"Are you sure?" he asked, an attempt to make sure she had not meant something else.

"Matthew, yes nah. You don't want? Don't you think I am beautiful? Don't you love me?"

Matthew sighed. She had skipped distances and had jumped into the murky puddle of love. He was young too and had always seen love as something special and unreachable, a feeling only made for Ramsey Nouah and Stella Damasus, for Richard Mofe Damijo and Regina Askia, and for all those attractive Indian actors and actresses, who took advantage of any available opportunity to sing and dance to songs of love and happiness. He did not think love was meant for houseboys and maids. When Chidinma threw the word at him like it meant nothing, like it was available to everybody, it felt unreal, but he was grateful. The idea that he too could share and play the game of love with an actual human made his stomach rumble.

"I love you," he said. "You are the most beautiful girl I have seen."

She smiled. "Let us do it then."

"Is it your first time?" he asked. She nodded.

"Try not to scream."

He pushed her against the wall and raised her skirt. In that standing positing, he attempted to insert his erect penis inside her, but it came off against the wall of her hymen. As he tried to force it in, she let out a scream, and he immediately put a hand over her mouth, panting in both fear and anxiety. "This is not a good idea."

"Why?" she asked him. "Someone will hear us."

"I promise I will not scream again," she said, pulling his shirt. "You will scream," he said confidently. "It is your first time." He pulled away from her and forced his penis back into his shorts. "I have a plan."

"What plan?" she asked.

"My oga and madam are travelling next week to the village. That means when I come back from the shop, I will be home alone. You should make out time and come in the evening. I will let you in through the back door, so that people will not see you. We will do *it* then. We will be more comfortable and I will play music to make sure no one hears us."

Chidinma agreed and waited for next week, barely sleeping at nights. It became difficult for her to have other thoughts. She would turn and toss around in bed, thinking of Matthew and of that evening under the staircase. All she wanted was to be with him, naked in bed. When next week came, to her disappointment, it was Matthew that travelled, not his oga. Matthew, she heard, had been sent packing for, over time, stealing hundreds of thousands of naira from his master's shop. He was even said to have had a bank account where he, through a friend, deposited his loot at a branch in Marina every Friday evening. What happened—what Matthew did or did not do—was not of concern to Chidinma. What bothered her was that she was never going to see him again. What would happen to the fantasies in her head? What was she going to do with herself and the desires that kept her awake, the promise he made to her?

Her sexual urge began to grow bigger, spreading gradually, like petrol spilled on a crooked floor, flowing into her days. Before, the urge had mostly visited her at nights, as she curled up in her bed, alone and pensive. But now, it was beginning to dominate her thoughts during her busy days. Discreetly, she started reading and watching images from copies of *Better Lover* magazine she borrowed from her friend Nkemakolam, a neighbourhood girl living with her aged uncle. She would fold the copies into squares, tucking them away in one of her bags like little abominations. *Better Lover* did not quell the urges; it multiplied them. The pictures in the magazines did not have much of an effect on her; they were mainly of naked women, designed to feed horny teenage boys. But the stories, which she devoted her time to read with interest, painted vivid and clear fantasies in her head, of what men and women did to one another in bed, of what women felt in bed. She read about different sex positions and about orgasm. *Better Lover* was not what she needed, she concluded. She needed to experience something more physical, something that involved the removal of clothes, something that involved another human, a boy. Edna missed all of this. That had always been her problem, an inability to see things happening under her nose.

These feelings, in the head and body of a teenager, without guidance, could only be held in for so long. They were tiny fragments of a time bomb hidden away in different parts of her body, and like all time bombs, they exploded, filling her with the fire of conviction that she needed to act out and experiment whatever she carried within. Matthew had given her a taste of the forbidden fruit and had disappeared; he broke her heart. She must forget him; she must find and eat her own fruits, the way she wanted, and if possible, share with others.

Chidinma did not have the freedom to look for these fruits outside, to seek out men, and she did not have that kind of courage to cause problems for Edna. So it was almost unavoidable that her experiments were going to start from her immediate surroundings. And her surroundings contained Edna's young twins, Neta and Jeta, the two people in this world she spent the most amount of her time with.

One afternoon in 1996, when Jeta was seven years old, she was alone with him in her room, playing Whot, while Neta read a novel in the sitting room. She started by tickling him, making the boy giggle and wriggle away from her.

"Come," she commanded him, tapping the carpeted floor. "Come sit beside me."

"No," he said. "You will tickle me."

"I won't," she assured him.

"Promise?" he asked, pointing at her.

She assured him again that she would not and he trusted

139

her, so he sat beside her. That was when she pulled him closer and kissed him. Jeta flinched, looking at her in confusion, he was no longer giggling. This was unlike those harmless pecks she would give him on the cheek, even in the presence of his mother. This was a deliberate kiss on his lips, full and wet. She moved again and covered his lips once more, and this time, he responded. She withdrew and asked him, "Do you like it?" He nodded and initiated it this time, sucking her upper lip like an unweaned infant.

The next day, she kissed him again, as he helped her fold his parents' laundry into the wardrobe.

"We need to play a game," she said to him, the tone of her voice hushed.

"What game?" he asked happily. "Is it like Whot?"

"No." Chidinma shook her head. "Nothing like Whot; it is more enjoyable."

"Let us play," he enthused, his smile widening. "What is it called?"

"What is it called? What is it called?" Chidinma mused, then snapped her fingers at him. "*Touch Me, I Touch You* is the name of the game."

"Touch Me, I Touch You," he repeated after her. "It sounds simple. I think I understand it." He touched her shoulder and waited for her to touch his, and she did, both smiling. He touched her face, expecting her to touch his, but she kissed him instead, snaffling the lead away from him. He played along and kissed her back. Then she lifted his shirt and sucked on his left nipple, for about five seconds, throwing him into another haze. It was another revelation, and he liked the feeling it gave him, but he did not understand this game, he did not know if it had rules and boundaries or not. He did not know if he was supposed to lift her own dress and play with her nipple the way she had done his. Something did not just seem right about it.

She dropped her right sleeve, baring her breast. Jeta's eyes dropped on it and remained there like it was a round, brown magnate and his vision was made of iron.

"Come on," she said. "Your turn." She grabbed his wrist and placed his hand on her breast. "Don't be scared, it's your turn."

"Okay," he accepted with a nod and started suckling her breast. She held his head down with one of her hands, while the other reached for inside his shorts and grabbed his penis, stroking it as gently as possible.

She started lifting her skirt before she heard Neta's call from the next room. "Jeta! Jeta!"

"Go and answer your sister," Chidinma said, withdrawing from him and pulling up her sleeve. "Did you like it, the game?"

"Yes," he said, his face downcast. This was a strange game to him. He liked the pleasure but did not understand why it made him shy.

"Don't tell your mummy that I touched your pee-pee, you hear?" She told him, and he nodded. "If you tell her or anybody about this game, we will not play it again. You want us to play it again, right?"

He nodded, raising his face.

"Good boy, Good Jeta." She rubbed his head. "Remember, tell no one, not even Neta."

Jeta left the room and, feeling the need to urinate, headed to the bathroom first, before joining Neta in their room.

Chidinma continued playing this game with Jeta, leading the child deeper and deeper into this pit of immature sexual gratification. One day, she lay him down and took his entire penis in her mouth, sucking as slowly as she could, impressed by herself that she did it well, as his little erection pointed up like a thick brown nail. He had liked it so much that he wished for her not to stop. She then encouraged him to return the favour, spreading out her legs to flash components of her pubic region before him. Prior to that moment, the only female genitalia he had seen was Neta's, the times they shared the bathroom, before they turned five and his mother stopped them from bathing together. Then, it had meant nothing to him, just a tool for passing urine, only different from his. The difference had been the only thing that confused him, until now that he was seeing Chidinma's, bigger, and crowned with a decoration of hair.

"It is okay," she said to him. "Just use your tongue and lick it.

You will like it."

Reluctantly, he obeyed, and did not like it. He pulled away, wiping his tongue with the back of his hand. He said it was wet and tasted salty, that he did not like the taste. When she told him that what he had tasted was normal, that it was called *juice*, he complained that it was not sweet and did not taste like Five Alive. But she urged him to endure and keep trying, making stupid and false-hearted statements like, "It is better than those sugary things. It is good for the body." She also threatened not to suck his *pee-pee* again if he did not obey. He liked it when she sucked it and did not want it to stop. He tried again, and gradually, he started getting used to it.

This game had continued, until Neta walked in on them one day, kissing and fondling each other. They broke apart when they noticed her standing by the door, her eyes seeking understanding.

"Aunty Chidinma, what are you doing with Jeta?" she asked, walking into the room. "What are you people doing?"

Though Chidinma knew that the twins trusted and loved her, she also knew Neta was smarter than Jeta, and the only way to make sure she did not report whatever she had seen to her parents was to give her a bite of the fruit, to make her share in its bond and commitment. Neta, no matter how sharp, was only a child, still innocent and pure in both thoughts and deeds, a relatively blank slate. So she took a long brown chalk and scrawled all over the slate, desperate lies about sex. She knew that all she needed to do was to make her points well, colouring them with some sham verisimilitude and conviction, for her points, being their first exposure to this sort of discourse, would become their truth. Moreover, their mother would always admonish them: "Always listen to Aunty Chidinma. Obey her and do all she says." She was Aunty Chidinma, their second mother, the big sister they did not have, and she knew that they believed that she would never lead them astray.

They believed her when she told them that there was nothing wrong with it, that they were just having fun and that they deserved to have fun, like people in the movies.

She convinced Neta to play this game with them and made them promise silence. The first day Neta participated, after they played, Chidinma bought them a pack of McVitie's Shortbread and made them promise secrecy. Then it became regular, quotidian even. They would all lay naked in bed, focused and lost. She taught them how to use their hands and tongues. She would lie in a supine position, her eyes closed, while the twins crawled all over her body, performing the acts they had learnt from her, kissing and caressing her, sucking her breasts and performing oral sex on her. The bond holding the three of them even became stronger. And though it was not enough for Chidinma, it was something. She enjoyed it and through these games, she lived some of the fantasies *Better Lover* had planted in her head, and she no longer saw Matthew in her dreams.

One evening, she encouraged the twins to touch each other, letting them know that it was normal, that it was harmless. They listened to her and acted according to her instructions while she watched. It started from kissing, then hands got involved, then tongues. As the days sped past and they got older, their minds had already been conditioned to see this as normal. It was the tilling of the abominable ground on which the seeds of their incestuous relationship was sown. They would carry on even after Chidinma got married to Big Ben and moved out of the house, and by the time they were fourteen, they had lost their virginities to each other. Of course, Edna missed that the love between her twins had been corrupted into a taboo.

Even when Jikora started complaining about the closeness of the twins, demanding that they stayed in different rooms, making clear attempts to always keep them separated, Edna still did not see it. She made it hard for him to say that which he feared. Maybe that was why the universe chose her, the cosmic staff pointed to her direction, for her to be the one that would walk in on them as they made out in bed. It was the cruellest of punishments, for she, if she was presented with options, would have chosen to die than be in that room that day, to behold the abomination. Someone else had been chosen to die, her husband. He would hurry into his car, speeding like he had not done since he was twenty-four. He would run a red light, running into another car, killing a man, depriving the man's wife and children of a husband and father. And just as the universe had designed it, he would cause his own death too, leaving his wife to deal with his loss and with the family of the man he had killed.

JIKORA DIED IN a car crash. That was what Edna told everybody. The story of a man who met his untimely death as he sped home to be with his beloved family was an easier story to tell. It was simple, and it was short. She did not need to explain to people what had caused his speeding, what had led to his death, what she had seen. That day had covered her with a haze of failure and guilt. A sense of failure emanating from the bitter acceptance that she had failed as a mother; a sense of guilt from the thought that she had not done enough to save her family from this string of tragedies. There she was, for all those years, thinking that she had done a good job, that her children had turned out good. When she asked them when it had started, this vile and reprehensible relationship, they lied to her and said it had started that same year, obliterating close to eight years of truth; a truth that contained their Aunty Chidinma. When she asked them how it had started, why it had started, why they chose to break her heart in this way, they had kept mute, refusing to trace that moment back to those days when Chidinma used them to make images in her head come true. The irony was that, as she sat waiting for her husband to get home, she kept saying to herself, "This thing would not have happened if Chidinma were still here. It would never have happened."

After she got the call that broke the news of the accident, she rushed to a hospital in Victoria Island, where the bodies of both men, her husband and the man he had killed, had been taken to. She met the wife of the other man, with another woman, crying at the reception. The woman wore a black sleeveless top and a wrapper around her waist. When the woman learnt of who Edna was, she made for her but her friend held her back.

"You see what you and your husband have caused?" the woman cried. "You have killed him, my own husband. Evil people, evil woman. I know you were sent to destroy my family. God will punish you."

Edna's legs felt heavy and weak. Her eyes ached. She wanted to drop on the floor and wail like the other woman. But seeing the other woman, the way she trembled in hysteria, the way she wanted to pounce on her and tear her apart, made her stronger than she was, stronger than she should have been. She stood with a frown on her face, a flurry of emotions engulfing her spirit. Her children were sleeping with each other. Her husband had died and had taken another life with him. She felt sorry for the woman in front of her, for the sorrow her own family had caused her, and she felt sorry for herself.

A week later, Edna traced the woman to her home in Festac, and again she was with that same friend she had seen with her at the hospital. Edna did not know why she had come, why she felt she owed this woman something.

"My name is Edna Okoye," she said to the woman, as she sat beside her in the sitting room. The woman remained quiet, only shaking her head. "I lost my own husband too. I understand what you are going through." The woman shook her head again and folded her arms under her chest. "I just want you to know that I am sorry. Personally, I am sorry. And on behalf of my dead husband, I am sorry that that accident happened."

When it was obvious that the woman was not going to speak to her, her friend led Edna to the door and told her, "She is angry. Nothing you say now is going to make sense to her. A lot of things are going to change for her and her sons. So this is not just about the death of her husband; it is also a matter of not knowing where to go from here." The woman's voice was soft, as pleasing as her pretty face; she held no judgement. Edna knew that the woman understood that whatever happened was not her fault, that she too carried her own grief like a heavy burden.

"Leave her alone for now. I think you should come back later.

Do you hear me?"

Edna nodded, squeezed the woman's hand and left.

She did not come back. She had her own domestic

problems to deal with, decisions she needed to make. And since she had decided to keep the secret of incest between her children to herself, she was all alone and needed to make her decisions unaided. She had thought about separating them, sending Jeta to her disciplinarian cousin that lived in Suleja. There, he would be enrolled into another institution to finish secondary school. All she needed to do now was to weave and package a perfect story, one that his cousin would believe. It was a good plan, separating the twins, she thought. Keeping them away from each other as long as she could was exactly what she needed to do.

Then the twins walked into her room one day, as she sewed a bed cover she had mistakenly torn during laundry two days before. Since that day that her husband died, she had barely spoken to them. If she had her way, she would have left the house for them. It broke her heart, whenever she set eyes on them. They walked into her room that day and dropped to their knees, their eyes already filled with tears before they started speaking. Edna looked away and started sewing vigorously, fearing that she would puncture one of her fingers.

"Mummy, we are sorry," Neta began. "Please, forgive us." Edna did not look at them. "We have wronged you, we know this. We are ashamed to even be here."

"This is the devil's handwork," Jeta said.

Jeta's statement immediately got the attention of his mother. She paused her sewing to cast him a harsh look, her red eyes rolling in inchoate anger.

"Don't say that, you stupid boy!" she barked. "It was all you, you two. There is no devil here, you hear me?" Jeta nodded. "You are the devil." She pointed the needle in her hand at him. "You better start taking responsibility for this crime you have committed against your body and against God."

Neta continued, "We know that this is our mistake, and we accept this. If there was a way we could take back time, we could have. It is unfortunate that we put you through this. I am ashamed of myself. All we ask is for another chance, your forgiveness. We have learnt and this will never ever happen again. Forgive us, Mummy."

She pulled the thread connecting the needle to the fabric and severed it with her teeth. "Your father died for this!" She pierced the needle into the roll of thread. "Your father is gone. He isn't coming back." She covered her face with her right hand and started sobbing. "He isn't coming back."

Neta got up and sat on the bed, beside her, and threw an arm over her shoulder. "You have to forgive us. Let us heal together, as a family," she said, her voice confident and mature, like that of an adult.

Those words she spoke held comfort, a comfort that Edna was desperate for. She lowered her head and placed it next to her daughter's chest, allowing her stroke her hair, while Jeta watched from where he still knelt, like a luckless outcast.

It was as if that evening put Edna's heart into a furnace and melted it alongside the anger it held. She remembered how she had wanted to have more babies without success. Neta and Jeta were the only offspring destiny had prepared for her. Her role as a mother was not to separate them, but to love them and guide them through life. They had to stick together; she was certain that if the dead could speak, Jikora would have frowned at her idea to send Jeta away to Suleja. She was the parent and was supposed to be responsible for her children. And no matter what they had done, no matter how flawed they were, they were still her babies, and they deserved a second chance from the woman that brought them into this world. The most important thing was that they had shown remorse great enough to give hope to her broken heart. It would not happen again.

II

When Neta and Jeta returned to boarding school for their final year in secondary school, Neta started to understand just how deep Jeta had gone into their relationship. When she told her mother that they would break the ties of incest holding them together, she had meant it. When she had asked for her forgiveness, she was willing to do anything it took to actually earn it. But unknown to her, she was speaking for herself only. Jeta was far gone.

One day, after classes, as other students went to their various dormitories, Jeta asked to see her. They stayed behind while others left. When they were alone in class, Jeta moved to kiss her. She pulled away and slapped him across the face. "Are you mad, Jeta?" She had never been this angry at him. "What is wrong with you?"

Jeta held his face, surprise taking over his facial expression. He was surprised; it surprised Neta that he was surprised. "What is the problem, Neta?" he asked. "Why did you slap me?"

"Why won't I slap you? Why did you even ask me to wait?" "Because I noticed that you have been avoiding me. I wanted to see you. Is it wrong to want to kiss my girlfriend?"

Neta grabbed her forehead, feeling the sudden impact of a belligerent headache. Jeta was calling her *his girlfriend* for the first time, meaning he was even defining this relationship, giving names, this thing they had promised their mother that they would kill and bury. Neta knew that defining things breathed life into them. "I am not your girlfriend," she said firmly. "I am your sister."

"And there is nothing wrong with my sister being my girlfriend, I am telling you."

"Don't you have a conscience? Our father died for this sin."

Jeta shook his head. "I don't agree with you. Daddy died in an accident. We did not kill him. And this is not a sin, I don't agree with you."

"He died because Mum called him. He beat the traffic light, did you not hear? Why do you think he was speeding? It was because of us. We did this, you and I. Now, we have to make it right. For us. For Mum. For Daddy. And for the innocent man he killed in that accident."

"Neta, this is just a trial period for us." He tried to hold her hand but she pulled away.

"We need forgiveness from God. We have sinned, a terrible sin.

What has happened to you?"

"We have not sinned, Neta," Jeta disagreed. He went ahead to point out consanguineous marriages that were acceptable in history. "Even in the Bible, there are several cases of righteous men who married their sisters and cousins. Abraham married his own sister, Sarah. Are you saying Abraham was wrong? Remember, God always visited

Abraham and spoke directly to him in the Bible. God was in support of his union with Sarah, his sister."

Neta held her head with both hands. "I am finished," she said. "Why are you thinking like this?"

"Because I love you, Neta," he said. "I cannot live without your love."

Neta shuddered at the mention of *love*. She searched his eyes and found no joke in them. Jeta was serious; he believed he loved his twin sister, after everything that had happened, after all the promises they had made to their mother. Neta stood up and dusted her palms. "This unusual kind of love is unacceptable. Love me like a sister, not as a girlfriend." Her voice was subdued now. Jeta's heartbreaking admissions had weakened her. "Don't ask to see me after class again, until you come to your right senses. I am going to the girls' dorm." She turned and started walking towards the door.

"Neta, don't go," Jeta pleaded. "Please, don't go. I know you love me too. Let us make this work."

She looked over her shoulder at him, wondering how she let things get to this point, her eyes holding both confusion and pity. A part of her had always felt there was something wrong with what they were doing, but Jeta had always shown no remorse. His total lack of guilt, and how happy it seemed to make him, made her unsure. But whenever she set eyes on Jeta, images of their father's face flashed before her eyes. She could not believe that Jeta thought they could move past all that had happened and carry on. She did not understand it.

"You need deliverance, Chukwujetalum," she said and walked away.

She wanted him to know that she was serious and that they were never going to be like they were. From the way Jeta spoke of love and called her his girlfriend, she knew he had been blinded and deafened a long time ago. She needed to make a statement that involved real action, not the mere movement of her lips.

So she said yes to Tobe, the son of a wealthy politician, a boy from the science class who had been asking her to be his girlfriend from their days in Form Four. Other girls in her dormitory had always said that Tobe was tall and handsome. They huddled together to discuss him, how cute they thought he was, how he appeared to have eyes for only Neta.

"Why do you keep rejecting this handsome boy?" they would ask Neta.

Neta did not understand why they all felt it was important to point out that Tobe was good-looking. She did not think that he was as handsome as the girls said; she did not even care much about that. What she cared about was Tobe's exceptional brilliance. Throughout their stay in the school, Tobe won numerous awards during Speech and Prize-Giving Days. In JSS 3, Tobe had won the Cowbell Mathematics competition, both at the regional and national levels. The principal and teachers of the school always spoke of him with pride. Because of him, Cowbell had erected a giant billboard in front of the school gate, recognizing the school for producing a national winner of their annual competition. It improved the image of the school and that meant they were able to attract more students during admissions. Tobe himself was granted a scholarship that would see him through secondary school and through his years in any university he got into. When their Junior WAEC results were out, Tobe scored thirteen A's in as many subjects, a record in the school's history. Neta had always admired him but could not give him the chance he had always asked for because of what she had with her brother. Jeta had always known of Tobe's interest and would always warn her: "Stay away from that boy. He is up to no good."

When Neta said yes to Tobe, it was not because he was tall and handsome, it was not because he had been chasing after her for years. It was because she had always admired his intelligence and because she wanted to prove a point to Jeta, to teach him a lesson he was supposed to learn by himself but was too blinded and cut-off from reality to understand.

Tobe was over the moon the day Neta held his hand and said to him,

"I accept now. I want to be your girlfriend." When he returned to his dormitory that evening, he told every boy who cared to listen that Neta was now his girlfriend. The first time they kissed, he also told the boys. He told them that it was, so far, the best experience of his life. He told them that Neta was the best girlfriend a boy could have; he told them that she was sweet and intelligent. Days later, when the story seeped through to Jeta, it had already been altered and distorted.

"Tobe is telling people he kissed your sister," one of the boys told him. "He said your sister is sweet." The boy's voice carried an intentional gravity, one that was created to galvanize Jeta into action. The story infuriated Jeta for two reasons. One: Neta's relationship with Tobe was a clear indication that she had moved on from him. He did not want to accept it. Two: It felt like Tobe's story had stripped him of his dignity. Tobe was kissing his sister in dark classrooms and was telling everybody about it. And when they told him what Tobe had said, that his sister was *sweet*, his heart sank. It was not like he did not understand that *sweet* in that context meant nice and kind, but he was peeved at Tobe for kissing his sister, and the only imagination that came to his head from the story was that of his sister as a succulent snack, a giant human lollipop, saccharine and chocolate-flavoured, with Tobe licking her off sloppily, with neither respect nor fear.

"You let him kiss you?" Jeta asked Neta the next day after class. "And so?" Neta asked. Her face held a complete lack of care to whatever Jeta had to say.

"He is my boyfriend. He is allowed to kiss me."

She stressed the word *boyfriend*, pulling it like the string of a crossbow, then releasing it, a poisoned arrow to Jeta's chest. She wanted him angry enough to get his own girlfriend.

"You don't know what you are doing, Neta. He is telling everyone in the boys' dorm that he kissed you."

"And what is wrong with a boyfriend telling his friends about a kiss he shared with his girlfriend?"

"He said you are sweet. Why are you allowing him disrespect you?"

"It is none of your business. He is my boyfriend; that is all that matters."

When Jeta noticed that conversations with Neta about Tobe had hit a wall, he confronted Tobe in his class one day during break time. "You have to stay away from my sister," he said, standing over him.

Tobe looked at him reluctantly and continued flipping through the pages of Osei Yaw Ababio's *New School Chemistry*. Jeta picked the textbook and slammed it on the table. "I am talking to you!"

"And what would you do if I don't?" Tobe responded, standing to initiate a staredown. "What would you do?"

"You are asking me that?" Jeta asked, pushing his forehead against Tobe's. "You are asking me that?"

Tobe goaded him further. "Your sister is in love."

The mention of the word *love* struck Jeta in the head, disconnecting the wire that held his self-restraint in place, and he threw the first punch, a cracking right hand that caught Tobe's right cheekbone. Tobe replied with a punch of his own. Jeta ducked and the first fist swung over his head, but he did not miss the second, it was to the nose. They immediately came together, attempting to wrestle each other to the ground, while other students gathered to watch. It was the mention of a teacher's name that broke the fight. "Mr Lanre is coming! Mr Lanre is coming!" they heard one of the students warn. Mr Lanre was the chemistry teacher, the class they were meant to have after the break.

Then Jeta said to the hearing of everyone, blood dripping from his broken nose. "Let us meet at The Arena. I challenge you." He stuck out his little finger at Tobe.

Tobe immediately locked his own finger with Jeta's and pulled it out. "I accept your challenge," he said, sticking out his tongue to taunt Jeta the more. "This time, I will break more than your nose."

THE ARENA WAS one of the two refuse pits dug at the back of the boys' block of dormitories. The first pit was already in use: students discarded plastic waste during sanitation for incineration afterwards. The other pit was bare and unused. In one year, it had become an abode for violence and brutality, it had become a place where scores and wrangles were settled without interruption, where boys resolved their disputes like gladiators, to the entertainment of everyone, but with fist fights that did not bend to any rules. With a pinkie swear, challenge and acceptance were consummated. Whenever a fight was taking place, boys would form a circle around the pit, watching the parties involved as they punished each other inside the pit. The fights usually came with a promise of no interruption or interference. The aim was to give the fighters all the time in the world, with encouragements and cheers, to fight until they were thoroughly exhausted. Fights in The Arena, most times, ended animosity between boys, as the fights were always to the finish, till a clear winner had emerged or all energy had been sapped.

Even the girls had heard about The Arena. They had also heard about Onaeko, the acclaimed champion of The Arena, who loved to fight naked and had the most fights and wins.

When Neta heard that Jeta had challenged Tobe to a fight in the pit, she tried to stop it. After she tried to convince Jeta not to fight and failed, she tried to get Tobe to pull out.

"You will not fight in that stupid pit," Neta told Tobe, a day before the scheduled showdown. "I don't know what is wrong with you boys. Must everything result in a physical fight?"

"But he challenged me. He started it."

"You taunted and goaded him! You broke his nose. He is just a jealous brother, protecting his sister. I expect you to be the mature person and ignore him."

"It is more than that," Tobe said, turning away, causing Neta's heart to race. "He hates me. It is not just about protecting his sister; Jeta has always had a special hatred for me, and you know this. Remember, he punched me first. He caused it."

Neta walked up to him, rubbing his back as he looked out the window. "You need to pull out of that fight."

Tobe turned to look at her. "It is not easy. I already accepted his challenge in front of everybody. The date has been fixed; it is happening tomorrow evening."

"And so what? Nobody is going to beat you if you don't show up."

Tobe forced a smile. "No, nobody will beat me, but they will do worse. They will turn me into an object of ridicule. Nobody breaks an acceptance to The Arena. It would have been better if I did not accept."

"I don't understand you boys and these stupid rules. They are annoying. I am telling you to end this madness. Do not fight my brother. You are not like this. Don't let him turn you into what you are not. What do you think the teachers will say when they discover that Tobe, the boy who is supposed to be a shining example, the model student, is fighting in pits?"

"This is not about the teachers. This is about honour, about my name. I cannot renege on my word. I have to fight. And moreover, what kind of boyfriend would that make me if I chickened out?"

"A good one. I am begging you, Tobe, don't fight for me. I don't want this to happen, don't you get it? What honour are we talking about here?"

"But Jeta is willing to fight for his sister. I need to show him that I can fight for you too."

Neta grabbed his wrist. "You said it yourself that Jeta has always hated you. So, for him, this is not about me. It is about whatever hatred you think he has for you. And for you, I think it is just about your ego. Don't lie to yourself and say this is about me."

Tobe pulled her closer to himself and held her by the waist. "Jeta has always hated me, but it has always been because of you. He knew I had been interested in you from day one. This is about you, Neta. It has always been about you." He stroked her right cheek. "My love."

Be "Leave me alone, *jor*," she said and slapped away his hand. "Your love that you cannot listen to."

"You worry too much. This fight needs to happen. I don't want to lie to you that I can pull out of it, then go ahead and fight. It is just a simple fight between two boys. Fights happen all the time in this school. Squabbles need to be settled. It is not like people break bones or die in these fights."

"The fact that it has not happened does not mean that it cannot happen. People actually break bones from fights. People actually die."

"You and I know that will not happen."

"What if you lose? What happens then?"

"Don't worry, My Love," Tobe said, covering her in a hug. "You don't have to think about it. It will all be over tomorrow."

Tomorrow came and boys gathered, forming the usual circle around the pit. Onaeko, the champion of the pit was even present. He was one of Tobe's supporters, one of the boys that Tobe always helped during exams. He was there to cheer him to victory. The boys watched Tobe and Jeta as they stood inside the pit with fists clenched and pointing towards each other's face, staring into each other's eyes with hatred and anger.

"You will stop talking shit about me and my sister after today," Jeta said loudly, rains of his spittle flying onto Tobe's face.

"You cannot do more than a dead rat."

Again, Jeta threw the first punch, and the fight started, drawing cheers and excitement from the audience. It had started with different combinations of well-calculated punches from the two boys. Then it graduated into a show of reckless fists and kicks. Tobe surprised everyone. Before then, they had always seen him as this slim and weak boy who only cared about mathematics. But what they saw at The Arena was different. Tobe overwhelmed Jeta with a relentless combination of punches and somehow found ways to avoid most of those that Jeta threw. Just within a few minutes, Jeta's nose was bleeding again and a welt had developed on his forehead. Tobe was clearly winning the fight. People started chanting his name. The chants were the problem; they led him to believe he was Jean Claude Van-Damme. Spurred by those chants, he spun and attempted an audacious back kick. Jeta caught his errant leg and with one quick kick, swept his other leg, sending Tobe to the ground. This allowed Jeta get into a tight mount, from which he rained fists and elbows down Tobe's face. The punishment continued and when it looked like Tobe was going to turn him over, Jeta adjusted and maintained his dominance by immediately switching into a back mount, wrapping his legs around Tobe's waist and grappling him around his neck. Desperate to free himself, Tobe threw blind elbows to Jeta's body, but they were weak, too close to generate any real power. When one elbow hit Jeta in the chest, causing him real pain, Jeta was infuriated. He planted his feet on the ground of the Arena and immediately wrapped his arms around Tobe's waist. Tobe tried to throw more elbows to catch Jeta's face behind him, but Jeta lifted him off the ground and slammed him, headfirst. The boys went quiet. Jeta stood panting. Onaeko jumped into the pit to attend to Tobe. He had stopped moving.

Tobe's neck was broken. He died shortly after he was rushed to the school clinic. Jeta was arrested, his subsequent conviction for manslaughter ensured by Tobe's politician father.

In those early years of Jeta's imprisonment, as she cried her eyes out, Neta came to believe she hadn't tried enough to stop the fight. She thought about the tools she had but failed to use. She should have threatened to end their relationship if Tobe did not agree to shun the fight. She should have reported the intended fight to one of the teachers. She blamed herself for Tobe's death, just as she blamed herself for her father's death. Her twisted relationship with her twin brother had caused both. She thought that she did not do enough to save herself and her brother. Jeta was myopic and did things for immediate gratification. Her mother always told her that although she and Jeta were twins, she was his elder sister.

"Remember to always watch over that your Coconut Head brother," she often said.

But she had failed her mother. It was why she resolved to stay away from sex at the university. She had stuck to her resolution until the night Derek walked in on them with a pistol.

12

As a child, Peter had wanted to be many things, at various stages. At first, he wanted to be Superman and constantly imagined himself flying in unison with birds of the air. But after watching Peter Parker, his namesake, leap from building to building, shooting webs from his wrists and performing awe-inspiring heroics, during a cartoon episode of Cadbury's Breakfast Television, he knew he wanted to be Spider-Man. He wanted to become this Peter Parker, this unassuming college student that moonlighted as a superhero, beating up bad guys and turning webs into grappling hooks. Gradually, the fantasy started to take over, bouncing around the chambers of his brain like a luchador competing for a wrestling prize. Then it flew out of the ring and landed into his dreams. He started seeing himself fly in his dreams; the dreams felt so real that he woke up carrying a tiny delusional conviction that he could, as a matter of fact, jump around like Spider-Man. One day, Anita Sweet told him about what she had read somewhere, how Peter Parker got his powers, how he was bitten by a spider that changed his life. The next day, he tracked down a cellar spider relaxing in its web, up the wall of their veranda. He seized it carefully and placed it on his arm, expecting it to bite him, to inject him with its venom, or whatever magical secretion present in spiders that endowed humans with abilities that defied scientific rationalization, but the spider did not; it was more interested in getting away. When it crawled off his arm and landed on the concrete floor, he tried to pick it back up but it autotomized its hind legs, making him think that his touch had harmed the spider. He gave up on it and let it scamper away, convinced that this fragile creature whose appendages yielded to a mere touch could not possibly be capable of injecting him with superhuman fluids.

Peter soon passed that stage, naturally breaking out of that world where children dwelled in brainless fantasies. He realised that it was not possible for a human being, either through magic or scientific transformation, to fly and weave spider webs. This realisation came with an easy acceptance that Peter Parker was, and would always be, a mere product of cinematic animation; *film trick*, like his mother would say. His dreams had immediately shifted to something more real, something that did not involve capes and webs. To football. He had started thinking that he would, one day, don the national team jersey with pride and make his mark in international tournaments, like Kanu Nwankwo did at the Olympic Games in Atlanta. All those years of kicking *felele* around with his younger brother in his father's compound had stuffed his thoughts with hopes and dreams.

These hopes quickly vanished when he gained admission into secondary school and started playing a more competitive form of football, realizing that he was not as good as he thought he was. It was this acceptance that had reminded him of his long-standing affection for Saint Obi, how his classmates would form circles around him to listen to him narrate movies which Obi had starred in, and from that love hatched another dream, a dream to be an actor, just like Obi. He did not particularly have a profound interest in acting, neither did he think he would make a decent actor. He had just wanted to follow his love for Saint Obi into being like him. The dream had grown so strong that when his best friend in secondary school, Paul, created the P-Square gimmick, for them to act and behave like Peter and Paul Okoye, it had felt like an imposition. Whenever Peter tried to imagine himself as a musician, these thoughts were always immediately effaced by his admiration of the actor.

When it was time to sit for JAMB exams and prepare for university life, Peter wanted to study theatre arts, just like Saint Obi. He believed that it would only be fair to develop and hone the necessary skills needed to follow in the giant footsteps of his idol. He kept hoping and believing until when it was time for him to fill his JAMB form and he mentioned it to his mother.

"Are you okay, this boy? Which one is theatre arts again?" she said. "We are talking about real courses and you are talking about theatre arts. Come on, put medicine there." The *come on* was a threat, sharp and vicious, a knife to the throat. When Paul told him that he too was applying to study medicine and surgery, it was easy for Peter to choose it as his preferred course, and as he stayed at home waiting for Unizik, he began to imagine himself as a doctor. In his dreams then, he always saw himself in hospital wards, on a white overall and a stethoscope hanging around his neck, talking to his patients assuredly. Sometimes, he saw himself in theatres with masks on, performing unknown surgeries. He decided he would embrace medicine and put his best into studying it. He wanted to be a better doctor, not like those ones his mother always complained about, those ones that always put money first before the lives of their patients. His mother would be proud of him.

But like malignant forces of failure, Unizik and a man called Daddy Ebo conspired to kill those doctor dreams of surgeries and hospitals. Paul's admission to study medicine and surgery had worked out. It was Paul who introduced him to Daddy Ebo, that deceitful devil who claimed to be a Roman Catholic priest at a parish in Umunya and was supposed to have the right connections at the university. Daddy Ebo had defrauded him of one hundred and forty thousand naira, money that his mother could have used to support her business. He then disappeared. Convincing himself that Paul did not have a hand in the scam was difficult. And the fact that Paul's dream of being a doctor was still alive made it incredibly difficult for Peter to come to terms with what had happened; the situation ruptured their friendship forever. Unizik offered him Pure and Industrial Chemistry instead, his name included later in the supplementary admission list. He accepted it because he knew it was better than staying at home, and he did not have that sort of burning passion for medicine that would make him obstinate to the point of vowing that it was either it or nothing else. So he packed his bags and boarded one of the buses at The Young Shall Grow terminal at Maza-Maza, to Awka, to study a course he knew nothing about, one that he would never bring himself to love.

His experience during his industrial training broke the little interest he was beginning to develop in chemistry. After the training, he told Amandi, "I cannot practise chemistry. I don't think I want to be a lab rat that will just be imprisoned in a room full of chemicals, carrying out meaningless analysis and tests. It is a boring life that I don't want any part in."

When it was time for Youth Service, after his state of mind had been bruised by the events that took place in Unizik, after he had survived a gunshot to the chest, after his relationship with Neta looked like it could never be repaired, he went into the NYSC camp, like most of the other graduates from different universities, unsure of what he wanted to make out of his life, unsure even of what he wanted from life. He knew he did not want to practise chemistry but did not know what he would rather do. He had never thought about banking until NYSC posted him to a bank. After Youth Service, the bank offered him a full-time job and retained him. That was how it all started.

After his employment, Peter started to understand that being a banker was more than the fancy suits and starched shirts; it required a great deal of hard work and commitment for one to be recognised and climb up the ladder. He wanted to enjoy it, to love that which he now called a profession. He poured his heart into it and gave it his best. But the job was extremely demanding and caused his life to deviate from the normal. He found himself consumed by it all, the work, the pressures. So much that he sometimes forgot how to really live, how to love, how to be happy. That young boy that had wanted to be Spider-Man, that young boy that had dreamt about being a footballer, that young boy that had seen himself cutting and stitching patients up in theatres, that young boy that had spent four years in Unizik, studying chemistry, that young boy that had wanted to be Saint Obi, was now trapped within the professional walls of the banking industry. Gradually, it started to seem his life was all about his job, with very little time spared for Winnie, with very little time available for his periodic visits to his mother's apartment, with very little time for social networks.

He often wondered how today's university students studied and prepared for exams, with the distractions of these social networks. During his days in Unizik, there had been a lot of other distractions, but the only tools available for remote socialization had been text messages and phone calls. They did not have to deal with the distractions of BBM and WhatsApp, with the distractions of Facebook.

It had been eight months since he last logged into his Facebook account. It was an account he had opened years ago, for the primary purpose of finding Neta who seemed to have disappeared into thin air. His efforts did not yield results; it was difficult to find who did not want to be found. He had, three years ago, come across a Facebook account with the name *Angela Okoye*, with no profile picture and minimal information about the owner. The account had only one post, and when Peter read it, he was certain that it belonged to Neta, because the post was about literature:

> *You are a writer*, it said. *It is only by retaining full consciousness of what you are that you can understand life and its expectations better. Most nights, untold stories in your head will keep you awake. You will not be rich, not*

as you want. You will not be as famous as a rockstar. But
you have something better...through your characters, you will
live a thousand lives in one. Through them, you will travel to
countries without leaving the confines of your room and the
vastness of your solitude. And you will tell your stories.

He had immediately sent a friend request to the account. But when he checked again the next day, the account had vanished. He knew it had been deleted; he knew it was Neta still running away from him. The last time he saw her before he heard about her reading was when she visited him at the hospital, as he recovered from wounds resulting from the bullet Derek had buried in his body. She had told him, "I think we should stop seeing each other. We can't recover from this."

"We need to pull through this together," he had said to her. And she had nodded. What he did not know then was that her mind was already made up and her statement had been a notification, not a call for permission. She left that hospital that day, never to be seen again for years.

When he logged into his Facebook account, a few days after that night he spent with Neta, and saw a message from Paul, he was not sure how to feel about it. Paul had written formally, calling him by his full name, "Peter Idenala. How are you? I am in Lagos. I would like for us to see. It has been a long time."

The last time he spoke to Paul was before they gained admission into Unizik. The discussion had been about Daddy Ebo, when Peter's name was not on the list of students admitted to study medicine and surgery. That day, they traded words of bitterness and fire. Paul's last words to him were "you can go to hell, if you like", words he could never bring himself to forget. The last time he saw Paul was more than eight years ago, during the second semester of their first year, they had been in the same class for the compulsory ICT training at their school's Afrihub building. They finished the training and received their certificates of proficiency without speaking a word to each other. From the second year, Paul went off to the permanent campus for medical students at Okeofia, and Peter never saw him again. The last time he heard anything about Paul was four years ago, when he heard that he had graduated from medical school and was a resident at the Nnamdi Azikiwe University Teaching Hospital in Nnewi.

Peter clicked Paul's profile picture on Facebook to take a closer look at the face of the woman that sat beside him in the picture, both wearing big smiles. He could tell that the woman was his wife. Seeing that Paul was online, he immediately replied, "It is good to hear from you, Paul. Where in Lagos are you?"

"Ajao Estate," Paul responded immediately. "You?"

"I am on The Island."

"I am coming to The Island later in the evening."

When evening came, Peter drove to Ahmadu Bello Way, to a restaurant called Goddies, to meet with Paul. When he walked in, he sighted Paul seated at a maroon plastic table, with a steel fork in hand, dismantling a plate of pounded yam and oha soup. Peter stood, peering at him, certain that it was him. Though he had added a little weight and now had a face full of beard, Peter knew that it was Paul, the best friend of his childhood. "Paul," he called.

Paul reacted to his call, raising his now smile-covered face. As Peter approached his table, Paul dropped his fork and stood up. He grabbed Peter and engaged him in a hug, ignoring a hand Peter had extended to him. "How are you, Peter?" he asked, grabbing Peter's arm.

Peter nodded. "I am good, Paul."

"Sit, sit," Paul said, pointing to the seat across to him. "What do you want to eat?"

Peter sat and answered, "I am fine. No need to bother yourself." "Beer?" Paul asked, and Peter hesitated. "Come on, why would you reject beer from an old friend?"

"My girlfriend is coming over to the house this night. I don't want to return home drunk, useless and overfed. I just wanted to see you." Peter beckoned to one of the waitresses. "How are you? Where are you practising?" He turned to look at the waiter. "Please, get me water." The waiter nodded and walked away.

"A hospital in Awka."

"Really? Are you back to Awka?"

Paul smiled. "Awka is like home to me. And you know what they say about home; it is where the heart lies. After my housemanship and NYSC, I tried to get back into the teaching hospital at Nnewi, as a full-time doctor, but it didn't work out. I wrote some exams, but it just did not work out. Then I met an old doctor in Awka who took me in and put me in charge of his hospital. I run the hospital for him. We have a sharing formula of the gains from the hospital operations." Paul pushed his plates of food to his right.

"Interesting," Peter said. He received the bottle of Eva water from the waitress and thanked her before returning his attention to Paul. "That's great. What brought you to Lagos then?"

"PLAB," Paul answered. Seeing the expression on Peter's face which suggested he had no idea what he meant, he explained further. "It is a medical licensing exam that one needs to pass before one can practise medicine in the UK. Professional and Linguistic Assessments Board."

"PLAB," Peter said, as if he was attempting to memorise the word. "Why are you writing a UK licensing exam? Are you leaving the country?"

"Yes, I am." Paul nodded. "There is no hope for doctors in this country."

"Why do you all say that? Why are all the doctors attempting to leave?"

"We are not valued here. We are not being paid well, both private and public sector doctors. I cannot spend all those years in school only to be receiving peanuts as salaries. I have to leave this country."

Peter sipped from his bottle of water. "In a way, I think it is a good thing that you doctors are leaving."

"Why do you think that?"

"Think about it: the only reason you guys are being undervalued is because of your population. Doctors are just too many."

"Are you sure we are that many?"

Peter nodded. "Yes, I think so. And these universities keep injecting more and more each year, into an already crowded space. When a doctor rejects a job offer because the proposed salary is too low, there's another waiting to accept that same offer, even for a lower pay. When you guys keep leaving, there will be a scarcity of good doctors. Then doctors can bargain better and receive more value. More value, more money."

"That's another angle to look at it from. But that is not my only reason for deciding to leave. My wife is already there. She is a doctor too. She is living and working there. I need to join her."

Peter nodded. "You have to. I saw on your Facebook profile that you were married. That is good news."

"Yes. It is a young marriage. Staying apart does not do us any good. If everything works out and I pass this exam, I will join her by the end of the year."

Without beer, the permanent crack in their friendship, which they had been attempting to cover with discussions about doctors and emigration, began to resurface, burying their attempts in a hollowness of silence. They had grown too apart that it was now difficult to engage in those endless streams of discussions, like they did when they were younger. Peter ordered another bottle of water and watched Paul finish his food in silence.

"I heard you were shot," Paul said, desperately cutting through the silence. "I am sorry about that. I am sorry that I did not try to visit you, but I followed the case and I was relieved to hear that you survived. I am sorry that I was not there for you."

Peter gave off a dry smile. "There is no need to be sorry. We were not talking then. We were not friends; there was no need to pretend."

Paul heaved a sigh. "What happened to us? Why did we destroy our friendship?"

"You know what happened, Paul."

Paul's voice transformed into a whisper. "Peter, I swear on my unborn kids, I had no hand in that scam. Daddy Ebo scammed us all. My admission was luck; somehow, I scored above the cut-off score they set for medicine. Daddy Ebo did not make that possible. He swindled us both. The regret I have is that I was the one who introduced him to you. I was only trying to be a good friend. For that, I must ask for your forgiveness."

"You did not think you needed my forgiveness then. What has changed now? You claimed no wrong and did not think you needed to accept any responsibility for what had happened. You said I should go to hell."

"I said that?" Paul asked in disbelief, pointing at his chest.

"Yes, you did. You said I should go to hell. What has changed now, Paul?" Peter was speaking and smiling.

"I was a child, Peter. We were children. I have lived with this burden on my conscience for years now. I understood how hard things were for you and your mother then. I understood how you had to depend on that Mr Sweet for money. I made you and your family waste that kind of money by bringing Daddy Ebo your way. Your hope of studying medicine was dashed; it was you who got swindled. You deserved to be angry at me the way you were. I should have been more considerate, more humble, and more tolerant. We were kids, Peter. I see my mistakes now. You must forgive me, brother. For the sake of the childhood that we shared, the experiences we went through together. You must forgive me."

Peter looked at him for a while, then smiled again, that

same dry and forced smile. "It is okay, Paul." He knew there was no point holding on to this decade-long grudge against Paul and the truth was, deep down, over the years, he had leaned towards the feeling that Paul could not have connived with Daddy Ebo to orchestrate such evil against him. Deep down in his stomach, he knew that Paul, that boy he played in the rain with, did not have that kind of heart. "I forgive you. I am good now, I am doing fine. It was not like I had any real passion for medicine; I was only trying to make my mother happy."

Before they left the restaurant, Paul asked him, partly joking, "What about the lady you took a bullet in the heart for?"

Peter smiled. "The funny thing is that after six years, I met her again, just last week. Can you imagine that?"

"Are you serious, Peter?" Paul asked.

"Yes *oh*. I am serious."

"How do you feel about her now?"

Peter shrugged. "Still the same, bro. She still has my heart. She disappeared from my life with it."

"And what do you want to do about that? What about the girlfriend you said was waiting at home for you? Does she know about this woman that has your heart, this woman you almost lost your heart for?"

Peter shook his head and bit his lower lip. "No, she does not have a single idea."

"And what do you want?"

Peter sighed. "I don't know, man," he said. He knew that he wanted Neta, and whenever he mustered courage big enough to listen to his feelings, they always suggested to him that he needed her in his life. He knew that he wanted her, but admitting it to himself, or anyone else, scared him sometimes.

Paul put a hand on his shoulder, making him remember Amandi, how he always held his shoulder. "Peter, you were like a brother to me," he said. "We have had our issues, but I still love you like a brother. I will not lie to you." He patted his shoulder and withdrew his hand. "If someone holds your heart, if someone holds that sort of importance in your life, you would be nuts not to do everything within your human and natural capacity to be with them. You would be nuts."

As he drove back home from Goddies that evening, Paul's words remained with him, almost like they filled the air around him, like Paul was in his head and was, at the same time, seated next to him, singing them like a song: *You would be nuts not to do everything within your human and natural capacity to be with her.* He was driving home to meet Winnie, waiting at home, but he knew he no longer wanted to be around her. He tried to form breakup lines in his head, but they cut into discordant strings of nonsense. It was hard to breakup with someone who had not done anything wrong, who did not look like they deserved to be broken up with.

When he got home, Winnie helped him out of his clothes and boiled water for him to have his bath. When he stepped out of the shower, she served him dinner, a light combination of boiled plantain and fried egg. As he sat in the living room, eating and watching her as she watched him with a smile, his heart started racing. Those breakup words he had planned to speak, no matter how disorganised they were, retreated down his throat. He could not do it, not today. Winnie had not done anything to deserve this kind of treatment.

She cleared the table when he finished eating and did the dishes. When she returned to the living room, she took his wrist and led him into the room. He followed her without contests, like a lamb being led to the slaughterhouse. Before she undressed him, she undressed herself, her naked body filling him with that rush of desire like it had always done. This time, she put herself in charge, rejecting and thwarting all his efforts to take control. When he understood that she wanted this, something different, to lead him through this ride, he allowed her, soaking up all the pleasures her touches offered. They did not make love; she made love to him.

So, it confused him when she spoke to him, stroking his chest as they lay in each other's arms. "This is the last, Pete. I am leaving you."

Peter sat up to look her in the eye and make sure she had been serious when she spoke. "What?"

"I am leaving you, Pete," she repeated, sitting up too, pulling the blanket up to her waist. "I have to go."

Peter chuckled. "Where is this coming from?"

"There is someone my mother wants me to get married to. I met him. He is a good man and is ready to have me. I have made my decision, but I needed to let you know because I respect you." She reached for Peter's hand. "Believe me, this is hard for me, but I think I deserve to be loved. I need to give someone else a chance. I don't want to waste any more time with you."

"Your mother does not know me. She cannot just

arrange for you to marry another when she has not taken her time to meet me."

"You did not even want to see her. I told you she was in Lagos,I wanted you to meet her, but you did not want that. I was waiting for you and you were nowhere to be found. You disrespected me."

"I told you, I was busy at work."

"Spare me that, Peter. I am not a baby. I know when a man is not mine." She touched Peter's cheek. "You need to let me go. If we keep seeing each other, I won't be able to let go because seeing you sparks up these feelings that I cannot hide. I am not tired of you. I am just afraid that I will get lost in this and ruin my life."

Peter stood up from the bed and shook his head. "I don't want to accept this," he said. His words were not confident, but he felt compelled to express some form of resistance.

"You know what I am saying is true. You only wear your romantic form at night, giving me intimacies and pleasures that I have never felt with anyone before you. But I can barely recognise you by day. You don't even think of me when I am not around you. You do not miss me, you do not want anything serious with me. A clever girl would run, but I have stayed. Let me be the fool for love this time, I said to myself. I knew it was unhealthy to stay, but I kept hoping that you would change and become mine one day, just as much as I wanted to be yours." Tears were already streaming down her face. "I don't want you to think that you did anything wrong to me. I knew what I was getting myself into. You did not make promises you did not keep." She stood up from the bed too, wiping off tears from her face. "Loving you was never a mistake, but I have to let you go now. I cannot force you to love me. You hide behind your banking job, but the truth is that you cannot love anybody."

"Why are you saying these things?"

"You are lost, your heart is lost, and until you find the person you lost it to, others will keep suffering for it. I don't want to suffer anymore. I am leaving."

She started dressing up. He sat on the bed, watching her. He wanted to speak, to say things, to beg her to stay, that he was going to make efforts to be a better lover, but he knew he would be lying. He knew that by deciding to leave, she had done him a favour and had made things easier for him. He knew she was right; the right thing for him to do was to let her go. His heart was lost and he needed to be with the one that had made it hers. He needed to be with Neta.

13

The next Saturday, days after Winnie broke up with Peter, days after he met with Paul at Goddies, Neta called.

"There is a rat in my apartment," she said quickly, sounding flustered. "A big one, Peter."

"Really?" Peter asked, not sure if his disbelief was about the rat, or about her calling him to talk about a rat.

"Yes, Peter," she said.

"How did a rat get into your apartment?" Peter asked.

"I don't know, Peter. I need you to buy rat poison while coming later this evening."

"I did not say I was visiting today." Peter found the strength to say, excited that she wanted him around.

"Today is Saturday," she said, the agitation in her voice had died down. "Do you have a meeting with your MD?" Her voice was low and playful.

Peter laughed. "Okay, I will be at your place later today. But don't you think you should get a trap instead? With a rat poison, the rat dies in a hidden place and the smell is always hideous."

"The rat is big; it will drag the trap along."

Peter smiled. "Okay. You will have your poison."

"Thank you, Saint Peter," she said.

Peter's smile widened. "You are welcome."

That evening, Peter bought the rat poison she had asked for. He drove to her place and met her as she stood at the balcony, feeding her parrot. Peter stood behind her, a smile on his face, watching her.

"It would not talk," she said, still attending to T.T.

"Is it male or female?" Peter asked, walking up closer behind her.

"It is a male parrot."

"How do you know?"

Neta emptied the plate and dropped it on top of the cage. She closed the cage and turned to face Peter. "From the features. I did some reading."

"If you wanted it to talk, why didn't you go for a female?" Peter said, his lips retrieving into a grin.

Neta hit him on the chest. "What do you mean by that? I have seen men who talk more than women." She left him and walked off, into her bedroom, and he followed her.

"Here," he said, handing her over a plastic bag. "The rat poison you asked for."

She received it from him, looked into it and dropped it on her dresser. "Thank you, Peter," she said and sat on the bed. "You are a life saver." Then she got up from the bed, picked the bag and kept it under the bed. "One needs to be careful with these things."

"Why do you need to be careful with it?"

"Isn't that obvious; it is poisonous, Peter." She sat again on the bed. "My father used to say that *ihe n'egbu oke n'egbu mmadu*: that which can kill a rat can also kill a human."

Peter sat next to her. "I do not agree with you. I don't think this poison can kill a man."

"I am telling you something, but you won't listen now. You cannot afford to consume this. It is also dangerous for you."

It turned into an argument, one that culminated into Peter picking up his phone to dial Paul's number. "My friend is a doctor," he said. "He should know better." And just like that, Paul was his *friend* again. He called Paul and put him on speaker. "Paulo, how are you?"

"My brother, I dey oh. You?"

im alright," he answered impatiently and""I'm alright," he answered impatiently and jumped to his reason for calling. "I am arguing something with someone and I need you to settle this. She thinks rat poisons can kill humans too. Please, tell her how wrong she is."

"They can actually," Paul answered, disappointing Peter. "It depends, though, on the potency and quantity. With the right potency and right quantity, it can kill a human being?"

"You see?" Neta said happily. "You never listen."

"Who is the person you are arguing with? Who is speaking?" Paul asked.

Peter glanced at Neta before answering. "Neta. It is Neta." "Neta? The girl that stole your heart?" Paul said; his voice carried a big smile.

"Bye, Paul," Peter said and cut him off. He looked at Neta and their eyes met. "Paul can talk nonsense, don't mind him."

"Which Paul is this?" she asked. The smile on her face had waned. "Paul from your secondary school?"

"Yes."

"I don't understand it. You did not speak to him in Unizik. How did you reconnect?"

"We did not. We still weren't speaking. I just met him last week after all those years. He came into Lagos to write an exam he called PLAB."

Neta nodded. "I know PLAB. He is relocating to the UK?" "Yes, he is. His wife is already there."

Neta looked away and sighed. "You told him I stole your heart?" "Don't listen to him. He was just joking."

Neta looked at him and their eyes met again. "You told him I stole your heart," she repeated, and this time it was not a question.

Peter stood up and started pacing the room. "Yes, I did," he admitted. "But you already know this. You have always known this. What have you not done to me, ehn? You stole my heart and disappeared with it for more than six years. Then you killed me in your book."

Neta smiled and stood up. "No, I did not."

"You did. You wrote that I was shot in the chest. You wrote that I lay on the floor, unmoving. You ended it there. Everyone who reads your book would interpret it to mean that I died. Who gets shot in the chest and survives?"

Neta held his shoulders. "You, Saint Peter. You are a survivor. What I wrote in a book has nothing to do with that; it doesn't change that. People who read it can interpret it in whatever way they want. Besides, it wasn't even your name. I keep saying this to you, there is no character in that book named Peter." She stroked his arm. "And don't think you were the only one whose heart was stolen. I know I don't admit things easily, but you have my heart too, Peter."

"Are you sure, Neta? You were willing to go decades without seeing me. And I checked my safe, I don't have anybody's heart in it. How do I believe you?"

She wrapped her arms around his waist. "My therapist is certain that my happiness lies with you."

"Which one is therapist again?" Peter asked. "Why are you seeing a therapist?"

Neta shrugged. "That is what lost people do," she said. "Stop saying that."

"But it is the truth. I am but a lost woman on a lonely path. My only companion has long been my void of a heart, inflated dreams." She held Peter's face, piercing into his eyes again. "You are a big part of my dream, Peter. I have spent years running away from it, thinking I could wish it away, because I needed to forget all that happened in school. I thought I could move on from us, from Derek's death, by keeping you away from my life. Staying away from you came with at a big emotional cost. You were right, Peter: I was a coward. I should have stayed. We should have faced it together. I shouldn't have thrown away what we had because life visited us with a couple of tragedies. I should have put our feelings and love first as you have always done from day one. I apologise for all these years, Peter. For everything I put you through. For the bullet you took because of me."

"Shh, shh." Peter put his index finger across her lips. "You can't blame yourself for that. I don't blame you. It was not supposed to happen."

"Every day, I keep thinking things would have played out differently if I had listened to you that night when you warned me not to open that door. Almost like you saw it."

"I didn't see anything, Neta. I was not man enough to face Derek. I was nervous and scared. I did not think he was standing at the doorway with a gun. I did not see anything."

"Still, I should have listened. If I did not open that door, he would have left. The next morning, whatever he smoked would have cleared from his eyes. It was all my fault."

Her eyes were getting clogged with tears.

"Don't blame yourself, Neta." Peter planted a kiss on her forehead, then on her lips. She tightened her grip around him as they kissed, tears flowing down her cheeks. He withdrew from the kiss and started wiping tears off her face with his hands. "I cannot live without you, Angel." It felt liberating calling her *Angel* again after so many years. "My mother has invited me to the house next weekend. She said she will be making new yam. Come with me, let us go and see her."

Neta pulled away from him, sniffling and rubbing her nose. "Why? Why do you want me to meet your mother?"

"What are you afraid of? Are you afraid of being my wife?"

"Are you serious right now? How do you jump into things like this?"

Peter grabbed her right wrist. "I am serious. Of course, I am serious. What is the point waiting? It has been established: we need each other. We will both be happier people if we are together. Let us make it permanent. I know I am not perfect. There is still a big room for improvement. I will carry all my emotional and mental belongings and move into that room, like I have always done for you. Things will be better this time, Angel. We are no longer children. We now have a better understanding of how life works. Let us try again, please. Marry me."

"These decisions are not that simple, Peter."

"You can take your time and think about it." Peter was talking desperately. "I will give you time, but you must come with me to Yaba next weekend to visit my mother. I want her to meet you. Would you do that for me?" He pulled her closer. "Your biggest and most fundamental impediment is that you constantly overthink things. You always want to be in control of your feelings and emotions. But that is not living. Living is knowing that sometimes, we need to lose control of our innermost selves. If love demands to be felt, let us feel it. If life demands to be lived, let us live. And if living, being who we are, means that mistakes have to be made, let us make them, for it is through them that we learn and become better people. I have grown to understand that the worst kind of life is that which we live in fear of feeling, which we live in regrets from the past." He ran his fingers down her hair. "You used to quote some guy to me when we were in school, remember? Life is to be lived, not controlled."

Neta smiled. "Ellison," she said. "Ralph Ellison."

"That's the one." Peter nodded. "Unizik is in the past. True, mistakes were made. True, friendships were broken. True, we lost people who were close to us. But we cannot shut out the feelings of our hearts because of this past. It is gone, we have to move on, we have to live. We cannot play that *pack* of our lives *bart*." Peter smiled before he corrected his last sentence. "Sorry, we cannot play that *part* of our lives *back*."

Neta smiled too, then started giggling.

"What? Why are you laughing? Come on, Neta. Everyone makes that mistake."

"I know," she said. "Do you know what it is called?" Peter shook his head. "Does it have a name?"

"Mm-hmm. It is a common error in English language known as spoonerism."

Peter drew her to himself and held her in a warm embrace. "Spoonerism," he repeated. And just like that, it felt like they were back in school, young and in love. She was teaching him words and grammar, like in the old days.

14

Just as it had been in recent times, the days raced past and the weekend that Neta had agreed to meet Peter's mother came. That day, after Peter left, she had called her mother on Skype and told her about this man she dated in school that had proposed to her, about this man that wanted her to meet his mother as soon as possible.

"Do you love him?" her mother had asked. "Does he love you? Are you certain?"

"Yes, Mum," Neta had answered, her lips curled in a smile. "Does he have a stable job?" Her mother had pressed further.

"Hope he is not one of these boys that are into internet fraud. Yahoo-Yahoo boys."

"Mum, he has a good job. He is a good man, and he loves me above everything else. You will like him."

Her mother had sighed and said, "Okay then. You can go and see his mother. You deserve to be happy. You have been through a lot in this life. I wish I were in the country with you right now."

Neta was in her study with Esther, waiting for Peter to come and pick her up. Esther was fiddling through the books in the shelf, checking them one after the other. "Neta, come and give me a book to read," she said.

"Lai lai," Neta responded from the seat where she sat. "The last one I gave you, you are yet to return. "You still have my *I Do Not Come to You By Chance*. You need to return that one before I can give you another one. I am sure you haven't even read it."

"Neta, you are being stingy. Stingy over a book."

"That is your problem. Hear the way you say it like it means nothing. I don't buy these books cheap. But even if I did, they are my books, my possessions. The fact that I took out money to buy them means that I attach value to them. Even after reading them, I love to still have them on my shelf. That is why I don't understand it when some people borrow my books and don't return them." She pointed at Esther. "People like you. You think it's not important. To you, it is just a book. When I lend you a book, it stays on my mind until I get it back. It's like a monumental debt I'm being owed."

"Okay o." Esther withdrew her hands from the shelf. "I will return your book and take another one."

"But you don't read them. Why do you bother? It is not solely about returning them; it is also about reading them, reading them the right way."

Esther stepped away from the bookshelf. "Wonders shall never end," she said, jamming her palms together. "All this plenty sermon and grammar because of book. I am happy that you have found someone. I am happy that you will soon get married. You need to understand that there are more important things to life than these books. I am happy."

"Esther, let us not jump like this. I have not even agreed to marry him."

"And you are going to see his mother? Neta, your problem is that you don't embrace good things when you see them, almost like you do not think that you deserve happiness. Why are you like this? It is these books. Someone needs to throw all of them away."

Neta smiled. "Your plan is to collect them one after the other without returning any, until they are all missing, ehn?"

"Neta, I am being serious now. What is your problem? You need to change. Accept that young man and whatever he is bringing, you will be happy you did. And I told you to wear makeup, you will not listen, this girl."

"I don't need more makeup, Esther. The powder is fine."

"You are going to see his mother for the first time. First impressions matter. Wear contact lenses, you will not agree. That is how you will be carrying eyeglasses up and down."

"I don't want her to think that I wear makeup all the time when it's not true. I don't want her to see me as fake. I want her to see me the way that I am." Neta blew a breath. "I am just nervous, Esther. It is not like I have done this before. I've never gone to see any man's mother."

Esther went behind Neta where she sat and wrapped her arms around her. "Don't be nervous, love. You will be fine. I want this for you and I want you to want it for yourself because it is love. And love is beautiful. You need to embrace it."

Neta smiled and rubbed one of Esther's arms. "Thank you, Esther. You have been a good friend."

Twenty minutes later, Peter arrived. He left with Neta, while Esther remained in the house, watching TV.

TOY WOMAN, AS expected, had aged, just like Peter's mother, but she was still beautiful and her face still glistened when she smiled. Peter's mother had always told Peter that Toy Woman was a friend sent from heaven. She said she was the only one that stayed after her husband died and all the money stopped coming.

"She still stayed when we became poor," she had said to Peter. "When it was clear that being friends with me no longer came with a promise of financial and material gains, she stayed. All those other leeches that called themselves my friends disappeared; they left me to my fate. Prisca stayed with me through my most difficult times, even when that man killed your father. She was with me at the hospital, after the burial, through my tribulations and struggles."

When Peter arrived at his mother's apartment with Neta, Toy Woman was present. They all exchanged pleasantries and hugged one another. Peter introduced Neta as "Chukwunetam, the girl I told you about", prompting his mother to give Neta another hug. "How are you, my daughter?" she asked, her face overtaken by a wide smile. She introduced Toy Woman to Neta.

"This is Prisca, my very good friend." Toy Woman smiled at Neta and immediately told her how beautiful she thought she was, causing Neta to drop her face in diffidence.

They all walked into the sitting room where they sat at a table to eat a meal of hot yam porridge and greens. It was difficult for Peter's mother to make three sentences in a row without finding ways to squeeze *Prisca* into it. "Peter, help me thank Prisca," she said, lifting the lid of the big bowl that contained the yam pieces. "She travelled to the village and brought new yam for me. Eat it and see how sweet and soft it is." When Peter tried to dish from the bowl, she slapped his hand. "You need to pray first, this boy." She turned to Toy Woman who had her eyes fixed on Neta, as if she had been paid by Peter's mother to observe and scrutinize her, to see that which she might miss. "Prisca, do you know that this boy no longer goes to church?"

Toy Woman immediately turned to Peter. "Peter, is that true?"

"You don't need to listen to him," Peter's mother cut in. "It is true. This is not the way I brought them up. His brother is a youth leader in his parish in Abuja. But with him, I don't know what happened in that school I sent him to, that university." She turned to Neta. "Chukwunetam, hope you go to church." Neta nodded. "Which church do you attend?"

"Catholic, ma," Neta said politely, a smile on her face.

"Good. That is great to hear," Peter's mother said, a sudden excitement taking over her voice. "You must make sure you change him. You must pull him out of this path to hell he is on."

"Mummy!" Peter called out. "Ahn-ahn! Just because I don't go to church on Sundays, God will now condemn me to eternal damnation? It is not that serious nah."

"Shut up, this boy," his mother barked and he stifled a laughter. "It is not a joking matter. The Bible says that we must remember the Sabbath day and keep it holy. It is an instruction from God. What happens to people who don't obey God's instructions? They go to hell. All your life, I have been trying to teach you, but you don't listen. You cannot keep living your life without being in a close relationship with the Creator. Do you even still pray?"

"Yes nah, I pray," Peter lied. He stopped praying a long time ago, after Amandi's disappearance. What happened to Amandi destroyed whatever was left of his faith in God. He did not think God was fair to Amandi. They were all children, growing, making mistakes and learning. Amandi's HIV infection was an unfair price to pay for the lessons of youth. He blamed himself for the things he thought he could have done to prevent it that he did not do, but he also blamed God. His mother once told him that God wanted the best for them, that his guardian angels were always with his children, protecting them from harm. Where was Amandi's guardian angel when he went into bed with the one that infected him? Or was it that Amandi was not God's child? He began to pull away from God and from the church until it got to the point where he felt he had completely lost the face of God, where he was beginning to question his existence. Now, whenever he knelt or closed his eyes in an attempt to pray, he could not find words. He did not think God was listening to him anymore. His mother did not know that even Neta could not do anything about it. The few times she dragged him to church after Amandi's disappearance in school, he went with her to make her happy, he was not thinking of God because he always left his mind at home. And there was no way he could delve into that heavenly realm of spirituality where he was supposed to be free and lost in communion with God and his angels without his mind.

"Peter, you have to be praying," Toy Woman said. "Prayer is the master key that opens all doors. Things are happening in this world. You cannot live in it like there is no God. You need to be strong spiritually."

Peter nodded and made one of those promises he had made to Neta and his mother countless times, one of those promises that he used to end conversations about God and attending mass.

"I have heard. I will improve, I promise."

"That is what you will always say," his mother said. "You promise these things and you fail. After everything God has done for you. How many people survive gunshots to the chest? What more do you want him to do for you before you start to appreciate him? God loves you. He is calling and trying to reach out to you every single day. All you need to do is walk into his arms, but you have refused to do that!" She turned to Neta. "Did he tell you that they wanted to kill him years ago, in that godforsaken university, ehn?"

Neta nodded. "He did," she said, looking at Peter as the smile on his face waned. "I have seen the scar." *Poor woman*, she thought. *If only she knew I was the reason her son was shot. Poor woman.*

Peter's mother sighed and said to Neta, "Chukwunetam, please pray for us before our food gets cold."

Neta nodded and clasped her hands. "Father Lord, please bless this food before us, through Jesus Christ our lord." They all echoed *amen* and started eating, dishing food into their individual plates from the big bowl.

Through the meal, Neta answered questions thrown at her by Peter's mother about life and about work. When she told them that she was a fulltime writer, Peter's mother found it interesting. She told Neta that for her, the best book she had read, written by an African, was Buchi Emecheta's *Second Class Citizen*. They started discussing the book, stating what they thought the protagonist's strengths and weaknesses were. Peter listened to them, nodding and not contributing to the conversation, happy that Neta was getting along with his mother. Toy Woman too did not join the conversation. Her eyes were still fixed inquisitively on Neta, observing her as she ate. The times Neta looked her way and their eyes met, she maintained eye contact with her, making Neta uneasy. Neta stopped looking to her direction but still felt the weight of her eyes.

"Your face looks familiar," Toy Woman said calmly to Neta.

"Really?" Neta asked with a smile on her face.

Toy Woman did not return the smile. She looked worried and a little spooked. She turned to Peter's mother beside her. "Her face looks familiar," she said to her.

Peter's mother took a curious look at Neta. "Is it possible you have met her before?" she asked Toy Woman. Toy Woman leaned in and whispered something in her ear. Her mouth opened, suggesting a sudden realisation. "It is true oh, she looks like her."

"Looks like who?" Peter asked, curiosity rising in his throat.

His mother ignored him and asked Neta, "Nne, where are you from?"

"Anambra," Neta responded. "Agulu."

"You see?" Toy Woman said. "I told you she looks like her. I noticed it the very moment she walked in."

Peter's curiosity transformed into worry because he could see the seriousness in the faces of the women. He looked at Neta and saw that through her calmness, confusion was beginning to take over her. "Mummy, what is going on?" he asked.

And again, his mother ignored him and asked Neta, "Nne, what is your surname?"

"Okoye," Neta said slowly, her eyes rolling in confusion.

"Ifu go ya?" Toy Woman exclaimed, snapping her fingers. "Have you seen it?"

Peter's mother moved to the edge of her seat. "Is your mother, by any means, Edna?"

Neta's eyes widened. "That is my mother's name, yes. Edna is her name."

Peter's mother sighed and dropped back on her seat. "Where is Edna now?"

"She is in the US. How do you know my mother?"

Peter's mother stood up and walked into the room, her hands on her head.

"Aunty Prisca, what is going on here?" Peter asked Toy Woman. "How do you know her mother?"

Toy Woman looked away. "Go and ask your mother. She is in a better position to tell you."

Peter stood up and walked into the room, leaving Neta and Toy Woman to sit through the tension and awkwardness that had saturated the environment.

Peter met his mother sobbing in her bedroom. He sat beside her and asked. "What is going on? I am confused."

"That girl must leave my house now," she said. "Take her home."

"I need an understanding first. This is a girl that I am going to marry."

His mother grabbed her head again with both hands and cried, "Chai! Edna has found me again. This woman, this woman, what did I do to you in this life? Why are you after me?"

"Mummy, talk to me!" Peter was giving in to his anger. "What is going on here?"

"You cannot marry that girl." "Why?"

"Because you don't know her. You don't know anything about her family."

Peter took his mother's hands. "Mummy, I need you to tell me what you know," he begged. "Please, Mummy."

"You should ask her how her father died, the date he died. Her father was the man that killed your own father in that accident." Peter freed her hands, his face tightened into a grimace of shock. "Her mother is Edna Okoye. I met her at the hospital and she also visited our home then. Chukwunetam is a splitting image of her. She was the vessel our enemies used to get us. I thought she was done, now she is after my sons. You cannot marry that girl."

"Are you sure about this?"

"I am very sure," she said and buried her face in her hands, sobbing. "They killed your father, Peter. They put us through all the hardships we went through over the years, they destroyed our family. Take her home, Peter. Please, take her home. Please."

Peter nodded and stepped into the sitting room. "Let us go, Angel," he said to Neta. Neta immediately stood up. She wanted to be away and far from here. The air no longer felt sufficient.

"Thank you, Aunty Prisca," she said.

"Bye, bye," Toy Woman said without looking.

Peter and Neta remained in silence as they drove back to Neta's apartment, their hearts filled with thoughts and questions. Neta only spoke when the car drove to a halt in front of her apartment building. "What the hell is going on, Peter?"

"How did your father die?" asked Peter.

"In a car accident," Neta responded. "We talked about this in school."

"I see." Peter looked away. "It is true then. They are right." "What is true, Saint Peter?" Neta asked, touching Peter's shoulder.

"You don't tell me anything, Neta." Peter's face held imminent anger. "I don't know anything about your family. You keep everything about your past like a deep secret."

"Why are you talking like this?" Neta asked. "I told you how I lost my father."

"Your father was the man my mother told us that killed my father years ago. Your father ran that red light that caused the accident that killed my father. Toy Woman recognised you; she said you look exactly like your mother. Apparently, everything they said is true. Even after twelve years, my mother has not forgiven the man that caused the whole thing, neither has she forgiven his wife, your mother."

Neta felt her heart gaining weight. "Are you serious about this?

Do you think this is true?"

"Of course, it is. You heard them mention your mother's name."

Peter shook his head. He was struggling to hold on to a particular feeling. He felt disappointed from the undeniable realisation that convincing his mother to accept Neta would be a herculean task. Then there was anger rising in his belly towards Neta for telling him so little about her family, about her past, but he did not want to embrace this feeling and express it the way it was coming to him, throwing any tantrum he could find within himself. He believed that if Neta had been more open about her family, if she had shared more from her past, they would have, at some point, realised that their fathers died in the same accident. He decided it was best if he went home. "I should just go home."

"Are you sure you don't want to come in?" Neta asked, her voice a plea. "You should come in and rest a little while."

"I need to go home," Peter said, more firmly this time. The last time he had been this firm with her was when he was still asking her out in Unizik. "Let me go home."

Neta knew that she needed to let him be alone. She, too, had her own confusions to deal with, questions she needed answered. Without uttering more words, she found her way out of his car. She did not say goodbye to him when she exited his car. She did not kiss or hug him. As she walked towards her apartment gate, she heard him drive off, his car engine revving away, but just as she had already promised herself, she did not look back. She had also promised herself not to cry. She was beginning to accept the reality that tears had never solved anything for her; they would not solve this.

She found her apartment keys under the foot mat, where she had asked Esther to keep them before she left. When she opened the door that led to her sitting room, she saw her parrot, T.T, in its cage, on the centre table in the sitting room. She sighed and dialled Esther's number.

"Hi, Love," Esther said. "My number one writer."

"Hi, Esther."

"How did it go with Peter's mother?" Esther asked. Neta could feel the weight of her voice over the phone, drenched in excitement and curiosity.

Neta nodded. "It went well," she said. "Very well. We will talk about it more when we see."

"You don't sound okay. Are you sure all is well?" The excitement in her voice had been immediately replaced by concern. "Do you want me to come over now?"

"No, dear. Let us talk when next we see."

"So, why did you call me? You don't want to *gist* me over the phone, so why did you call? You are missing me? For once, say it with your mouth, say that you miss me."

She sat on the couch and pulled the centre table close to her, her eyes fixed on T.T as it stared back at her. "You left T.T in the sitting room, Esther."

"Oh, I forgot. I was just playing around. I have been wanting to ask you, why do you call the parrot *Titi*."

"It is not Titi, but T.T, like *double t*. The parrot is tongue-tied, so I named it T.T."

That was when she heard the parrot talk. "T…T," it said, mimicking her.

"Are you there, Neta?" "Esther, T.T just spoke." "Are you serious?"

"Yes, I am. It said *T.T.*" Neta leaned forward, towards T.T and said calmly. "T…T."

"T…T," the parrot repeated with its robotic voice.

Neta gasped in excitement. "How are you?" she asked the parrot, but it repeated *T.T* instead.

"It is speaking, yes. I can't believe this." "I told you, what that bird needed was time and training. You lacked patience. That bird would have been singing and conversing with you by now if you had made out a little time to train it properly." "But I have never owned a bird before, I have never owned a parrot. I don't have the skills to train him." It was the first time she was referring to the parrot with a human personal pronoun. The fact that it had spoken, to her, meant it was more alive and human than she had thought. This meant that neuters could no longer be used to address it. "I don't even have the time for that." She observed T.T, as it moved its head back and forth. "Can I call you back, Esther?"

"Okay," Esther said. "Speak more words to the parrot. Let it learn new words and even sentences."

"I hear you, Esther. I will call you back after I have showered and spoken to my mother. We have a long gist."

"That reminds me: When you left for Yaba, some man came to look for you. He looked like a madman, lean and with bushy hair. He wanted to wait for you but I was having none of it. He was saying things that did not make sense."

Neta stood up from the couch and started walking towards her bedroom. "Who was that? What was he saying? What did he say his name was?"

"He said his name was Angelo, that he is your brother. When I looked into his eyes, I saw you. You two look alike *oh*.

Do you know him? You have never said anything about a brother."

Neta's heart skipped and a wave of dizziness took over her. She immediately knew who it was. So when she heard a knock on the door, she ended her call with Esther and ambled towards the door, imagining what he looked like now. Slowly, she opened the door, and just as she had expected, he was standing in front of her, grinning.

He had grown and changed through the years, but she was certain that it was him. She could see through the beard and rashes that covered his face. His smile was still the same. His twin brother was out of prison and was standing in front of her.

"Chukwujetalum," she called, a little bemused and close to tears. It felt like she had a ghost standing in front of her, a malnourished ghost.

"Neta," he called and moved towards her. "Aren't you happy to see me?"

She grabbed and hugged him as tightly as she could. They remained in each other's arms, crying over shared, unrealised dreams.

15

The main thing Neta remembered about shadows was that Jeta had been fascinated about them when they were children. From this curiosity flowed a stream of questions. He would barrage her with irritating and childish questions about shadows, where they came from, how they were formed, what they represented. His short-lived obsession ignited her own interest. When she was not answering any of his unreasonable questions about shadows, she was observing him fool around.

One night, she walked in on him slapping and kicking his own shadow cast on the kitchen wall by a kerosene lantern. "Go away," he repeated playfully, giggling as he opened up his body, his legs wide apart, his fists clenched and pointing towards the wall, like a martial artist posing before a fight. Another night, as they returned home from Block Rosary Crusade, he tried to outrun his shadow cast on the ground as it followed him relentlessly, sprinting away and leaving Neta walking behind him and laughing at his stupidity. When Neta eventually got home, she met him seated on the dining table, gasping for breath and gulping cold water from a cup.

"Get off that table," Neta said to him. "You know Mummy does not like us sitting on tables."

Jeta got down and sat on one of the seats. "It is not possible to outrun your shadow. It is part of you," he admitted.

"You make me laugh, Jeta," Neta said. "Of course, you cannot outrun it and you cannot hit it. Your shadow is you and you are it."

These days, whenever she thought about her past, she remembered her own words: *Your shadow is you and you are it.* When Peter told her, days ago, that the past was gone and they needed to move on, she did not believe him. It would have been comforting to believe that the times of life rolled with a magic eraser that rubbed away and neutered sour memories of the tragedies and mistakes from the past. It would have been liberating if the past did not count. She needed it more than everyone else. She wanted to believe him, that it was possible to leave the past in the past, but she knew it was not true. She knew that the past, like a towering shadow, was so powerful and overreaching that it even moved years ahead and that the only thing certain about the future was that the past would be present in it. For one not to be able to see one's shadow, one must be prepared not to see anything at all. For one not to be able to remember the past, one must be prepared not to remember anything at all. And for one not to remember anything at all, one must be prepared to die. That was the only way out, to walk down the path of death, to the unknown land of no return. She knew that whenever she found herself in this land, the only thing she would be grateful for was that it had ended, this torture from the past.

Her past had haunted and hunted her for years. She had gone through school and life, carrying its events in a box of silence, thinking that it was safer not to share, not to push the lid open to people she did not trust. And even when she trusted, she still held this box shut, for she felt revealing what she carried in this box would leave her exposed to human judgement and criticisms because she believed she was personally responsible for everything her past had stored away. It was true that Aunty Chidinma had caused the incest that existed between her and Jeta, but Neta felt responsible for it. She felt responsible because she knew that she should have put an end to it. She could have; all she needed to do was report what she had seen that day to her mother, that day that she walked in on Jeta and Aunty Chidinma playing *Touch me, I Touch You*. Even then, she knew something was not right about it, but she trusted Aunty Chidinma. She allowed herself be convinced that it was normal; she allowed Aunty Chidinma convince her to join them in the game. The game had felt good, better than whatever physical pleasure she had ever felt before. That feeling was like a drug, one that she and Jeta had become addicted to. It was the kick of this drug that led them to the sin of full- blown incest. She allowed Jeta to convince her to continue because deep down, a part of her did not really want to stop. It felt too good to be stopped. Yes, it was Aunty Chidinma that started it. They were just children, normal twins that just wanted to play and talk about shadows, but Aunty Chidinma had robbed them of their innocence, and had replaced it with a knowledge too heavy and dysfunctional for their young minds to bear. Neta blamed herself because she let it all happen. Some days, she wanted to defend herself, that she was only a child and could not have done much to stop it. That way, it would have been easy for her to deal with, to throw all the blames she carried under the bus of childish innocence and naivety. But her conscience would not let her, because she knew that she knew then, even as a child, that it was wrong. She should have spoken up. She should have told her mother and reprimanded Jeta, the same way she always watched over him, the same way she had firmly told him that his obsession with shadows was stupid. The biggest stupidity, however, was that she was sleeping with her brother, that she had carried on with it.

It was true that her father died in a car accident. He had ignored a red traffic light while speeding home to his dear family, and had paid with his life, and with the life of another. It was an accident; that was what happened, what everyone was told, what everyone believed. Accidents happened all the time. This was a lie, Neta told herself. It was not a simple accident. She knew this and saw the same feeling in her mother's eyes months and years after the accident. She did not see it in Jeta's eyes: he had been totally disconnected from that acceptance of blame that was built with remorse and heartbreak, a knowing too strong that it matured into insomnia and self-resentment. That accident had happened because her father was rushing home to answer her mother's distress call. The only reason that distress call had happened was because her mother had caught her in bed with her twin brother. If the incest had not existed, her father would not have had any cause to leave his office at that time, he would not have run that light, he would not have died that day. It was also her fault that the other victim of that fateful day had to die as well.

When they returned to school and Jeta still wanted to be with her, in that immoral and incestuous way she believed had killed her father, she affirmed what she had seen in his eyes after their father died; a complete lack of remorse, a painful disconnect from reality. She wanted to teach him a lesson, that what they were doing was wrong and abnormal, but he did not want to learn. As if he had condensed air at the doors of his eyes, he was blinded by sex and what he had called *love*. She was desperate to teach him, to open his eyes to the evil they had done themselves and their parents. She was desperate to teach him this lesson, even if it meant breaking his *coconut head* and forcing the lesson in. Tobe was the machete needed for her to achieve this. Tobe had died because of her, because she used him.

She took the life of that bright young boy. She was responsible for his death, just like she felt responsible for Jeta's imprisonment. These were all ramifications of the incest. So if the incest was her fault, as she let herself believe, she killed Tobe and sent Jeta to prison. This was the weight she put on herself throughout her stay in Unizik, as she tried to hide in solitude and in literature.

She had thought that she had seen it all, that her heart could take no further weight. She thought so until that unfortunate night when Derek walked into her apartment brandishing a gun. It was even easier for her to accept that Derek's suicide and the attempted murder of Peter were her fault. It was easier because, for the first time, people agreed with her. The news had been all over school, two boys fighting over a girl. When Peter opened his eyes and was recuperating in the hospital, she visited him and cried at his bedside, knowing that her mind was already made up. She was going to attempt to disappear from her past. She knew she would fail eventually, but she wanted to try. She would walk out of that hospital that day, cutting Peter out of her life. She would go about whatever life she had without ever visiting Jeta in prison. For years, she went through this self-deception, but the weight in her heart did not give in, memories from the past was constantly with her. That was why, after she graduated from Unizik, when she decided to write her debut novel, she could only write about her past, the one story that burdened her heart. She could not bring herself to write fiction the way she had always wanted, purely fiction, not disguised memoir or autobiography.

When her novel, *The Angel You Know*, began to gain acclaim within the literary circle, that box she had always carried along with her, the one in which she stored away events from her past, cracked open, and like desperate apparitions, people began to emerge to haunt her. Peter was the first to resurface through the crack, carrying a torch of hope and a promise of love and happiness. But Derek's ghost clung tightly to one of Peter's legs and escaped the box with him: Peter's presence made Derek's memories fresh once again in her mind, but the promise which he held in his hand, of love and happiness, was supposed to mute the jarring sounds these memories returned with. What she did not know was that two other ghosts held on to Peter's other leg as he forced his way through the crack: her own father's ghost and the ghost of the man that had died with him in that car crash, the man she now knew as Peter's father. These ghosts began to haunt her after she went to Yaba with Peter to see his mother, after that unfortunate discovery. And that night, after she opened her door to find her lost brother,

Jeta, standing before her, Tobe's ghost emerged with him, a powerful reminder that her past was her and she was it.

Apart from a thick beard, a receding hairline and the other changes that came with physical maturity, it appeared Jeta had not changed much. He was still that little boy who thought he could elude his own shadow and disconnect himself from his past. He now preferred to go by his middle name, Angelo. He said Jeta was dead, that the name reminded him of the privation and violence he experienced in prison, of the devil's attempts to ruin his life. He put it all on the devil, it was easier to do that, very typical of him, to attribute the consequences of his misdeeds to an invisible supernatural being, with horns and a tail, that could never be present to speak for himself. He was not like Neta, his heart was nothing like hers. It was not a sponge that soaked up and retained self-blame. It had never been in his nature to accept responsibility for his actions. He had not changed much; he was still that little boy who was in love with his sister.

Yes, he still loved Neta. He told her so as they sat in silence in the sitting room, after she watched him devour a meal of Semovita and hot vegetable soup, his favourite kind of soup, that she made for him as he took time to have a long warm bath and clip his nails.

"Do you remember this?" Neta asked, tugging at the bracelet Jeta had sent her years ago from prison, when she was still in Unizik.

"I still love you, Neta," he said, his voice deep and genuine, breaking Neta's heart again. "All these years that I spent in that prison, it was the thought of you that kept me strong and going, the thought that I would be in your arms once again." He reached and grabbed Neta's hand, stroking the beads of the bracelet.

Neta closed her eyes, her chest rising and relaxing in a deep breath, in a desperate attempt to contain her emotions and the feeling of anger rising in her system. The feel of his hand against hers felt like a sting, his words were like a dagger driven into her heavy heart. "How did you even find me?" she asked. She had just wanted him to have a good bath, to feed him and allow him have a long sleep, to give him his first night of peace and comfort in over a decade. But his distasteful confession of love, after everything that had happened, disappointed her all over again. He did not deserve peace. "How did you know where I live?"

"I remembered my way to Aunty Chidinma's boutique here in Surulere. She was happy and shocked to see me. She was the one that told me you stay in Surulere too and gave me your address. I made her promise me that she was not going to give you any prior notice. I wanted to surprise you. Before then, I had gone home, to the old house, hoping that I would see either you or Mum, and was told you moved out. I heard Mummy remarried and travelled out of the country." He leaned forward, towards Neta. "What kind of mother does that? What kind of mother abandons her son in prison and elopes with a man?"

"Don't talk about her like that!" Neta snapped, withdrawing her hand from his grasp. "She did not elope. She fell in love and got married. Normal love, Jeta; love between two adults who are not related by blood."

When Edna, their mother, met Chuck, an American oil executive who was vacationing in Lagos, she had told Neta about him.

"He is a good man," she had said. "This is the closest I have come to happiness since your father died."

Two years after Neta graduated from Unizik, Edna told her that she was remarrying, that Chuck had asked for her hand in marriage, that she was contemplating moving to the States to live with him. Neta had encouraged her because she saw that Chuck made her smile. "You have to go with him, Mum. Give this a chance."

"But what about you? I can't leave you here."

"I am a grown woman, Mum. Plus, I can always visit. You are not running away. You need to open up your heart to love again. You deserve to be happy."

"What about your brother? Who will be visiting him in prison?"

Neta did not visit Jeta in prison, not for a single day. At the beginning, his mother deliberately kept her away from him.

"Seeing him in prison will cause you a great emotional burden. I don't want that on you. You have to move on with your life. I will do everything possible to get him out. Time shall come for you to visit him. Not now."

When Neta graduated from Unizik, her mother then tried to get her to visit Jeta in prison, but she refused. Unizik had loaded her heart with tragedies that she had not imagined. Seeing Jeta in that state, locked up like an animal, would have harrowed and damaged her beyond repair. She continued staying away from that prison, and even after she and Chuck succeeded in convincing her mother to leave Nigeria, she did not visit Jeta and no one told him that Edna was traveling out and would stop visiting. After Edna travelled, she tried all she could, through phone and Skype calls, to get Neta to visit her brother, but she had kept on procrastinating.

"She just stopped visiting!" Jeta said, raising his voice to meet Neta's. "She did not tell me she was travelling, she just stopped visiting."

"Jeta, we put that woman through a lot. We caused her a lot of pains, every misfortune she had known, we brought it, and you are here judging her for giving herself another shot at happiness. You need to grow up and start thinking like an adult."

"I am a child now?" Jeta asked angrily, pointing to his own chest. "I am a child now?"

Neta shook her head and sighed. "Mum did not tell you that she was leaving because she did not want to break your heart. I made a promise to her that I would start visiting you. I was supposed to tell you that she had remarried. My visits were supposed to make up for her absence."

"Then why didn't you visit, huh? Why didn't you? Before Mum stopped visiting, I kept asking her about you and she kept promising me that you would visit. You betrayed me, Neta. After all we went through together as children."

"I was scared, Jeta!" Tears started to roll down Neta's cheeks. "I was scared that the guilt would kill me. I feel responsible for what happened to you, what happened to us. I could have stopped it all. I had the power to stop it all."

Jeta took her hand again. Lowering his voice, he said, "None of this was your fault, Neta. It was the devil's handwork. Tobe should not have died. In school then, boys fought all the time, some even with weapons. I don't understand how a fist fight led to someone's death. Can't you see that the devil's hand was in it?"

"Oh, Jeta. The devil had nothing to do with this; it was us. A sexual relationship was never supposed to happen between us, but we let it. That was the beginning of all these problems. Can't you see? That is why it breaks my heart when you say you still love me. Back then, we could make excuses for ourselves, that we were children, but there is no justification for this madness now. Let us grow up, Jeta. This discussion should not even be happening. It is madness to talk about that sort of love between us, after everything that has happened. Please, Jeta."

Jeta scratched his head and held on to Neta's hands.

"I can't live without you, Neta," he said, his voice heavy with seriousness. "The thought of being with you again was the only thing that kept me sane all these years. If loving you means that I have not grown, so be it. Our love should be one that conquers. Please, don't leave me now. My body and soul needs you now."

Neta withdrew her hand once again and started wiping tears off her face. "I am going to bed," she said, getting on her feet.

"Please, Neta. Spend the night with me, I miss you greatly."

"Oh, Jeta." Neta shook her head for the brother it seemed she had lost. "I am off to bed. Let me know if you need anything. Manage the small mattress in that room. That room is actually my study. I will move my bookshelf tomorrow. But you cannot stay here for long. We need to make other arrangements for accommodation." She walked away, into her room and bolted the door.

16

It was still difficult for Peter to describe what it felt like to be shot. The main thing he remembered was that the bullet had hit his upper left chest with an impact that he had never felt before. The force sent him crashing to the ground so quickly that it felt he was already on his way down even before the bullet had hit him. When he went to ground, he neither writhed in pain nor struggled for his life. He gave in to the bullet as quickly as it had hit him, accepting that it was his time, certain that he was going to die. He did not know death too well, but he knew that it took whomever it wanted to take. He did not want to go down as one of those humans who died fighting death, whimpering and screaming in fear. So, he waited patiently for death and whatever it was people said came moments before it. He had once heard that one's life flashed before one's eyes before one's death. He waited for this flash, expecting to immediately see his entire life roll before him in a film of whiteness and light. But the flash had disappointed him and all he saw was a blurry image of Derek standing over him, shouting down at him. Derek was close to him, even hunching down towards him, but it felt his words were coming from hundreds of meters away, indistinct and inaudible. What he heard well was Neta's cry as it mixed in discordance with Yanni's tunes seeping from a CD-player. When he heard another gunshot, he believed Derek had shot him again, though he did not feel any impact this time. He gradually began to close his eyes in peace and acceptance. *This is it*, he had thought. *I deserve this fate. I will take it like a man.*

The next time he opened his eyes, images were still blurry, but he could see nurses swarming around him as a doctor assessed his wounds. He was convinced that he was in heaven, not that he had died and made heaven, but he was in heaven to answer for his deeds on earth, and the doctor and nurses were merely attempting to stabilize him for judgement. He knew he was doomed to hell; there was no need for the judgement. His last deeds on earth had included betrayal of a friend and the sin of premarital sex. As soon as he felt the sedative needle pierce his arm, he shut his eyes once again, to get more rest and sleep before he met with God for His final judgement, before He cast him to that land burning with sulphur, that land his mother had always spoken of. He tried his best to be a good person, to make heaven, but had failed. He had fought this heavenly race and lost; there was nothing else he could do. It was now beyond him.

When his eyes opened again, he found himself in a quiet hospital ward, on a bed, his nostrils stuffed with nasal prongs as he received an IV infusion. He was expecting to see God, the way he had always imagined Him, that aged Caucasian on an immaculate robe, with white beard and hair, surrounded by grace and blinding light. But all he saw was Neta standing by his side. Maybe Derek shot her too, he thought. Maybe that second gunshot he had heard as he lay dying on the floor was meant for her. Maybe she was here too, in heaven, they were here together, to answer for their deeds in life.

"Neta," he called weakly. "Neta."

She nodded and reached for his hand. He could see that tears were dripping down her face. "Derek shot you," she said.

"I remember," Peter replied. "I know." He sighed through a pause. "Am I dead? Are we dead?"

Neta stroked his head gently. "No, love. You are not dead. I am not either. We are still alive. This is a hospital."

"He did not shoot you?"

Neta shook her head, blinking out tears. "No, Peter. He shot himself. He took the gun to his head and pulled the trigger. I could not stop any of it. I immediately called for help, and my neighbours came to help."

Peter nodded, taking the news with full pain. "Is he...?"

"Yes, he is dead. He died instantly."

Peter shut his eyes, struggling to control his angered breathing. "And you? You are okay?"

Neta stepped away from him, wiping tears off her eyes. "Not really, Saint Peter. Not really," she said, shaking her head. "I am leaving."

"Wh-wh-what do you mean?" Peter stuttered out the question. "I think we should stop seeing each other, Peter. We can't recover from this."

"We need to pull through this together," Peter managed to say.

Neta smiled and rubbed the back of his hand. "You are stable now. The doctor has attended to your wound. He said you will be fine. I have called your uncle. He will be here shortly. I am leaving and I will not come back. Too many bad things have happened. We cannot be together again."

That day, he watched her walk out the door without speaking further, without saying anything more to convince her. He was tired and confused and did not know that she was going to disappear, never to be seen for six years.

Peter's uncle, Polycarp, visited from Nnewi that same day, as Neta had stated, and stayed with him through the night. In the evening, when the doctor walked into the ward to speak to him and Uncle Polycarp, he noticed that it was the same doctor Amandi had referred him to when he was desperate to have Senno's unborn baby aborted, another glaring reminder of his sins. The doctor had a big smile on his face, even broader than the one he had the first time they met, making Peter fear that he recognised him, and would always think of him as that licentious boy who paid for the liquidation of innocent babies in the womb. His heart started to race to the thought that the doctor could bring the topic up, exposing him to his dear uncle. To prevent this from happening, to occlude the embers of incipient recognition, he did not acknowledge or return the doctor's smiles.

"How are you, Peter?" the doctor asked him, still smiling. "How do you feel?" Peter gave a slight nod of the head without responding with words. It was a deliberate strategy to dissuade this man from bringing up the circumstances of their first meeting in this small world.

Peter listened as the doctor told Uncle Polycarp how

lucky he was to be alive. The doctor said the bullet to the chest had gone through-and-through and had neither hit any vital organ nor broken any bone. The gunshot also had not resulted in a loss of a substantial amount of blood. But he had told them that the bullet had created a sucking chest wound. Peter had no idea what he meant by that but heard when he said, "He was lucky that the students that brought him here had the sense to tape the wound up. His lungs would have collapsed completely. We had to give him supplemental oxygen as we tried to stabilize him."

The doctor went ahead to tell him that there were still two fragments of the bullet in him. "He was shot with an Awka-Made gun, I have seen several cases of it. It is even a miracle that the bullet itself passed through and exited. Attempting to remove the fragments will cause more harm than good. He has to live with them for now." He patted Uncle Polycarp's shoulder. "Your boy is lucky. I cannot say the same of the boy that shot him. He destroyed his own brain, dying instantly. I still don't understand it."

"Thank you, Doctor," Uncle Polycarp said, removing his washed-out black cap to scratch his big head. "Who paid for all this? Did you attend to him without payment?"

The doctor smiled. "The young girl that was here with him made the initial deposit that we asked for. She ensured we had the police report we needed, as fast as possible, before we commenced real treatment. I also heard she had been at the scene and was the one that called for help. If you ask me, your nephew owes that girl his life. She did the right things at the right times."

When the doctor left, Uncle Polycarp turned to Peter.

"Peter, what is all this?" he asked, anger and sympathy mixed in his voice. "You want to kill your mother? Why are you getting into these troubles? What if the bullet had hit your heart? You would be under the ground by now. What did you do to that boy? Why did he shoot you?"

Peter sighed and began to speak his lies slowly and carefully, "It was a cult hit. They mistook me for someone else. I am sorry, Uncle. I did not ask for these troubles."

Uncle Polycarp grabbed a seat and sat by Peter's side. "I may be getting old, but I am not stupid," he said to Peter, his eyes fierce and piercing. "This was the exact same thing you said when you appeared in Nnewi two years ago, badly beaten like a common criminal, to the point that you lost a tooth. The exact same thing! I did not believe this story then, but I let it go. I wanted to give you the benefit of the doubt. You lied to me then, Peter, and you are lying to me now. I ask again, what happened to you and who was the young lady that called me?"

Seeing that Uncle Polycarp had caught him in his lies, Peter decided to tell him the truth, some parts of it. He told him that Neta, the girl that had called him, the one the doctor said saved his life, was his girlfriend. He told him that the boy that shot him was a bitter and jealous ex who could not handle the fact that Neta was in love with another boy.

Uncle Polycarp removed his cap again and hung it on his right knee. His face looked like a man who was searching for ways possible to sugar hurtful words. "Are you saying you got shot because of a girl?" he asked, his lips vibrating in disappointment. "They sent you to school to study and you are busy chasing girls *up and down*. I am sure those boys that beat you up years ago did so because of a woman." Peter sighed without saying anything to either accept or deny the brazen truth Uncle Polycarp's last sentence came with. "I am calling your mother right away." Uncle Polycarp began to frisk his pockets for his cell phone.

"Uncle, please," Peter begged, his voice still weak and defeated. "It will break her heart."

"I cannot cover up for you this time, Peter. This is serious; you could have died. I cannot keep this away from your mother. She would never forgive me if she found out herself. I have to call her."

"Please, allow me to tell her myself once I get to Lagos. I am done with school, even defended my project. After recovering from this, I will travel home and I will tell her. It is better that way."

"How do I know you will tell her?"

"Please, Uncle. I promise you. You can call her a week after I have travelled to confirm if I told her or not. Please, trust me."

AFTER RECOVERING, PETER kept to his word when he returned to Lagos, but he did not tell his mother that he had been shot because of a girl. He did not even mention the name *Neta* to her. "I have something to tell you, Mum," he said to her the night he returned to Lagos, the tone of his voice serious and deathly. "Okay?" his mother said, her heart already swarming with trepidation and anxiety. "What has happened?"

Peter unbuttoned his shirt to show her the patched up wound on his chest. "I was shot, Mum."

"You were *what*?" she stood up and approached him where he stood. Floundering, she peered at the wound and into his eyes. "Tell me you are playing a trick on me."

"I am not," Peter answered. "I was shot."

"What do you mean, Peter? As in, someone shot you with a gun, a real gun?"

"Yes, ma." He knew it was time to lie again, to pour a glass of cold water on the bombshell he had just dropped. "The bullet was not meant for me. They mistook me for someone else."

His mother became frantic and started touching him all over, examining his body. "Are you alright? Are you okay?"

"I am fine, Mum," Peter tried to make her fears go away. "The bullet hit and went through, without any major damage. I have fully recovered."

His mother put her hands on her head. "This boy will not kill me." She was already crying and screaming at him. "You want to kill me. First, you lost your tooth to them, now you want to lose your heart too. I sent you off to that school, intact and whole, alive. What did I do to deserve all this from you, Peter? Are you sure you have not joined those secret cults in school?"

"That is the last thing I will do, and you know." Tears were running down his cheeks too. "You taught me better than that."

"I taught you to stay away from trouble, to know God and just stay safe. You have not learnt, Peter. I doubt that you have. I should have listened to Mr Sweet and sent you to a private university. He was willing to pay, but I was worried that

I would make him spend more than was necessary on your education. I didn't want to be a constant burden to him. I think he was right. I should have listened to him. I don't understand these children and their cults." She looked away as fresh tears began to pour. "Your father...none of this would have happened if you father were still alive. We had already agreed that you and your brother would go to university abroad." She looked up to the ceiling. "Life, what did I do to deserve all this?"

Peter held her wrist and said assuredly. "I am fine now. There is nothing to cry about, nothing to worry over now. I am done with school. I am back home now, with you, exactly where I belong."

It was the first of the numerous times they would discuss this incident. That night, Peter overhead her on the phone, talking to Toy Woman. It was Toy Woman that told her that someone was after her son, that the wicked hand of the devil was in it and he would not stop until he took Peter, just as he took her husband. The next day, she invited a woman they called Sister Vero, a member of the Catholic Charismatic Renewal. Before Sister Vero arrived, she already told Peter to prepare to receive the protection of the Holy Ghost. She told him that Sister Vero could see beyond the ordinary and called her 'The Woman with Spiritual Eyes'. "You need deliverance, Peter," she told him. "Sister Vero is very powerful, the right person to pray for you and cleanse you of the sins and evils that useless school has bathed you with."

Sister Vero came at night, a lanky, unassuming woman with colourless eyes, holding a yellow Good News Bible to her chest. That was when Peter's mother made it known to him that Sister Vero had come to conduct a vigil of prayers and deliverance. Though Sister Vero said few words as Peter's mother introduced her to Peter, her eyes remained on him, haunting and curious. Even as they ate dinner and readied themselves for the spiritual battle ahead of them, she kept his eyes on him, like she already could see evil spirits and the devil's spell hovering all around him.

"Why did they shoot you?" she asked Peter, causing a palpitation of his heart, that heart that had recently dodged a bullet. It took him a few seconds before he responded. He knew he was going to lie; he knew he had to lie, to this woman who stared at him like she had already seen his entire life. What if she had already seen what happened that night and was testing the extent of his sinfulness, expecting him to play into her hands and break the simplified version of the Ninth Commandment by lying brazenly?

"Mistaken identity," Peter said. "Those cult boys." He answered her only with simple noun phrases, with as few words as possible. In this his short, troubled life, he had learnt the invaluable lesson that whenever the threads of lies were spun and drawn out for too long, they responded by weaving into superfluous and difficult words, straining the fibre taut, to a breaking point.

Sister Vero's transformation, when they plunged into the vigil, scared him. She began to vibrate and jump around energetically, her eyes tightly shut the whole time. Peter's mother prayed and sang praises with her. They sang and prayed on top of their voices for hours, with Sister Vero cutting in at intervals to introduce different prayer points and shouting, 'Pray! Pray!'. She eventually ordered that the prayers be stopped, opening her eyes to stare again at Peter, the look this time was more intense, more domineering.

"You," she said, pointing at Peter like he was an unwanted spirit. "Come here. Kneel down here."

Peter obeyed. Kneeling in the middle of the room as Sister Vero laid a hand on him and spoke in tongues, reminding him of the movie, *Living in Bondage*: that scene where Andy Okeke knelt in a stream to be bathed and cleansed, as a protection against the ghost of his wife. For Peter, the major difference was that while Andy Okeke was cleansed with incantations and goat blood, Sister Vero was cleansing him with incoherent words and spittle.

Peter knelt there, half-expecting to be overtaken by the spirit of God, to fall to ground and wriggle as this foul spirit Sister Vero spoke off left his body, but all he felt was the force from Sister Vero's hand, pressing his head, sinking his body to the ground. She did not stop until he yielded and went to ground, his eyes closed. She knelt beside him and spoke more, with her hand still placed on his forehead. This time, she was saying actual words, about God taking control, covering him with the Blood of Jesus.

After the vigil, they sat, reflecting on what Sister Vero called *her revelations*, waiting for daybreak.

"Peter," Sister Vero called, this time the look in her eyes was normal, more human. "How are you?"

Peter nodded and glanced over at his mother as she shook her head and waved to the ceiling, still muttering prayers. "I am fine," he said. "Thank you."

Sister Vero turned to Peter's mother. "Your son is fine in Jesus name."

"Amen!" Peter's mother responded.

"All the plans of death and damnation The Enemy has for him have been destroyed this very night. The yoke has been broken in Jesus name."

"Amen!"

Sister Vero went into another short song of worship and Peter's mother joined her. The song was brief this time. "Your son's relationship with God has been bent," she said to Peter's mother. "When I was praying, I saw a vision of Peter turning his back on God. That is why he has been exposed to attacks from the devil."

Peter's mother snapped her fingers repeatedly. "It is that school, Sister Vero. I should not have sent him to that school. What do we do now?"

Sister Vero smiled and raised her shoulder. "You have nothing to worry about. That was why I said *bent*, not *broken*. And that was why I said that he was the one that turned his back on God, and not God on him. In my vision…" She paused and outstretched her arms towards Peter. "…God had his arms like this, stretched out and welcoming, begging your son to come back. There is hope. All your son needs to do is to fall back into his arms, like you have trained him, be close to his Maker and Saviour. He is the son of God. God cannot forsake him." She turned away to look at Peter as he sat with his face downcast. "He has stopped attending mass and has stopped receiving the Body and Blood of Christ. He needs a spiritual refortification."

"Peter, is Sister Vero speaking the truth? You no longer go to church?"

Peter did not answer, he did not even raise his face to

look at his mother. It surprised him how spot on Sister Vero had been. The new wave of fear swarming in his stomach was that Sister Vero had seen his lies too, the circumstances of his shooting and was going to pull the lid off the cauldron of his lies.

"Sister Vero, what can be done to remedy all of this?"

Sister Vero sighed and said, "I will give you prayer points and verses from the Bible you will read every morning and night with him, prayers that will bring back God's favour in his life. But he needs to decide within himself to come back to God. That relationship has to be rebuilt; it has to be made permanent, for without Him, we are nothing. Peter needs to understand this."

When Sister Vero left, Peter's mother had an extended conversation with him on the importance of knowing God. She made him promise her that he would go for a confession next Wednesday and asked him to go and get some sleep. That morning, as Peter threw himself on his bed, mentally and physically drained, he heaved a heavy sigh of relief. The vigil had ended and he felt disappointed in himself that he had not felt any form of spiritual uplift. He had not felt any spirit leave him. He had not felt anything resembling the presence of God. All he felt was relief, relief that it was all over, that he had lied and this woman with spiritual eyes had not found out.

For years, Peter went about his life, carrying the bullet wounds and fragments, and the soreness they held, as an unwanted reminder of Unizik, of his mistakes and their consequences, of the unfortunate events that took place while he was an undergrad. The bullet entry wound also made it unbearably difficult for him to forget Neta, put her in the past, and throw her and the depressing thoughts that came with her memory into that same forsaken space where he had successfully forced Senno, Udoka and Oluchi into. Within this space, he enjoyed total control over memories. Memories stored in this space knew their place and lacked the guts to intrude into his life; they only crawled to shore when they were deliberately invoked by him and were always quick to withdraw and shrink back into their respective corners within that space. That was Peter's space, the one place in his mind that he had unrivalled control over, where he was king. But Neta refused to live in it, and the bullet wound was just one amongst the numerous vessels through which she visited Peter's head and disrupted his activities whenever she pleased, without warning.

The acceptance that she would always be in his head only meant that he would always hope to see her again, to be with her again. What he had for her was a consuming love; he could not squash his feelings for her.

He would always try to forget her but would always fail as many times as he tried. After she walked out of the hospital, before Uncle Polycarp arrived, the next time he heard anything about her was during Youth Service. He was serving in Lagos, while she was posted to faraway Borno. Then, he had hoped that they would see again, as soon as possible, and did not care if it meant that he was going to wait for when Youth Service was over. She had shocked him when she remained unreachable after one year. Soon, a year became two, then two skipped to four, and then six years swept past without any information about her, not even on Facebook. Peter was frustrated at how possible it was to love and understand someone so much, but yet know little about them; nothing of her family and friends. When they were together in school, he knew that she did not keep friends, and even if she did, they had no mutual friend. It was also a reminder to him that the only real friends he made in Unizik, Amandi and Derek, were either dead or missing. Connections to string together to try to find her were limited, and his job in banking did not give him that sort of freedom needed to be fully invested in searching for her.

When the years continued to race by without any sign of her, Peter began to think that she had stayed back in Borno after NYSC, maybe she had found something worth holding on to at the north- end of the country, a perfect excuse to hide and be away from him. Maybe she had even relocated out of the county, and he had lost her forever, just as he lost Anita Sweet. That was why he felt like a starving pauper who had just discovered that his thatched hut was sitting on top of a gold mine the day he sat at her reading, watching and listening to her speak. That night that he drove her home— and they slept in each other's arms, like in the old days of Unizik— brought a deep feeling of peace and hope. He knew that she, in his arms, was the key to his happiness, the missing piece that, all these years, had strained his life, making it impossible for him to love another. Winnie was right when she told him that his heart was lost, that he needed to find the person he lost it to.

Two days after Toy Woman's inquisitiveness exhumed memories of Peter's father, the circumstances that led to his death, as well as the involvement of Neta's father in it, it was gradually becoming clear to Peter that blaming Neta for this discovery was a big injustice. She was not her father, she had not even been in the car that day, and she could not have known that the man at the other end of the crash was Peter's father. She had no blame in this, neither did she need forgiveness from anybody. It was he who needed her forgiveness. He was being inconsiderate and irrational for allowing undue feelings of anger contaminate the clarity of his judgement. And the truth remained that he could not imagine his life without her. Yes, her love had put him through a lot; it had frustrated him and taken him to the brink of death and back, but he liked where he was with her; he liked the promise her love carried, the beam of a dawning future, a blazing light at the end of the tunnel. He was not going to leave her. His mother and Toy Woman would have to live with this fact.

These thoughts in his head culminated into the acceptance that he needed her forgiveness. So, he bought her flowers and a creative non-fiction book about success and happiness, Andy Andrew's *The Traveler's Gift*. He retrieved an old picture of him and her, which they took at Chuckies, the first time he ever took her out, and scribbled its back full of lyrics of a song titled *Two Waves* and slotted it in-between the pages of the book. He stated that it was a song from the movie *Final Whistle*. Saint Obi's character had sung it to his love interest:

You are the melody; you are my life. You are the woman for me. Living without you is a punishment. I will hide you from the eyes of the world. Let's meet like two waves and promise never to part.

You are the one, my love. My heart belongs to you. I will follow you till the end. Let's meet like two waves and promise never to part.

THE FLOWERS, A bouquet of white and red roses, and the wrapped-up copy of *The Traveler's Gift*, rested on the passenger seat as Peter made the drive to Surulere, to Neta's apartment, after a dull and lifeless day at work; a day that ended with his boss inviting him over to his office to discuss his pending transfer to Ghana, once again. "When will you be ready to move?" his boss had asked, this time, making it sound like Peter had no choice and did not have the right to turn down the transfer. "I have thought about it deeply and I concluded that I cannot recommend another person to HR for this move. It is you that I need there; you are the right man for this job. When will you be ready to go?"

"Can I get back to you on this by the end of the week, sir?" Peter asked diplomatically. He was in that uncomfortable position where the simple word his heart was pushing up his throat had become too heavy for his mouth to speak, a definite and unmistakable *no*. Neta and the beautiful prospects of love and life with her had made him more decisive—he did not want to be transferred to Ghana.

His boss nodded and spoke further, "Peter, you are still young, unmarried and without children and no domestic encumbrances. You should not hesitate to grab opportunities such as this. Over there, you will be the most senior Risk Management staff. Responsibilities like this will help you grow and become a better professional. This move will groom you for leadership."

As his boss gabbed on and on, Peter struggled to keep his mind focused on the conversation they were having, away from Neta and the visit he had planned to her apartment. He already had a mental plot on how it was all going to play out, the subtle ways he was going to use to ask for her forgiveness. Like an uninvited preacher, he would knock on her door, bearing gifts and a smile. She would open her door to him, and he would hand her the flowers. Still standing on her doorway, he would say to her exactly what the florist he met online had said to him: "Store them in a vase full of salt water. They live longer that way." He imagined that she would receive the bouquet from him, smiling and scenting the sweetness of its petals. He would then hand her Andy Andrew's book and say, "Well, I haven't really read it, but I hear it is a great book. I know a part of it talks about faith and happiness. I need you to read it and apply its principles to your life. I need you to be happy, Neta, because that is how you make me feel." He would point her to the picture hidden in-between the pages, telling her that the words behind it, written in cursive, spoke where his own words failed him, that they better explained what she meant to him, *his melody, his life, the one his heart belonged to*. He would take her hand and promise never to leave her, never to think of leaving her, to stick with her every step of the way, to love and fight for her. He would call his mother and ask for another visit, another chance to get her to either forget or ignore the past and accept Neta. He imagined that a plethora of emotions would well up inside Neta, moving her to tears. They would kiss and hug, a long, tight, comfortable and peaceful hug, and their worlds would be well again, even better than they had ever been.

But it did not play out like he had imagined it. When he knocked on her door, she did not answer, but someone else did. It surprised and startled him that the door swung open to reveal a half-naked man attempting to wither him with his eyes. Peter immediately stepped back, thinking that he had definitely knocked on the wrong door. It had to be!

"Who you be?" the slim man asked, tugging at the waistband of his boxers, the only piece of clothing he had on. Peter's eyes followed his hands, catching a glimpse of the outline of his penis as it dangled inside his boxers "Wetin you want?"

"Neta," Peter responded, still unsure of what was going on. "I am here to see Neta."

"Who you be?" the man asked again, hostility and mistrust trailing his words.

"I am Peter," Peter answered. "Where is Neta?" He was now recovering from the shock, gaining the confidence he needed to demand answers, to speak like a boyfriend who had just found a half-naked man in his partner's apartment.

"What do you want from Neta?" the man asked.

"Excuse me, who are you?" Peter asked, as politely as he possibly could in the situation he had before him. "And what are you doing in Neta's apartment?"

"Since you care so much about my name, I go tell you." The man stepped forward, covering the space Peter had created when he first saw him. "My name is Angelo. I am her brother. Now, what can I do for you? What do you want?"

"Brother?" Peter asked, not sure if he was expecting an answer.

He was thrown right back into that haze of shock and confusion he had just emerged from. "Brother?"

Jeta nodded and stretched out his arms towards Peter. "I guess those are for her. Can I have them?" And like a man in a deep trance, Peter obeyed and handed the bouquet and book over to Jeta. He watched Jeta sniff the flowers like a hungry he-goat, like they were meant to be eaten. "Who you be, who are you to her? So I can tell her. She is not around at the moment."

"Peter," Peter managed to say. "Just tell her it is Peter."

"Peter," Jeta said with a derisive grin. "No, I will not call you Peter. I will tell her it was Mr Flower that brought the gifts." He laughed briefly at Peter and at his own statement before plunging into a sudden seriousness, pointing a firm finger at Peter. "Leave my sister alone, do you hear me? Stay away from my sister, or I will hurt you. I swear to God, I will break your bones."

Peter did not say another word to him. He did not haul his own words to challenge Jeta's affronts, neither did he shudder or twitch in fear. The incomprehensibility of that moment had debilitated him. He had known Neta forever and she had never mentioned anything about a brother. She had, on few occasions, spoken about a father and a mother, never about a brother. Where had he surfaced from? Why did he look malnourished, with outlines of his bones so visible that it looked like a man on a cheap skeletal costume? Why was he so angry and hateful towards him, someone he was meeting for the first time? Why did he want him to stay away from *his sister* even before getting to know him? What was wrong with this man? He remained in this state, his mind covered in this puddle of confusion, as Jeta called him 'Mr Flower' one more time and grabbed his crotch before slamming the door shut in his face.

Then a cold sensation gushed within him like his blood

had turned to refrigerated water. He did not understand what just happened and could not tell why this *brother* was grabbing his crotch at him, but he knew something was wrong. He knew that this evening *dream* had, and needed, a bigger explanation. He could not help but put his mind to desperate work. First, he considered the possibility that this was a hoodlum who had harmed—even killed— Neta and had illegally taken over her apartment. But the undeniable resemblance between this man that called himself Angelo and Neta, his Angel, laid a clearer imagination to the truth. His lips were as full and his nose as pointed as Neta's. His eyes might have been scornful and hostile, but they were Neta's eyes too. He was certain of it. Maybe he was indeed Neta's brother, only that he was mad. As he walked back to his car, he dialled Neta's number and it went to voicemail. That was when he told himself that he would go home and wait. He told himself that he would return, possibly call the police, if he did not hear from Neta within the next twenty-four hours. But if she was alive and unhurt, he was sure that she would come to him. He would wait for her. He was certain that she would come bearing answers.

PETER WAS RIGHT. Neta came to him. She knocked on his door that same night, holding the picture he had placed inside *The Traveler's Gift*. He embraced her and kissed her neck when he let her into his apartment. He wanted to be patient and understanding with her. He had bottled up all the feelings his meeting with Jeta had created in him. He knew she had answers; he wanted to get them as calmly as possible.

"This note," Neta said calmly, revealing the note at the

back of the picture. "Do you mean all these things you write and say to me?"

Peter scratched his neck. "I am disappointed that after all these years, after all we have been through, you can still ask me that. Yes, the words in that note are from *Final Whistle*, like I stated in it, but they don't describe how I feel about you any less. You have no idea what you mean to me, Angel."

When she smiled, her smile was tight and thoughtful. "This movie, *Final Whistle*," she said. "You once sent me words from it in a text years ago."

"Yes," Peter responded, unflinchingly peering into her eyes. Her eyes held a sadness that he had seen before, even in his own eyes when he looked into the mirror; it was a sadness that he knew only love could bring about.

"Can you remember the words, what you wrote?"

"Yes, every single word. It is like reciting the alphabets, like singing the national anthem."

"But the national anthem is not that easy for a lot of people." She moved closer to him and held his right arm. "I want to hear the words again. Say them to me."

He started speaking, almost robotically, "I feel so lonely when you are not around me, for your presence makes me feel on top of the world. Please, my love, don't go away. Come back to me…"

She cut in, making him stop, surprised that she knew the words. "You are my strength when I am not strong, my sight when I cannot see. Love of my life, I feel so strong when you are with me."

"*Standing by my side,*" Peter corrected her with a smile. "I feel so strong when you are standing by my side. You remember."

"Yes, Saint Peter. I remember everything, everything you have ever said to me. I remember."

"But you ignored the text when I sent it. It broke my heart." Neta stroked his arm. "I was trying to get away from you, for the sake of Derek, but you kept coming. You remember what I told you after we let that guy take this photo of us at Chuckies?"

Peter nodded. "You warned me never to let Derek see the picture."

"I was always worried about him." She paused to look at the picture. "See how happy we look here, yet I still feared that we were doing something wrong. Why did you keep coming?"

Peter shrugged. "I was helpless. It was love; there is no other explanation I have for it. I was certain that I could not live without you then. You can say that I was fighting for my life."

"What about Derek? What about his own life? Don't you think our lives would have been better if we had put a stop to this love then?"

Peter wagged a finger in her face. "No, no," he said. "You don't know that. We don't know that."

"But Derek would still be alive."

Peter pulled her closer and touched her hair. "You don't know that. This is life, people die. We made our choice, to build this love. Derek made his choice, to shoot me and kill himself. We have let ourselves carry this guilt for years, but it has to stop now. We are not responsible for his death; we need to put him in the past and live."

"Seven years ago, I tried to run away from you, and I

failed. A year after, I attempted again. It seemed like I had succeeded, but you found me again. All these years, as I hid from you, as I avoided Facebook because of you, as I grappled with the guilt of Derek's death, the solid truth was that I never stopped loving you, not for a single day. But this love hurts. Why does our love hurt so much?"

Peter took her face in his hands and kissed her lips. "We can make it better, Angel. I have made up my mind, it is you or nobody. We will go and see my mother again. She and Toy Woman…She and her friend need to stop drivelling on about what happened in the past, what was never your business."

"The past is part of us, Peter. Stop making it look that simple, that we can just drop everything that happened and move on. The past haunts me, Peter. It comes every minute, with pain and venom. My past is heavy and rough. I wonder why you love me so much. I am not worthy of this kind of love. I don't deserve you."

Peter smiled. "What are you saying, Angel? Stop lying to yourself. We know it, even the universe knows it: I am the one who does not deserve you. I am the one who should feel grateful for your love. You are everything a woman should be. You are kind and amazing. Your beauty is otherworldly. You have your life figured out from the first day I met you. You inspire me. You make me a better man. I can't ask for anything more."

Neta blinked and tears poured freely. "You don't understand, Peter. I have done bad things in the past. My life has been one big punishment for all the wrong I did."

"Don't speak like that!" Peter rebuked her. "You don't

know what you have, what others wish they had. Back in school, all the girls wanted to be like you. My fellow guys envied me because you were my girl. You are an angel, Neta. My angel."

"That is the point, Peter. People have always seen me as that immaculate girl, living in her perfect little world. I am the cynosure of their eyes and they put me on a pedestal. But there is more. There is a darkness they don't see. I am no angel, Peter." She pulled away and turned her back on Peter. "Things are not always the way they seem."

Peter closed the gap she had created and put a hand on her shoulder from behind. He sighed before he spoke, "I don't know what you think you have done in the past, but you have not killed anybody."

"Something worse, Peter."

Now, fear was beginning to rise in Peter's belly. "What is it that you did that is worse than killing?"

"Something that is not murder but has killed people, and still it won't stop." She turned around to face Peter again. This time, she was no longer snivelling. Her eyes had lit up with an unusual fire of acceptance and confidence, peering into Peter's like they were about to stare two holes into his head. "Something that killed your father."

Peter withdrew his hand, the one he had on her shoulder. "What are you saying? My father died in an accident. And even if your father caused it, it does not make you liable because you are his daughter."

"The only reason my father was speeding beyond limits, the only reason that accident happened was because my mother made a frantic call to him to come home. He was coming to see what she had seen, what I did."

Peter folded his arms under his chest. "What did you do, Neta?

Please, tell me."

"You met someone at my house, right?"

Peter nodded. "Angelo. He said he is your brother? Is he?"

"Yes, he is my brother, my twin brother. His other name is Jeta, and he just got out of prison." There was something about Neta's eyes and the tone of her voice that bothered him. He knew she was serious. "There are so many things you don't know about me, so many things I have kept from you. I am sorry, Peter."

"What happened, Neta? What did you do?"

Neta kept her gaze at Peter, searching his eyes for his fears and thoughts. "I am sorry, Peter," she said again.

"What did you do?" Peter asked her again, his voice drenched in fear and impatience.

She sighed and said bluntly, "Jeta is my twin brother and I used to sleep with him."

17

Peter's mother always spoke about life with undiluted confidence, as if she had a superior understanding of it, like she was the maker and giver of it, and had some form of authority over it. Some days, she stated categorically that life should be all about God; she said He was the only thing that should matter, doing the right thing and seeking His face, striving to make heaven. She always wanted Peter and his brother to attend mass on Sundays and receive Holy Communion; she said it was the only channel through which relationship with God was strengthened. She told them that Jesus made it known that without eating his flesh and drinking his blood, one would not have life; that a life lived without God was no life at all. But other days, she admitted that life was about other things, like love and happiness. She said a life without love and happiness was bound to be empty and meaningless.

Whenever she spoke about happiness, she always stressed that it was the most important thing on earth and should be pursued ahead of wealth and material things. She called material things *fading* and *worthless*. She spoke about happiness as if it was a low-hanging fruit, blessed with essential vitamins and succulence, invaluable but cheap and reachable at the same time. She called it a choice, and said it was for free, that all one needed was to keep a close relationship with God.

"In relationship with Him, happiness is guaranteed, even in poverty and death," she once told Peter.

When Peter was a child, when happiness from family love and stability still bathed him daily like spring water, he had believed her. He had believed her until that year that they had lost his father. Then he realised that happiness was not a choice, not as his mother had made it seem. Happiness was not something to be controlled or wielded to suit one's desire at will. He understood this because he tried to turn on that button, to allow happiness obliterate the stinging pain his father's death had formed in his heart, but it had not worked. Several times, when he was alone, he went on his knees and begged God to make the pain go away, but it had remained, torturing his young spirit. It was either God was not listening, or He was just taking his time, or his mother had lied to him and it was not easy to control happiness like she had always said. She had lied to him and to herself; he saw how grief conquered her following her husband's death, how she never fully recovered from the loss, how it took away a huge portion of her happiness, a huge portion of her being. So the death of his father ridded him of the lessons his mother taught him, of the things she made him believe, but it also filled him with an undeniable acceptance that he did not understand this thing called happiness.

Whenever Peter's mother spoke of love, she also made it about God. She said it was the greatest law in heaven. She only spoke about love in its purest form, that kind of love that was devoid of sex and sin; the love of one's family and neighbours, and the love of God himself. She never ever discussed the kind of love Peter saw in movies, the kind of love that entangled men and women, boys and girls, trapped in romantic complications. The kind of love that, more often than not, led to sloppy kisses and premarital sex. Maybe she did not talk about this love because she thought it somewhat contaminated, a convenient excuse for sin. She could not condemn it outright either, because she knew that this sin, ironically, was the foundation of some of the things in her life that she considered beautiful, things like her marriage and children. She too had been part of this sin of premarital sex covered with the excuse of love; it would have been unfairly hypocritical of her to condemn it. That was why she chose silence and did not want to be the one to quell his son's curiosity about it. When Peter started developing adolescent feelings for Anita Sweet, he certainly knew it was something different. He would eventually, after Anita had left the country, call it love, that sort of love his mother never spoke about. When he met Oluchi, he witnessed something resembling it and he liked how it made him feel. He felt it again when he met Neta, only that it was stronger, a force that filled him with the undeniable acceptance that he did not understand this thing called love.

It was true that Neta's love gave him hope and happiness, and improved different areas of his life, but it hurt him a lot of times and punctured his peace of mind. When she told him the truth about a brother she used to sleep with, he was stunned like he had never been before. More stunned than he was when Amandi told him of his HIV status. When

Amandi disappeared, leaving him distraught and confused, it was easy to blame God for being cruel enough to let such misfortune befall Amandi. And, even till this day, there were days when he still wished it had all been a dream, that Amandi had been found and that doctor in Awka had made a huge misdiagnosis. Two years ago, he ran into Nnanna, Amandi's cousin, and learnt that Amandi was yet to be found, that his parents had not given up hope.

So he blamed God for Amandi's disappearance, even doubted his existence. But he could not blame God for Neta's confession, for whatever it was that happened between her and Jeta. At first, he did not want to believe it so he tried to help her deny it.

"You don't know what you are talking about," he had said to her. "It is not true. Please, tell me it is not true."

To his disappointment, it was true; as true as Amandi's disappearance. She continued speaking, explaining why Jeta had killed a boy, why he had gone to prison. He wanted to ask her why, to try and understand why it happened in the first place, but he was too shocked and heartbroken. When he spoke, he begged her to leave his apartment. For the first time ever since he met her at that birthday party in Unizik, he did not want to be around her. He needed to be alone. He called in sick and took days off work.

He remained alone, drowning in his own thoughts, until his mother called him two days later and said to him: "Mr Sweet called. He has invited us to a dinner tomorrow."

"Please, Mum, I am not in the mood to go anywhere tomorrow." "Peter, your younger brother is not in Lagos. You have to go to that dinner with me," she insisted. "That family did a lot for us, to put you through school and ensure we had a decent roof over our heads, after your father died. When they invite us for dinner, we have to be there. And besides, Mr Sweet specifically asked about you."

The next evening, Peter drove to Yaba and picked her up for the drive to their old neighbourhood in Festac, where the Sweets still lived.

"You are losing weight," his mother said, a few minutes into the drive out of Yaba. "Are you sure you are eating? I have told you to come to the house every weekend to take soup that you can keep in your fridge, but you are doing big boy for me.

"I am eating, Mum," he said. "I am just a little stressed out."

His mother reached out and touched his neck with the back of her hand. "Your temperature is a little high," she said. "When was the last time you went for a check-up."

She withdrew her hand but kept her eyes on him.

"Nothing is wrong with me," Peter responded. He wanted her to leave him alone, and he felt bad for it; that he wanted his own mother, this woman that would literally die for him, this woman who loved him unconditionally, not minding that he was not biologically hers, to leave him alone. "I am fine. How is Toy Woman?" He tried to shift the topic away from himself.

His mother scrunched up her face and cast him the same look she always wielded as a weapon when he was a child, the one that jolted children to good behaviour and self-correction. "*Ngwa*, call her by her real name," she demanded calmly.

Peter grinned. "I am sorry, ma. Aunty Prisca. How is Aunty Prisca?"

His mother sighed and sank into her seat. The mention of Prisca's name always covered her with an aura of peace and fondness. "She is fine. God is still blessing her. He will keep blessing her."

Peter swallowed and continued driving. He was expecting it; his mother always waited for the simplest of excuses to shower Toy Woman with prayers and blessings. "Good."

"Something is wrong with you," she said. "You are not happy. Are you mad at me because of what happened the last time you visited? Is it because of Chukwunetam?"

Peter shook his head and smiled. Somehow, she was right. Yes, he was not happy, and it was because of Chukwunetam. But it was not because of what happened the last time he visited his mother; it was because of what happened the last time Neta visited him. It was something he could never tell his mother, not even with a gun pointed against his forehead.

"I am happy, and I am not mad at you."

"Peter, Neta looks like a good girl, I know this. All I am saying is that there are many other good girls out there. I can even find one for you if you want me to. You do not have to marry someone whose presence will constantly and painfully remind your mother of the death of her husband. And that her mother, that woman, Edna, is not a good person at all."

"What did she even do exactly?" Peter asked. "She lost a husband too. It was not her fault."

"I met her twice, Peter. We did not really speak at the hospital, because I was going crazy then. She later came to the house to see me and I did not talk to her. Prisca was with me then. Prisca told her to give me time to heal, that she should come back. Peter, she left and never came back."

"But she was mourning her own husband too, Mum."

"Her own husband that killed your father! They brought this misfortune; she should have made more effort, shown more concern. Like I said, Neta might be a good girl, but that her mother is not *it* at all. Mba kwa."

Peter nodded, briefly wondering if his mother would still stand by her words, that Neta was a good girl, if he told her that she used to sleep with her brother, that she was the reason he got shot in school. "Did you tell the Sweets about this?" he asked her. "Is that why they want to see me?"

"No. The Sweets have nothing to do with this. It is our decision to make, you and I. This is a lifetime commitment. We cannot afford to make mistakes." She touched his neck again. "God will see us through this."

As usual, Mr Sweet and his wife were excited to see them. The dinner table had already been decorated with shiny enamel bowls holding rice, salad and chicken. Peter and his mother, Mr and Mrs Sweet, sat at the table as the maid, a teenage girl that wore a steady smile, as if it was stitched to her cheeks, dished out food into their individual plates.

Peter sat, observing Mr Sweet as he whispered something into his wife's ear and the two of them exploded into a booming laughter. The Sweets were ageing gracefully. Peter always admired how happy and satisfied they always seemed.

"Peero," Mr Sweet called out to Peter, who was sitting

across to him. "How is your banking job?" Mr Sweet's energy had not withered down the years. There was still light in his eyes and he still showed great interest in Peter.

"Fine, sir," Peter replied. "Very fine. And how is business?" "Good has been good, Peero. Business is fine. Are you sure you are happy with this banking job?"

Peter nodded. "I am doing okay, sir."

"And are they increasing your salary as expected?"

"They are trying, sir."

Mr Sweet sighed and said to Peter's mother, "Tell your son that if he ever gets tired of the bank, he should let me know. I will link him up so he can go into business. He cannot do this work forever, helping another man build his empire."

Peter's mother smiled and looked at Peter. "I am sure Peter will know exactly when to leave when the time comes. Let him gain the needed professional experience."

Mrs Sweet joined the conversation, speaking directly to her husband. "Please, leave the young man alone. You think everything is about business. You think once someone is not doing business like you, that they are automatically poor and miserable. The young man is doing okay, for his age. He has bought a car and has moved his mother to a better and bigger apartment in Yaba, away from this Festac you have refused to leave."

"What is wrong with this our Festac?"

"Darling, can't you see that the roads are gradually becoming death-traps?"

Mr Sweet laughed. "Okota is not far from you. You should visit there and see what death-traps look like, then you will know that Festac roads are a blessing."

"I heard they have started work on that road," Mrs Sweet said. "Moreover, the state of Okota road does not still eliminate the fact that our roads here in Festac are getting worse. And crime rate is on the increase once again?"

Mr Sweet faced Peter to involve him in the discussion. "These are national issues. There are crimes everywhere. There are crimes in Yaba too, and the place is over-crowded. They have their bad roads too." All Peter could do was nod to Mr Sweet's points.

"You are getting me wrong," Mrs Sweet said. "I am not saying it must be Yaba. There are places on The Island."

Mr Sweet shook his head. "So, we should carry the house to The Island?"

"We can sell it and buy another one. That was what Nnamani and his family did."

Mr Sweet shook his head again and smiled. "This woman. Let us leave this discussion alone. You will not win this one." He looked at Peter's mother. "Your boy is doing great. All I am saying is that he should not spend his youth pursuing short-term accomplishments. I am talking about the future, about sustainability. We all need to create our own worlds."

"Everything counts," Mrs Sweet said and turned to Peter. "You are on the right path, Peter. I am sure soon you will start talking about marriage, isn't it?" Her face relaxed into a smile and she flashed her eyebrows at Peter.

Peter smiled back at her and looked at his mother. "We are working on it."

"*Oya*, time to eat," Mrs Sweet said, seeing that the maid had finished dishing out the food. She looked at the maid. "Are we set now?"

"Yes, ma," she answered. "Which drink should I get? Should I get the fruit juice, ma?"

Mrs Sweet turned to Peter's mother. "Should she get juice for you, my dear?"

"Yes, please," Peter's mother replied. "Thank you." Mrs Sweet then asked Peter, "You will have juice too?"

But Mr Sweet interrupted Peter as he opened his mouth to answer. "No juice, please," Mr Sweet said. "Peter and I will have some alcohol. Let her get us that American wine."

"Darling, that wine is a French wine, and it was bought here in Nigeria. I don't know why you call it American because the person that bought it for you just returned from the US. And are you even sure Peter wants wine?"

"Wine is fine, ma," Peter responded and turned his attention to Mr Sweet who had just tapped his hand.

"Don't mind what she says. That wine is a gift from an Americanah, so it is American," Mr Sweet said with a slight laughter. "A young lady that I have known for years returned from US and brought it as a gift, because she knows that I like wine."

"What is the name of this wine?"

"I don't even know. I just know that she went into details, describing it, stating how old the wine was, why it was better than any other I had ever had. These Oyinbo people and their grand descriptions. I just like to drink wine; I get confused when they go through so much trouble trying to describe things I do not understand."

They prayed and started eating while the maid went off to get the juice and the bottle of wine. Mr Sweet delved right back into the topic of career and money as they ate, forcing Peter to keep his attention on him. When the fruit juice appeared on the table, Mr Sweet was still talking to Peter. When a wine glass rested in front of Peter, he was still listening to Mr Sweet. But after he had a quantity of wine poured into his glass, he looked up to say thank you to the maid but he was stumped. It was no longer the maid. His eyes followed her as she poured wine for Mr Sweet. He looked around to see if his mother saw what he had just seen, but his mother was chatting away with Mrs Sweet. Mr Sweet was still talking, urging him to taste his wine. He took his eyes back to the girl as she dropped the bottle of wine on the table and asked Mr Sweet, with an American accent, "Should I leave it here?"

"Yes, my dear," Mr Sweet said, tapping her back. "We will help ourselves from here."

Peter continued looking at her as she tried to make her way out. She was pretty, her skin dark and smooth, and her lips tiny. When she looked Peter's way and their eyes met, Peter's heart skipped. Then she smiled at him and the dimples came alive. It was her! He was certain that it was her.

"Anita," he called her.

She smiled again at him and nodded. "Peter," she replied. "You look good."

Peter looked around again. This time, his mother and the Sweets were staring at both of them, grinning. They were all in on this, Peter knew now. He stood up and moved towards her, his heart making all sorts of movements. "When did you get back?"

251

"Two days ago."

Peter threw his arms around her in a warm embrace. She held him too. The contact of their bodies was a confirmation of the reality before his eyes. It was indeed her. His Anita Sweet.

18

All it took for Neta to open her eyes was a beep of her phone, calling her attention to a text she had just received. She reached for the phone by her side and picked it up. It was a message from Fabian Dani-Moore, editor of *The Angel You Know*.

"Congratulations!" it read. *"The Angel You Know just made the shortlist! Two weeks left for the winner to be announced. I wish you the very best."*

Neta sat up, resting her back against the bedhead as she typed out a simple response to his text: *"Thank you, Fabian. Let's keep hope."* She was supposed to be happy. But she felt monumentally despondent. Days had passed since she told him the truth about her and Jeta, since he asked her to leave his apartment. Days had passed and he had not called to say anything; he had not even sent a message. She was beginning to doubt Debola, her therapist. He had promised her that she would feel peace, that she would be free. It now seemed like he had lied to her.

When Jeta returned from prison and moved into her apartment, uninvited and unwelcomed, she had opened up to Esther about her brother that just returned from prison.

She had told Esther of a normal fist fight between two teenage boys that led to an accidental death of one, nothing more. She had not lied but her truth was incomplete. She was scared of Esther's judgement. She needed to speak to someone who would not judge her.

That was how she had ended up speaking to her therapist about it. Debola was professionally incapable of judging her, she had thought. He might be disappointed and think her past distasteful, but she knew he would neither show nor voice his feelings. He could think and feel whatever he wanted. She just did not want to hear them.

So she had opened up to him and told him everything that had happened in her past, about the incest and everything that had happened because of it. Just as she had expected, he did not judge or rebuke her shortcomings. He gave her exactly what she had come for: audience and advice. It was Debola that had encouraged her to speak to Peter about it. "You say you love this man, that he has asked you to marry him," he had said to her. "You have to tell him the truth. You owe him that."

"It is not that easy for me, Doc. It is difficult to tell my fiancé that I was sleeping with my brother."

"You have kept this secret from him for so long. This is your chance to tell him. If you don't, he is going to find out later. These things always come out. Trust me, he will not forgive it then. This is your chance."

"What if he leaves me? I don't really want to lose him."

"It is a risk you have to take for your peace of mind. There is a freedom that comes with the truth."

Then he had asked her to tell him how the incest had

started between her and Jeta. She told him everything, about Aunty Chidinma and her games, blaming herself as usual, for not doing enough to stop it.

"Neta," Debola had called her. "You tell me these things and I sense that you have heaped all of the blame at your own doorstep. What about others? It is good to own up to our actions and take responsibility, but you cannot absolve others of theirs. It will kill you. Don't you think that Aunty Chidinma is the main person to blame, huh?"

Neta had shrugged. "I understand what you mean, but I don't absolve them of their blame."

"That is what it sounds like. In all my sessions with you, that is what I have noticed. You blame yourself for Derek's death, for the attack on Peter. Now, you are blaming yourself for this thing with your brother? Blame Aunty Chidinma for it. She was the older person; she took advantage of you and your brother. She abused you under your parents' roof. She was the problem."

As she sat on her bed, struggling with a recollection of the events that had marred these past few weeks, she did not feel free like Debola had promised; she felt defeated and damaged. From her room, she could hear voices emanating from the sitting room, voices of Jeta and two friends he met in prison, Larry and Leo, nicknamed *Leopard*. Just like Jeta, Larry and Leo had done time for manslaughter. Larry had stabbed a man to death during a street fight, claiming it had been in self-defence, while Leo was an apprentice at a mechanic workshop who ran over a little boy with a client's car that he was supposed to service. The three were out of prison, and every day they all gathered at Neta's apartment, to argue on top of their voices and finish her food. Neta found Leo more repulsive than Larry. His voice was always the loudest, and the way he licked his lips lecherously and undressed her with his eyes, whenever she walked past, made her sick. She had pleaded with Jeta, agreeing to pay for the rent, to move out of her apartment, but he was having none of it. She even helped him to get a job at a security outfit, but he had turned it down.

"I don't blame you," he had said. "You want me to be doing security work, ehn?"

Then, though she did not want to, she called her mother, and complained to her, that Jeta and his friends were suffocating her in her own apartment and had refused to move out. When her mother asked to speak to Jeta, he declined, just like he had done since he returned from prison. "That woman abandoned me in jail and ran off to the US," he said. "I hate her and I don't want to speak to her." It was because of them, Jeta and his friends, that Esther stopped visiting. She said she felt threatened by their presence. When Neta complained further to her, expressing her frustration and desperation to get Jeta to leave her apartment with his friends, Esther told her to find alternative ways and push him out. "You are the one that made them comfortable. You even converted your study to a bedroom for them. You even used your own money to make food for them."

"It was for my brother. I did not know he was going to bring his friends."

"But you are the one that is still making food for them. Since they do not want to work and they don't want to leave your house, start starving them. Hunger will open their eyes."

"I am worried about recidivism. If they are hungry, without money, they are likely to look for illegal ways to feed."

"Be there and be speaking English. *Recidivism*. Neta, you better starve these boys out of your house. You told me that they all went to prison for manslaughter, not robbery, not theft. They will not go out and start stealing, and it is not like they will commit manslaughter all over because they are hungry."

"These prisons harden people, Esther. They even end up becoming capable of anything to get by. I am worried about that. Jeta is still my brother, no matter what."

"It is your own safety that I am worried about. I cannot be around those boys. I don't know how you are able to do it."

THE NEXT SUNDAY, Neta paid Aunty Chidinma a visit. She had noticed that since Jeta returned from prison, Aunty Chidinma's calls had stopped. Before now, she would call every Sunday, asking Neta to visit and spend time with her and her children, Patrick, Small Ben and Samantha. Jeta's release from prison had, somehow, put an inexplicable stop to all that. But Neta was dying; she needed to be away from her apartment.

Neta sat in Aunty Chidinma's living room, and as usual, Aunty Chidinma did most of the talking. In her usual fashion, she prattled on about how proud she was of her children, telling Neta about their life progresses; how Samantha had passed her JAMB and WAEC exams in flying colours and was waiting to gain admission into the University of Lagos, how Small Ben was excelling in Mathematics and Physics.

"When Small Ben finishes secondary school, he will also go to Unilag, like his sister would," Aunty Chidinma said. "Their father keeps insisting on Unizik. I don't know what he saw in that school." She leaned towards Neta. "How was Unizik when you were there?"

Neta shrugged and sighed. Unizik held memories that always broke her heart. "What does Small Ben want?"

"That one? That one that is now doing big boy for me. He even said I should stop calling him Small Ben, that he has grown. He said I should be calling him Big Ben now, like his father. He is supporting his father. He wants to go to Unizik. I know that all he wants to do is to run away and be away from home."

"It is a good school, Aunty. Let them go there. Why don't you like it?"

"Chukwunetam, my dear, Unizik is too far for me," replied Aunty Chidinma. "I love my children close. That was how I fought with Big Ben, when he wanted to send them away to boarding school. I won that fight. I want to be responsible for them. I don't need anybody spoiling my children. I have watched over them myself; I did not have a housemaid, not for a day. So, if anything goes wrong with their upbringing, I can trace it back to the mistakes that I made myself. As a mother, it is heartbreaking knowing that you pushed your children into the hands of people that would destroy their lives. It is a regret that I cannot live with."

Neta forced a smile at Chidinma's hypocrisy. She was beginning to wonder why her mind had exonerated Aunty Chidinma all these years, of all the wrongs she had done to her and her family. She was beginning to wonder why she had remained in good terms with Chidinma, why she let herself carry the guilt. Aunty Chidinma knew the dangers of what she had exposed her and Jeta to. That was why she protected her own children like special eggs.

Now, as Neta sat, looking at Aunty Chidinma, forcing herself to laugh and smile to her stories, the love she had had for her all these years dissolved. She was reminded of what she had come here to do. It reminded her that she had come to look Aunty Chidinma in the eye and let her know that she remembered it all, every single thing she did to her and Jeta, every single thing she made them do to each other. She knew that Aunty Chidinma did not know that she and Jeta had carried on, turning it into a full-blown incest. She knew that Aunty Chidinma did not know the things it eventually led to, about how it had ruined their lives. Maybe that was why she went about her life, basking under the sunlight of her beloved children, totally free from pain and guilt. Neta had come to give her a slice of the weight she had carried alone all these years; she deserved it.

"I agree with you," Neta said to Aunty Chidinma. "People need to be careful in whose care they leave their children. People need to be careful."

Aunty Chidinma stood up. "You understand, my dear. I want my Samantha to grow into a good woman like you. I tell her this all the time."

Neta felt her anger worsening at Chidinma's myopia and ignorance. If her dear Samantha was broken and damaged, just as half as she was when she was her age, just finishing secondary school, she would not have survived it.

"I don't think you need to worry about Samantha. I

see she is growing into what you want, good and beautiful."

"Thank you, Neta. Let me get a drink for you. What do you want? Should I get Coke?"

"Water, Aunty. I don't feel like drinking Coke."

Aunty Chidinma walked into the kitchen and returned with a glass full of water. "What about Jeta?" she asked, as she dropped the glass on the table in front of Neta. "I am sorry that I have not asked about him." She took her seat beside Neta. "How is he?"

"He is good, Aunty. He is good. He told me he met you at your shop, that you directed him to my place."

"Yes, I did. I froze when I saw him. I didn't know what to say to him. He was not looking healthy. I had planned to visit you, to see him. How is he?"

"He is fine, Aunty. He just needs to recover."

"How is he mentally? Hope prison did not change him. I don't understand why they put that boy away for that long, for a mistake he made as a child."

Then it struck Neta that her opportunity had arrived. She needed to start speaking now. "Of course, it did change him. Prison always changes people." She drank from the glass on the table, finishing the content in one draught, and sighed, gathering courage for the next words she knew she was going to say. "He is no longer that small boy you used to play games with."

Aunty Chidinma smiled, her face tingling with nostalgia. "Those days we used to run around the house and play hide-and-seek. Good old days."

"I am not talking about hide-and-seek," Neta said, her voice shaking and rising. "I am not talking about that stupid game. I am talking about Touch Me, I Touch You. Do you remember that one, Aunty?"

Aunty Chidinma's eyes narrowed and her face tightened. "No, I don't know what that is."

"Of course, you do!" Neta stood up, and in that moment, all the restraint and respect she had had all these years for Aunty Chidinma disappeared and mixed with her anger. "You defiled us, and took away our innocence. Jeta was just a naïve boy that wanted to play. You destroyed him and you brought me into it because you wanted to make sure that I did not tell my mother. I remember it all, Aunty."

Aunty Chidinma's eyes quickly scanned the staircase and returned to Neta. "Neta, I am trying to understand what you are saying, but you need to bring your voice down. Big Ben is upstairs."

Neta chuckled. "You don't want your darling husband to hear your sins? All you care about is your family, after you have succeeded in destroying another woman's home. My mother trusted you. Jeta and I trusted you!"

"Neta, I don't know what has come over you. I don't know why you are speaking to me like this. Maybe I made some mistakes in the past, when I was still a child, but that does not mean that I destroyed your family. I loved your family like it was mine."

"Oh, you did destroy my family." Neta sat again and moved even closer to Aunty Chidinma. "You don't understand the extent of the damage those games caused. Let me break it down for you: Because of those games, Jeta and I started sleeping with each other, after you left. I am talking real intercourse now."

"Neta!"

"Oh, yes, we started sleeping with each other, after you got married and left our home. My mother did not tell anybody this, but she caught Jeta and me in bed when we were in secondary school. Then, she called my father to come home, that there was trouble at home, that she was going to kill us and kill herself. My father was on his way, speeding to get home as soon as he could, when that accident happened, the one that killed him."

Neta stood up again and paced the room briefly. "And it did not stop there. Do you even know the real reason Jeta went to prison?"

Aunty Chidinma shook her head.

"It was not just because he killed a boy in a fight. I was the main reason that fight happened. That boy he killed was my boyfriend. I had wanted to put an end to the sexual relationship between him and me, but Jeta was not having any of it. He still wanted us to be together."

"Neta, you have to calm down. You are angry. Let us discuss these things."

Neta ignored her plea and continued. "Then, I fell in love. A good man, someone that I have known from school. His name is Peter and he asked me to marry him. I was going to say yes because I love him too. But his mother would not let us get married, you know why? Because somehow in this twisted world, his father happened to be the man that died in that accident with my father!"

Aunty Chidinma's face had dropped by now. She was rubbing her palms together.

"All these years, I have blamed myself for all these bad

things that happened in my life. But, I am now beginning to trace all of them back to you. You broke my mother's heart and she did not even know that it was you. It has been you all along. My father died because of you. Peter's father died because of you. That boy Jeta killed, Tobe, died because of you. You may not have been directly responsible for their deaths, but you killed them all. You started it all, and I hate you for it!"

Aunty Chidinma shuddered and looked at Neta. "Don't say these things, Neta. I was a child then and you know it. It was the ignorance of youth. I have always loved you, Neta. I have always loved your family."

"You were fifteen or sixteen when you started playing these games with us, old enough to tell the difference between wrong and right. It was not ignorance, but wickedness. You went ahead with this evil, not minding the long-term effect it was going to have on us. You are the reason I have carried this guilt for years now. Jeta went to prison because of you! And you are the reason why he is still in my apartment, telling me that he still loves me. You have destroyed my life and I don't know how to even start forgiving you when I cannot even forgive myself for allowing it all to happen." Neta dropped on the seat and began to sob. "You destroyed my life. You took away my happiness."

Aunty Chidinma tried to reach for her hand, but she pulled away. "Do not touch me!"

"Neta, please, let us talk about these things. We need to understand each other."

Then they heard footsteps down the stairs, accompanied by Big

Ben's voice. "Kedu ife na eme?" he asked. "What is happening here?" He stood, looking at them, certain that something was not right. He could see tears on Neta's face and his wife almost sinking into the couch. "Chukwunetam, why are you crying?"

Neta stood up and wiped tears off her face with her hands. She glanced over at Big Ben and fixed her eyes on Aunty Chidinma, on her face as it contorted in fear. "Please, Neta. Don't," Aunty Chidinma said under her breath. "Please."

"I am fine, Big Ben," Neta said and started making for the door. "You can ask your wife what the problem is, but I doubt that she will tell you the truth." She left those words heavy in the air and walked away.

That evening, when she got back home, after she fed T.T, Neta walked into her room and powered her laptop. She opened up a blank MS Word document and began work on the manuscript of her second book. She titled it *An Unusual Kind of Love*; she was going to write a story about a girl in a sexual relationship with her brother.

19

Anita Sweet's unexpected return elicited something new and exciting in Peter; feelings that he had thought he would never be able to have towards another woman who was not Neta. That day, at the Sweets' residence, after they had dinner, he and Anita were alone at the balcony of the duplex, reminiscing about past experiences and playing catch-up. Even then, as she stood beside him, as they rested their arms on the railing of the balcony, a part of him still felt like it was a dream.

"Are you happy?" she asked him. "Have you been happy, Peter?"

"Of course, I am," Peter replied. "Why do you ask that?"

Anita smiled and looked away, staring into space. "Often times, we forget the most important question. We just ask about work, about family. Nobody asks about happiness."

She fixed her eyes back on Peter as he nodded to her words. "This is so unreal," Peter said. "I cannot believe this moment,that I am here with you, after all these years. I am excited and surprised at the same time. There is no reason to be unhappy at this very moment."

"I am happy too," she responded and turned to face Peter. "How many years has it been now? Like fifteen? You look the same to me."

Peter could not bring himself to take his eyes off her. His vision had been permanently nailed to her face. "What kept you away for so long?" he asked, still watching her smile. He sensed that the intensity of his look was making her nervous and uncomfortable, but he was too powerless to do anything about it.

"Trust me, I wanted to visit, but my parents insisted that there was no point. They preferred visiting me instead. My father kept saying, 'There is nothing in Nigeria. Just focus on your education'. When I was done with college, he said I should study for my masters before coming back. Luckily, or unluckily, depending on how you look at it, I got a job immediately I finished my masters, so I stayed back for longer. But once I got an approval to go on vacation, I knew I had to come down to Nigeria." She looked away and added, "You never asked of me."

"Anita, I wanted to. Even as child, I wanted to," Peter jumped to his own defence. "I just did not know how to. As I got older, it became even more difficult. I thought then that you had forgotten about me because you, too, never asked about me."

"I actually did, Peter," Anita explained, her voice slightly raised. "That means my parents did not pass my messages across to you. Each time they visited, I asked about you. I never forgot you. I knew when you gained admission into Nnamdi Azikiwe University, I knew when you got your bank job. I knew when you lost your father." She paused and rubbed his back. "I am sorry that he had to go like that, that early. He was a nice man."

Peter managed a sad and short-lived smile. "It is fine, Anita. Good people die too." He turned around and took the hand she had on his back. "That is in the past. What really matters now is this moment with you. It is good to see you again, Anita." He wrapped his arms around her, pressing his forehead against hers like they were performing the hongi.

Later that night, as he drove home with his mother, she said to him, a smile of accomplishment on her face, "Did you see how beautiful Anita looks now? That girl is the one for you, and you know this. You need to let Chukwunetam go."

His mother's words, and the renewed thoughts of Anita, kept him awake that night. His feelings for Neta had always been genuine and intense, but a relationship with her had always hurt. Even with all the hurt and hurdles they had had to face, a part of him still felt that he needed her to be complete. It was painfully apparent to him now that the six-year break created by Neta did not change much, because their reconnection had come with a hefty prize, a trail of discoveries that had led to more hurt. Their love had always been like this: It gave, but not unstintingly; it took more than it gave. And now, when he searched his heart, the hard truth was that, for the first time ever, he was beginning to have second thoughts about Neta. It was not like he no longer loved her; he was just certain that he loved Anita, too. Anita Sweet, the flame from his childhood that continued burning in his heart as he came of age. Even as he met and dated other girls, Anita Sweet was ever present, as a benchmark for his feelings. He was drawn to some qualities and features—including facial dimples—that Neta possessed because he had seen them in Anita and was searching for them. It was not that he did not want to be with Neta any longer; he was certain he wanted to be with Anita, too. Anita that his mother had accepted wholeheartedly. Anita that would give him peace of mind and was not a mysterious puzzle he had to live each day of his life attempting to solve. Anita that did not look like she hid away her life secrets in an impenetrable sack. Anita whose father did not kill his own father in a frenzy of senseless driving. Anita that was not sleeping with her own brother.

The next time he met Anita, he told her what was on his mind, what he was certain was on her mind too, what he knew their parents must have discussed. But before then, he asked her if she was dating someone in the US, and she said she wasn't, that she just broke up with her African-American boyfriend of four years, a man she called Blaise. She called him a *domestic partner* and said that their separation had been *messy*, because they had assets and bank accounts they owned together. She was open to Peter and told him that she had loved Blaise. She even told Peter about their trip to Germany last year, to attend a friend's wedding, and about some of the other good moments they had shared.

"Do you still love him?" he asked her, not bothering to find out why the breakup had happened.

Anita sighed. "We shouldn't have been together; we were not right for each other. It was time to end it."

When he told her that they needed to be together, that they needed to give their feelings a chance, she teased him and asked why he did not ask her out before she left for America. "Come on, Anita. I was a shy little boy."

"And how do you want to make this work?" she asked. "I will be heading back to US in a few weeks. What is the plan? What are we gonna do to the distance?"

"We will figure that out," he assured her. "The most important thing is that we both want the same thing and are willing to make it work. I don't want us to go into this just because that's what our parents want. I want us to go into this because we want it."

It was after they sealed their romantic agreement with a kiss that he decided he needed to be away from Neta for his new relationship to work. Though he knew that the right thing to do was visit Neta and tell her about what was happening, he was not going to do that. He did not trust himself around her, he did not know what would happen and he did not want her presence to discourage his resolve.

He walked into his supervisor's office the next day and accepted to be transferred to Ghana with immediate effect. He begged Anita to come to Ghana with him, to spend the remainder of her vacation in Ghana. She said *yes*.

20

Literature kept Neta sane. It was natural and easy for her to recede into it. She had wanted and expected Peter to be her peace, she had yielded to the acceptance that she needed him, but he now seemed unreachable. His reaction after she made her confessions and opened the box of secretes she had hidden away from him for years, covered her spirit with a cold blanket, damp with shame. Two weeks had passed; two weeks of Peter ignoring her calls; two weeks of her ignoring Aunty Chidinma's calls; two weeks of Jeta remaining an obdurate nuisance in her life, lying around in her sitting room, smoking and drinking with his infernal friends, Larry and Leo. Two weeks of Jeta consistently begging for food and love. She had continued to beg him to let her pay for a one-bedroom self- contained apartment for him, where he could freely stay and spend all the time he wanted with the knuckleheads he called friends, but he had refused her offer. One day, after she brought up the issue of the job she had been able to secure for him, the one with the security outfit, the one he had earlier refused to take, he plunged into a pool of anger and screamed at her, his words coloured with entitlement.

"Leave me alone! I don't want to hear these things. First, youproposed to move me and my guys into one small room, to put us back in prison. And now you want to demean me by turning me into a security man, so I will work long and odd hours, opening doors for people and embarrassing myself."

Neta wanted to quickly tell him that it was them, he and his friends, who had made her a prisoner in her own home, but she did not.

"Jeta, the job is to keep you busy. This idleness, the way you are living, is not healthy," She said to him instead. "The company of these people you call *your guys* will only destroy you. You need to get your life back."

"The one reason you are doing these things is because you want me gone. You want me gone so badly for Mr Flower to move in."

"Don't call him that."

"I will call him whatever I wish to call him!" Jeta yelled. "Mr Flower, that is what he is!" He tried to grab her wrist but she pulled away from him. "I have told you, Neta, we belong together. The only reason I survived that prison was because of you. You have no idea what I went through. But I was strong, I kept hope, because I wanted to see you again. You said that I need to get my life back. You are my life, the only reason that I am alive. Prison has taken away every other thing from me. I need you, Neta. I love you, like I have always done."

His words punctured her heart and defeated her, but not as much as the ones he said to her one night when he knocked on the door of her room, clad in just his underwear, begging to have sex with her. "It's been a long time, Neta," he had said desperately. "Help me. Just this night. I don't want to go out and look for a cheap prostitute. It is you I want; it has always been you. Only you. I have not been with any other person all my life. I need you tonight. Please, Neta."

It was after that night, after she had banged and bolted the door

in his face, that she decided she was going to make plans to leave her apartment, if he was not going to leave. She would have gone to stay at Esther's for a while, but was scared that Esther's curiosity would punch holes into her sadness and leak her secret. She did not want Esther to know the truth. She would have packed a few clothes and escaped to Peter's apartment, but she knew that Peter did not want her around for now. Her internal battles grew thick and broke into two dimensions: a part where her good heart assured her that, though weeks had passed, Peter was hers and would always return, no matter what. The other part was the non-sentimental awareness that reminded her that all the promises Peter made were before he learnt of Jeta. It reminded her that Peter was a normal human with feelings. She was not sure which part to lean towards, she was not sure which one held the truth. And it was the uncertainty that killed her. It hurt her even further, knowing that her confession to Peter, just like all told stories, must have triggered an unconscious visualization in Peter's mind. He must have imagined her naked, in bed with Jeta, lost in shameless sexual pleasure.

As she spent days, thinking about the pickle she found herself in, trying to decide whether to rent another apartment and escape with a few belongings so that before Jeta would realise that she had gone, it would be too late, she became closer to her parrot, and accepted its limited vocabulary, and poured her soul into that place that would always be there for her, immersing herself into reading African fiction while writing her second book. In her lifelong romance with writing, she had come to realise that a broken heart always meant that she would write and express her feelings better. Her stories were always personal to her, so she wrote them from her heart. And whenever her heart was broken, it was also open; like a fresh wound, it bled words. Literature did not make her forget, but it kept her sane.

That was why the reality of getting shortlisted for the National Literature Prize gradually began to bloat in significance to her. She began to feel that she needed to win the award. It would be a validation that she still had something that loved her unconditionally, a community that judged her differently. To keep her sanity, she concluded that she needed to constantly hear the validation that literature displayed in her face. So she communicated more often with Arese, the girl she met at her last reading, mostly giving her writing tips. She also started spending more time with Fabian Dani- Moore, her biggest fan, a man whose only discussion with her involved writing and expressing his optimism that she would be announced winner of the literature prize, the only things she wanted to hear.

The day the winner of the National Literature Prize was to be announced, Neta attended a book festival, to watch Dani-Moore render an energetic spoken-word performance of one of his poems that he had titled *Lead Us into Temptation*, a satiric criticism of African politicians and the connection between crime and bad leadership. Listening to Dani-Moore relaxed her, it even made her smile and jam her hands with other members of the audience, like she had no worries.

Dani-Moore came to sit beside her after his performance. "Thank you for coming to see me," he said, extending a hand.

She took his hand and smiled. "That was an amazing performance. When you perform, there is fire in your voice. One can tell it comes directly from your soul."

"You flatter me, Neta," Dani-Moore said and immediately switched topics. "The announcement is this evening."

Although Neta knew what he meant, she still asked him, "What announcement?" She wanted him to name it and breathe more life into it. She needed to hear it and she needed to believe it.

"Come on, the National Literature Prize."

Neta bobbed her head. "Oh, it's true." She hissed at herself. "I even forgot."

"You know you will win, right?"

Neta shrugged. "I don't know, Fabian. The other two books are great reads. I have read them."

"Your story, *The Angel You Know*, is authentic and real, a moving love story. It will win. I am sure the judges are not blind."

Dani-Moore's confidence satisfied her. He sounded like he was, somehow, privy to the results. She was not sure what the source of his optimism was, but she liked that it was there. She was grateful to know him, at this moment when her state of mind was more fragile than it had ever been.

On her way home from the book festival, she stopped over at a restaurant to have dinner and buy fruits for T.T. Ever since she gave in to Esther's advice, she had stopped making food at home. She wanted to starve Jeta and his ex-convict friends out of her house. She had no business feeding these men.

She had no business feeding them, but she could not get them out of her way. When she walked into her apartment later that night, they all lay on the floor of her sitting room, sleeping in various comfortable sprawls. Freshly wrapped joints littered the centre table, while the air was heavy with the stench of smoked weed. An empty bottle of cognac slept next to Jeta. She wondered how it was possible for them to always have alcohol and weed and still demand food from her. She wondered why they would not use whatever money they had to buy food, instead of using it to fuel their alcoholism and narcosis. But she ate a small part of her words when she sighted a plate under the table containing fragments of what looked like chicken bones.

Neta shook her head and picked her way through the bodies to enter her bedroom. They were messing up her home, they were looking for her trouble, but she was not going to play into their hands. Then Dani-Moore's face, and the hope that she was going to be announced winner of the Literature Prize, flashed across her mind. It consoled her that the prize money would be enough for her to move out of this apartment.

She had wanted to run a quick bath before she changed her mind and decided to feed T.T first. When she entered her kitchen to prepare T.T's food, she was angered to see that a mess had been made there. Because she had not cooked anything in weeks now, her kitchen had been clean and dry. Seeing how messy the whole place was, she knew that Jeta and his friends had cooked in it. They must have prepared the chicken they had eaten by themselves. Her assumptions were evident in the blood-stained feathers scattered in the kitchen sink. She took a closer look at the feathers and did not want to believe what her eyes had seen, what her brain was telling her. The feathers looked like they were T.T's. She immediately opened the kitchen door to the balcony where T.T's cage was and flicked the light bulb on. There was no T.T. The cage was closed and locked but it was empty. There was no way T.T could have flown away. She walked back into the sitting room and kicked Jeta's foot.

"Jeta! Jeta!" she screamed at him, startling him and his friends back to life.

Jeta sat up, rubbing his eyes. "Why are you kicking me?" he asked her, his voice sounding frustrated. Leo and Larry had their red eyes wide open now. Leo was on his feet while Larry sat on one of the couches, watching the drama that was about to unfold.

"Sis, welcome o," Leo greeted, punching a raised fist in the air. Neta gave Leo a look coloured with resentment. *Stupid Leopard with his stupid face.* "Where is T.T?" She turned her attention back to Jeta.

"T.T? Who is T.T?" Jeta asked, looking at his friends.

"Stop it, Jeta!" Neta screamed. "You are driving me crazy. Where is my parrot?"

"Oh!" Leo cut in again and snapped his fingers at Jeta. "T.T na the parrot name be that so?"

Jeta nodded. The next words he said to Neta would force her patience into retirement. "We have eaten the parrot." He pointed to the plate under the table. "Those are the parrot's bones."

Neta stood, fuming inside, not sure what to do, hoping that Jeta was joking even when she knew that he was not. They had eaten T.T and she needed to understand why.

"Why?" she asked.

Jeta got to his feet and faced Neta. "I cannot believe that you are asking me why. You locked grown men up for days without food. You have been starving us and feeding that stupid bird. To you, we are not humans. We are even lower than that bird. Of course, we ate it because we were hungry."

"Na true, Sis," Leo joined in again. "Hunger dey wire boys for here."

Again, Neta ignored him. "Jeta, what kind of rubbish is this?" she asked Jeta. "What did I ever do to you that you are making my life miserable?"

Jeta raised a finger in her face. "You chose that Flower guy over me, your blood. I have been there for you from day one. I went to prison because of you."

"You went to prison because of your foolishness, Jeta!" Neta riposted. "I am tired of blaming myself for your foolishness. I spent close to a decade, blaming myself, when all these things would have been avoided if you had just listened to me. You wanted us to continue living the same way, after our father had died because of it. I warned you against fighting Tobe, but you did not listen. All my life, I have tried to save you from yourself, but you are too stubborn to be saved, too foolish to be helped."

Jeta shook his head. "I accept," he said. "To you, I have always been your little foolish brother. That is what I still am to you. That is why you can't wait to get rid of me; you cannot tolerate me. You want to starve me to death, me and my friends."

"You and your friends ate my parrot!" She screamed at him.

"Because we were hungry!" Jeta screamed back, glancing over at Larry and Leo, as they nodded in assent. "If you were not being wicked and starving us, your bird will still be alive. How did you become like this, Neta?"

Neta felt the anger in her boiling over, she felt it rise and set her chest on fire. "Since you have decided to smoke your life away, you and your stupid friends have to leave my house tonight, or I will involve the police. I can see you all want to head back to prison."

"Fuck up!" Leo screamed and tapped Larry's shoulder. "Larry, did you hear her?"

"I did oh," Larry replied. "She said that we are stupid."

Jeta pointed a finger at Neta. "You can say all you want about me, but you will not disrespect my friends. They were all I had in prison, when you and your mother abandoned me to rot away. You have to apologise to them now."

"I will do no such thing," Neta said, staring into Jeta's eyes. "I will not apologise to stupid, good-for-nothing ex-convicts that killed my pet. You all need to leave now!"

"Chai!" Leo screamed and asked Larry again, "Larry did you hear her?"

Larry replied lazily, "Good-for-nothing. She said we are good- for-nothing."

Leo said to Jeta, "Your sister has insulted our lives. We no be human beings again."

It was then that Jeta grabbed Neta's arm and pulled her close. "Apologise to my friends," he demanded through clenched teeth.

"I will do no such thing," Neta said, attempting to free her arm from his grasp, but he held on as tightly as he could. "Let go of my arm, Jeta."

"You must apologise." He pulled her arm again.

And she slapped him across the face. She should not have, but she did. She did because she had always wanted to, to slap some sense into his head. She did because she had no idea that it would push him over the edge, and she lacked full understanding of what he was capable of doing to her.

It surprised her when Jeta slapped her back, a thunderous strike with the back of his hand, causing her glasses to take flight and crash to the floor. As she tried to speak, he hit her again with another slap, this one caught and tore her upper lip. She pulled away, holding her face and hunching in pain, shock written and drawn all over her. When she raised her face to look at Jeta, he was panting and sweating, his face contorted. When she raised another hand to hit him again, he grabbed her wrist, suspending her hand in the air, and flew into an incontrollable fit of rage and madness. He wrapped his arms around her waist and threw her on the couch. She tried to get up, but he remained on top of her, holding her down.

"Leave me alone, Jeta," she warned him. "You are manhandling me. What is the meaning of this?" It was when he slapped her again and started ripping her gown that she understood what he was trying to do. She began to struggle desperately, with all the strength and will she had left in her. This would not happen, she thought. It must not happen. "Jeta, stop it!"

Jeta would not stop, almost like he had been possessed, and all he wanted to do was take what he had hungered for for years. Soon, her gown was ripped open down the middle, revealing her underwear. As she started kicking and screaming out, she fell off the couch, Jeta with her. She tried to stand and run off, but he held her back and pinned her down again, punching her in the face this time. He was too strong for her. And her spirit was defeated when Larry crawled up and helped to hold her down. Then Jeta ripped away her underwear, her bra first to reveal her breasts, then her panties. This whole time, she could feel his erection poking her thighs. She made one last effort to get him to stop. "Jeta, I am sorry," she begged, tears rolling down her temples. "I apologise to your friends and to you. *Shebi*, it is apology you want? I apologise. Please, you cannot do this to me, let me go. You are my brother, my blood."

"You should have thought about that when you left me to die in prison," he said and reached for his boxers with one hand. "You should have thought about that when you were making plans to kick me and my friends out of your house, to allow Mr Flower move in."

Before Neta could speak again, he was already trying to force his penis into her. And when she felt the pain and him inside her, she knew that it was already late. She tried to struggle out of it, but Larry held her legs down and apart, while Jeta grabbed her wrists, thrusting in and out of her with vigour and greed. She screamed throughout the ordeal, her eyes on Leo, as he stood before her, licking his lips. Even though Jeta lasted for just about two minutes, before he deposited seeds into her, moaning and grabbing her shoulders, in a state of unbridled pleasure, it had felt like forever to her.

She felt a little sense of relief when he pulled up his boxers to the waist and stood up. She could not see properly because she did not have her glasses on, but she saw that he shook hands with Leo. She saw that he took a joint and a lighter from the centre table. She saw that he walked off, into his room, her former study, and slammed the door. When Larry let go of her, she sat up and covered herself up by pulling the two parts of her ripped gown together. She was relieved that it was over. But it was not.

"Leopard," she heard Larry call. "Hold her for me, let me do my own."

She looked up at them in disbelief. Then she got up and ran into her bedroom, but they went after her. As she struggled to bolt the door, Leo kicked the door open and she reeled backwards and jumped on the bed. The two men stepped in, their faces covered in disgusting smiles. Her eyes went to Larry's crotch and it seemed something was breathing and getting bigger down there.

"You cannot do this!" she said to them, pointing at Larry. "Jeta will not like this."

"Jeta is my brother," Larry said confidently. "I take whatever he takes. We ate your parrot together. Now, we have you together, just like brothers."

Leo proceeded to seize her, lifting and sending her down on the bed. Larry unzipped his trousers and came at her. Neta made up her mind that she was not going to let them; she would rather die than let them. Even though they had suppressed her power and she was physically incapable of stopping them, she started screaming the hardest she ever had in her entire life, in the desperate hope that someone might hear and come to her rescue.

"Shut your mouth, this girl!" Larry ordered, but she would not listen.She started calling out to Jeta. "Jeta, please help me!" she screamed. "Help me, Jeta! They will kill me." But Jeta did not interfere. She kept praying that he would badge in and make them stop, but her prayers were not answered. Jeta was nowhere to be found. He had betrayed her in the most hurtful of ways by remaining in his room. She stopped screaming and allowed Larry to have his way. Just like Jeta, Larry did not take long.

When she saw that Larry immediately switched positions with Leo, so that Leo could go too, her heart shattered. When she saw Leo's face as he licked his lips in excitement, she started screaming again.

"Sis, stop screaming nah," Leo warned her. When she would not listen, he started delivering devastating clouts round her face and shoulders. "I said shut up!"

His fist came with great pain, immobilizing her arms and knocking sounds out of her mouth. She stopped screaming because she wanted the pain to stop. She wanted it all to end. She stopped struggling and no longer needed to be held. She remained still, like someone who had gone into a trance, staring into space, but very conscious of what was happening. She saw when Leo got up to undress himself completely; he was the only one that undressed himself completely. She saw Larry as he stood, watching them as Leo returned to her and pushed his erection into her. After he had succeeded in knocking sounds and words back down her throat, calming her violently, he proceeded to rape her like it was consensual sex; he did not rush like the others. He moved his waist slowly, grunting like a pig and fondling her breasts. He even kissed her, slow slobbery kisses. Though she lay there like a log of wood, he kept his tongue on her inactive lips, licking them and wetting her face with saliva. And he was the only one that lasted. It must have been ten minutes, maybe more. It was so long that Larry had to ask him to hurry.

"Guy, you are taking too long," he said. "Do this thing make we comot for here."

His had been different, but just like the others, he came inside her. After he came, he kissed her cheeks before he pulled away.

"Thank you, Sis," he said. "We are grateful. No vex." Leopard was a bigger evil.

When they left her room, Neta remained on her bed, in that position she had been as these men violated her, unmoving, trying to work it all back in her head to understand how this night had escalated and ended with three men raping her and Leo eating her face. She lay there, her eyes fixed on her dresser, on the snow globe her father had bought her, memories and faces flashing over her eyes. She remembered her parents, all they did to keep them happy, how they all played and dinned together as a family. She remembered the young Jeta, how innocent and harmless he had been. It had looked like all was set then to ensure she had a normal and happy life. Then she remembered Aunty Chidinma and sighed uneasily. Aunty Chidinma caused everything, she reminded herself. She knew that she wanted to kill Aunty Chidinma. It was not a thought she wanted to hold on to, so her mind immediately skipped to Dani-Moore and his assurances, then to Arese, the aspiring writer that once called her 'The Future of African Literature'. She remembered Tobe, Derek and Peter, the other men that had been in her romantic life apart from Jeta, men that had loved her dearly, men who she believed had been unfortunate to have met her, men whose lives she believed she had either ended or damaged. It was difficult for her to hold on to the thought of a man, after what these men had done to her, but she tried hard to cling to the conviction that Peter was still hers. She needed that thought, she needed to hold on to that consolation. She took her mind back to Unizik, to the first day they met, at Elite Hostel, during Derek's birthday, remembering the look she had seen in his eyes, of love and promise. She loved that man with all her heart and was now convinced that she would not be able to live without him. She must see him as soon as possible, and she would not hold back again. She would tell him exactly what he meant to her, that he was now her life, just like she believed she was his. But thinking about Peter, always came with headaches from the past. Headaches like Derek. Headaches like Unizik. And at this moment, as she remembered Unizik, she remembered Amandi, Peter's friend that had contracted HIV in school. The thought of Amandi sparked movement in her. She sat up slowly. Her entire body and joints were on fire with pain and discomfort, like she had been cornered and pummelled by a professional kick-boxer. The distressing thought was about the possibility that these men had poured something else inside her. The idea of slitting her wrist flashed through her mind, because she was certain that she would never be able to get over what had happened to her this night. She felt powerless and worthless.

When her phone beeped, she reached for it and checked the text message that just entered. It was from Dani-Moore, saying, "Don't worry, Neta. Those judges are indeed blind. Your future and that of *The Angel You Know* are bright." She knew that the winner of the Prize had been announced and it was not her. It was a perfect crown to this night and the events that it had birthed. This same night that her parrot was killed and eaten. This same night that she had been beaten and brutally raped by her own brother and his friends. All she needed was Dani-Moore's text, strengthening her feeling at the moment, that she did not matter, that she was nothing.

She helped herself to her feet, grimacing in pain. She opened her door to catch a peek of the sitting room, and when she saw that it was empty, she walked out to look for her glasses. She picked up the glasses and what was left of her underwear. She saw that one of the lenses of her glasses had cracked. Then she heard voices coming from Jeta's room. They were discussing what had just happened. She heard Larry's voice first: "Leopard, you did not want to finish. You wanted to die there." Then she heard Leopard's: "It is not my fault. No be my fault. Jeta, your sister is very sweet." She heard Larry burst into laughter. She stood there with her eyes closed, fresh tears flowing freely, expecting to hear Jeta's laughter too, but it did not come. He waited to hear his voice, to validate Leo's statement, but his voice did not come. Then she expected his anger, for him to throw himself into a fight with Leo for laying hands on his sister, for saying that she was *sweet*, the same thing Tobe said, albeit affectionately, that drove him mad in secondary school, but he remained quiet. She imagined him smiling and smoking his weed, hardly giving a care about what they had just done to her. It felt like her insides were heating up and dissolving within her. The Jeta she knew only wanted her for himself and would never let any other person touch her. For him to lock himself up in his room and close his ears to her cries as his friends took her dignity away, meant that he was no longer her brother, just an ex-convict who hated her with a passion. It was only hatred that could make him do this to her. She felt like talking to someone, like picking up the phone and dialling her mother's number, but she knew that her mother would be driven to suicide, if she learnt what Jeta had done to her. So, she walked back into her bedroom, into her bathroom, and started cleaning up. She imagined that this night would have turned out differently if she had just showered and slept, when she had returned from the book festival, without looking for T.T. She began to cry uncontrollably as she lay in the bathtub, scrubbing her body with a bathing sponge, water from the shower mixing with and washing away her tears, wetting her dreadlocks. She had never been this hurt and confused in her entire life. She did not know how she was going to handle this, who she was going to tell, or the action she was going to take against them, when morning came. Morning came and the first thing she did was go to a nearby pharmacy to purchase contraceptives. After she paid for the drugs, she asked the pharmacist, a short endomorphic woman, "What can I do to prevent infection if I think that I have been exposed to a virus?"

"What type of virus?" the woman asked, leaning over the counter in interest.

"HIV, ma," Neta answered.

The woman stepped out from behind the counter and touched Neta's shoulder. "What is the problem, my dear? Did someone assault you?"

Neta shook her head. "No one assaulted me."

"Your face looks like you have been beaten up, and your lens is broken. First, you asked for Postinor-2. Now, you are asking how to prevent possible HIV infection. You were raped. Tell me who did this, and I will help. We need to get the police involved immediately."

"Nobody raped me, ma," Neta maintained. "Will you help me or not, about what I asked?"

The woman sighed and gave up, knowing that Neta had been raped, but respecting her decision not to talk about it.

"You need to be placed on drugs for a month. It is something called PEP," she told Neta.

"Can you sell these drugs to me?" Neta asked.

"I am sorry, I don't have these drugs here. You need to go to a hospital, or I can get them for you, if you want, but you have to return tomorrow."

"Is tomorrow not too late, ma?"

"No, it is not. You still have two or three days."

Neta thanked her and left, deciding that she would go to the hospital later for this PEP.

When she returned to her apartment, she swallowed the Postinor-2 pills at once, and drank a full glass of water. She locked the door of her room and started packing a few clothes. The sexual assault had pushed her to immediate action. She was not sure where she was headed, but she knew she could not continue staying under the same roof with these men. And she did not even know what was on their minds. What if they planned to come back, to rape her again?

A knock on the door startled her. "Neta, it's me," she heard Jeta's voice. "Please, open." His voice was gentle and charming, like how it used to be when they were children.

Neta zipped up the bag she had packed up and kicked it under the bed. She walked to the door and asked, "What do you want?"

"Please, Neta, I need to speak to you. Please, open the door."

She unbolted the door and walked back into her room, sitting on the bed. When she saw Jeta's face as he approached her, she knew that he had come to apologise. She watched him as he went to his knees.

"I am sorry, Neta," he said. "You have to forgive me. I don't know what came over me. It is the devil and the weed and alcohol. They messed with my mind. I should not have done what I did. I should not have let Larry and Leopard touch you. I am sad and ashamed. Please, forgive me."

Throughout, as he spoke and pleaded for her forgiveness, she did not blink or say anything in response to his words. She stared into space. She only moved when she shifted away from him as he attempted to touch her knee. What they had done to her was unforgiveable, just as much as it was irreversible. When it became clear to him that she was not going to speak to him, he stood up and walked away, throwing her one final mercy-seeking look before he disappeared.

She hurriedly went down on her hands and knees, to retrieve the bag she had tossed under the bed. That was when she saw the plastic bag containing tiny sachets of the rat poison Peter had bought for her a while ago. She recalled they even had an argument on whether rat poisons could kill humans or not. As she stood, peering into the bag in her hand, her heart started racing. Jeta was not making sense, the devil had no hand in what he and his friends did last night. This here, was what the devil could do, suggest appropriate punishment for people who deserved to be punished. In her moment of confusion, the devil had visited from under her bed and had handed her over a plastic bag full of punishment, opening her eyes to what she must do. She tied the bag up and threw it back under the bed.

Without entertaining further thoughts, she stepped out of her room and walked into Jeta's. The three men sprang to their feet, with lit joints in their hands, eyes on Neta, like they were expecting a judgement. "I forgive you," she said, looking at Jeta. "I forgive you and your friends."

"Are you serious?" Jeta asked.

"Yes, I forgive you."

A smile cracked Jeta's face. "Thank you, Neta," he said. "We are truly sorry."

Then Leo spoke. "Sorry, Sis. The thing been hold boys. It was difficult to control it."

It infuriated Neta that Leo called her *Sis*. It infuriated her that he spoke at all. It infuriated her that he was still breathing.

"It is fine," she said to Leo and turned to Jeta. "I should not have starved you guys. All this happened because of that. I also think I overreacted. T.T was just a bird. I should ask for your forgiveness too."

Jeta walked up to her and held her hand. This time, she did not withdraw from him. And when he threw his arms around her and kissed her cheek, though she did not return his gestures of affection, she did not push him away.

"Thank you for forgiving me," he said.

Before she left the room, she asked them what they wanted to eat. "What should I make for you and your friends?" she asked Jeta. "You guys must be hungry."

Jeta hesitated before he spoke. He looked at Larry and Leo, and they both nodded, even before he asked, "Do you guys want to eat anything?"

"Yes nah," Leo answered in excitement. "Is it until hunger kills us? And you know say we work well last night."

Neta's heart swelled up in anger. She sighed to control herself. "Let me make your favourite, vegetable soup," she suggested, her voice low and calculated.

"Do you have strength?" Jeta asked, genuine concern on his face. "Don't you need to rest?"

"I am fine, Jeta. I have rested. I will make the vegetable soup." Jeta shrugged and she walked away.

Wearing her glasses with a cracked lens, she left her apartment, to the market, to purchase the ingredients she needed for the food. When she returned, she entered the kitchen to clean up the mess Jeta and his friends had made with T.T's feathers and blood, before she started cooking. As she cooked, contemplating if she was in her right senses, trying to reach a final decision, she heard their voices from the room, Leo's the loudest as usual. They were chatting away and laughing like nothing had happened, like all was back to normal. Their laughter tipped over the lid she had used to cover and stifle her rage, and she began to tremble, an unmistakable conviction that all she wanted now was to shut their mouths and end their laughter forever.

She regained control of herself before the soup was ready. She boiled water and prepared ẹ̀bà before she served it out in three plates. She also dished the soup into three different beautiful and breakable bowls before she went into her room and returned with the bag of rat poison. Already possessed by hurt, she did not pause to think further. She closed the kitchen door and administered the rat poison into the bowls, one sachet for one bowl, convinced that it was what needed to be done. She put the plates and bowls of food in a tray and carried them into Jeta's room.

Her entrance filled Jeta and his friends with excitement as they helped themselves to their respective portions, thanking her. "Sis, this food look delicious," Leo said. "The aroma has been tormenting my belly since. You don try, Sis."

Neta threw Leo a plastic smile and everything he did to her flashed before her eyes again. The beatings. The kisses. The unending round of forced sex. This man actually thanked her after raping her. "Do you want more meat, Leo?" she asked him.

Leo looked at her, disbelief in his eyes. "Yes, Sis. Yes,

I want." She collected his bowl from him and went back into he kitchen.

She added a big chunk of goat meat into his soup and emptied another sachet of rat poison in the bowl. Then another. If anyone, among the three of them, deserved to die first and more painfully, it was this lip-licking animal that called himself Leopard. She returned Leo's bowl to him and he started eating, just like the others.

"There is water in the fridge. You can help yourselves to it when you are done eating." she said to them, scanning their faces one last time, wondering how stupid they were. How could they accept food from her after what they had done to her the night before?

"Wait, Neta," Jeta said, grabbing her left wrist as she attempted to leave. She turned and fixed her eyes on him to see if she could feel anything and stop him from eating the food, but she felt nothing. He was a wild animal now, not her brother. She did not feel even a smidgen of sympathy.

"Are you sure you are fine now?"

"Yes, yes," she answered, managing a smile before walking away.

She went back into her room and carried the bag she had packed.

As she walked out of her apartment, she reached for her bracelet, the gift Jeta sent to her from prison eight years ago and ripped it off her wrist. As the white and gold-coloured beads rattled on the floor, she heard their voices and laughter. She stepped out of her apartment and locked them in. And at this time when she was supposed to hate everything that looked like a man, she boarded a taxi to Ajah.

She was not sure what the consequences of her action would be, but she knew where she was headed. Peter had made promises to her, he had assured her that they would weather the storms together. No matter the atrocities of her past, she would always be his angel.

THE END

ACKNOWLEDGEMENTS

It is fundamentally impractical to remember everyone who, directly or indirectly, contributed to making this project a reality. While I will specifically mention some names, I am grateful to everyone who, in one way or another, has supported this work.

High Chief Peter Oge Obih (Okaka *na* Awka-Etiti) and his amazing family, for accepting, sheltering and feeding me years ago, when I first arrived at this unusual place called Lagos. Thank you for your kindness, for being there. I remember everything, like an elephant.

Onyeka Nwelue, for always being a source of inspiration to me, for remaining a paragon of resilience and creativity, for all your support.

The team at Abibiman Publishing, for giving this story another home, for your contributions towards the development of African literature.

Ozioma Nduka and Ikenna Nnanna, for taking up the unenviable task of reading the first draft of the manuscript, for your commendations and criticisms.

Dayo Amzat, for believing in me, and giving me a platform to grow professionally and personally.

Chigozie Obioma, for making out time to read the first few chapters of the original manuscript, for your comments and guidance.

Judith Egbare, Ijeoma Offiah, Ifeanyi 'Legend' Obi, Chris Anokwu, and every other person unfortunate to, at one point or another, listen to my rambling narration of this story. Thank you for your patience.

Doyin Samo and Yemi Kehinde, for always being there, for listening, whenever the music in my head becomes too loud and overwhelming.

Desmond Enechi and Lawson Omiunu, for the gifts of friendship and brotherhood, for being my backbone all these years, for tolerating my idiosyncrasies.

Ojeifoh Okosun, for being a big brother, for your interest in my life, for everything.

Tare Okwuasaba, Bello Kedji, Onyebuchi 'West' Odilibe, Segun Ajayi, people who were good to me when there was obviously nothing to gain.

Precious Nzeribe, my old friend and ornithologist, for the curiosities in our heads and for the love of the beautiful sport of mixed martial arts.

And Abiodun Ogunkoya, the therapist that pulled me back in 2019, when I was strolling beyond the boundaries of sanity.

This is our beginning.